Periscope Red

PERISCOPE RED

Richard Rohmer

General Publishing Co. Ltd.

Don Mills, Ontario

First published in 1980 by
General Publishing Co. Limited,
30 Lesmill Road
Don Mills, Ontario.

First printing

Canadian Cataloguing in Publication Data

Rohmer, Richard, 1924-
  Periscope Red

ISBN 0-7736-0080-9

I. Title.
PS8585.056P47   C813'.54   C80-094564-6
PR9199.3.R6355P47

ISBN 0-7736-0080-9

Cover design/Maher & Murtagh

Printed and bound in the U.S.A.

Books by Richard Rohmer

The Green North Mid-Canada (1970)
The Arctic Imperative (1973)
Ultimatum (1973)
Exxoneration (1974)
Exodus/U.K. (1975)
E. P. Taylor (1978)
Balls! (1980)
Periscope Red (1980)

1

9 March   7:05 A.M.

Beirut, Lebanon

A dense night fog had enveloped the silent port and its mutilated city, shrouding the shattered buildings and gutted streets. Now in the early light of dawn, the fog lifted to reveal the rubble of brick, concrete, and glass that spilled from the ruined towers. A light mist still swirled over the undulating sea. Through it, Said caught sight of the Beirut skyline as he sat hunched in the bow of the long, narrow rowboat, which decades ago must have been a lifeboat on some large, long-forgotten ship. As the craft moved slowly away from the shore, he shivered in the penetrating cold of the moisture-laden air which surrounded him and his companions. The thin material of his long black gown, his *aba*, offered little protection against the unaccustomed chill of the air.

As the shapes of the blackened, desolate buildings emerged from the misty darkness, their rectangular forms thrusting up from the bowels of the earth, Said's mind focused on the plan. It was his plan—all the details, all the training, all the scheming, the arrangements, the negotiations, and the objective. The goal, that was his, too. If he was successful—and he knew unquestionably that he would be—he, Said, would surely deal the mightiest, most powerful blow ever struck for his oppressed Palestinian brothers still in the refugee camps, those putrid, cancerous places in Lebanon where hundreds of thousands of nationless Palestinian Arabs had dwelt for decade after decade.

He praised Allah for giving him the genius, and with it the responsibility, to create and deliver this most massive revolutionary victory, one that would stun the world, rivet the attention of people everywhere on the plight of the Palestinians. His plan would make those indifferent, bloodsucking leeches of the Western world—especially the Jewish-Americans and that detested country that they controlled—take notice; it would compel them finally, once and for all, to recognize the Palestinian nation. Those Jewish-American imperialists would have no choice. None. They and their Western European comrades in oppression would have no alternative but to force the Israelis to give back every hectare of land, every building, every city, every port, all that they had stolen from the Palestinian Arabs in 1948, the year that he, Said Kassem, had been born in Haifa. Just one week after his birth he and his young mother and her parents were driven from their home by the British-backed Israelis.

Said's gaze rested on the black wool jacket of the man rowing the boat. The oarsman's back moved regularly as he skilfully lifted the oars out of the sea and swung them back and down in again, running the small, decrepit craft through the black, rolling water toward an as yet unseen destination.

When Said had gone to the harbor's edge the previous afternoon to hire a boat, he found this swarthy, squat and, like his vessel, unkempt boatman sitting on his beached craft waiting for business. A quick scan of the water revealed the nondescript coastal freighter Said had pointed out. It was standing about a mile offshore. The oarsman knew her well. Her owners were a group of Palestinian Arabs who had come to Beirut many years before. Unlike him they had prospered. Instead he, a native-born

Lebanese, a Christian Arab, had spent a lifetime working his father's boat—which was now his boat—off the Beirut beach and around the port. After one look at the anchored ship, he told Said he could take him there blindfolded, let alone in fog or a heavy mist.

Aft of the indifferent rower were three more passengers. Like Said they were dressed in dark, flowing robes. One of them was sitting on the seat immediately in front of the oarsman with his back to him. Hassan, too, hunched forward, his hands thrust through the sides of his gown in an attempt to hold in the heat of his own body.

The other two were crowded together in the stern seat. Their freezing legs and arms were pressed against each others' for warmth; their hands were hidden in folds of their gowns. In whispers they cursed the cold and their shared discomfort.

The larger of the two men at the far end of the boat lit a cigarette. The unexpected yellow burst of flame accosted Said's vision like a golden beacon in the lessening darkness, bringing his thoughts back to his surroundings. In the instant that the firelight played upon the angular, dark face of the thick-browed colossus of a man, Said wondered for the thousandth time how Ahmed and, for that matter, the other two, Hassan and Maan, the happy-witted soul pressed against Ahmed, would perform under the enormous stress of the high dangers to come and the risks he had promised them they would have to take in the name of the revolution and of the Palestinian Liberation Organization. They were PLO people, Arab freedom fighters. The task they were to perform was a PLO plan hatched from the fertile brain of a member of the PLO's Executive Council, Said himself, the right-hand man of the chief of the PLO. Said, it was rumored, might well succeed the chief if, Allah forbid, the leader were lost to the cause of the liberation.

For the past three months Said had trained these three men. Taught them everything he knew. Given them discipline and hard daily physical workouts, both in and out of the sea in which the final part of the plan would be performed.

In the main PLO camp, to the south of Beirut and some ten miles north of the Israeli-held Palestinian lands, Said had coached and instructed his recruits in everything he knew about the handling of automatic guns and knives and in the many ways of killing an enemy in close combat with no warning or noise. The ancient and refined commando tactics of hand garrote and other methods of silent murder were honed. Over the ninety-day training period, Said had run them countless miles, put them through hours upon endless hours of calisthenics, and kept them on a strict diet. The result was that at the end of the period, each of his men was lean and muscular. Even Maan, the roly-poly one of the trio, was slim and fit, although none of his jesting good humor had been lost in the process.

There had been extensive, thorough instruction in the handling of explosives, including their detonation by various means. Plastic explosives had been exhaustively covered, but no more so than the use of the special, incredibly powerful and sensitive device that they would use on their targets. It was not possible to teach them anything but the rudiments of radio electronics, the method that would be used to detonate their special explosive devices. Nor was it necessary, because Hassan was an expert. He had been selected as a member of the team because he was a communications specialist, with a Ph.D. in electronics from the Massachusetts Institute of Technology. However, as a precautionary measure, in case something happened to Hassan during the operation, Said had taught the other two the basics of the operation of the radio mechanisms that would be used to detonate the explosives at the right time.

It was the underwater work that in the beginning gave the three recruits the most difficulty. After long hours of working in the ocean, when they had become confident of themselves in their special gear, they found great pleasure in the new skills. Day after day, they had done classroom work on the handling of oxygen bottles, masks, and all the paraphernalia associated with scuba diving, although the task was made easier by the knowledge that during the operation they would not have to go to a depth greater than one hundred feet. After the blackboard sessions they would put their diving gear, with the inflatable speedboat and its motors, into the huge van that had been allocated to them for the training period. Then they would bounce off across the rough roads westward from the camp to the wintry shores of the Mediterranean.

During their training months of December through to the end of February, that sea of ancient history would greet them in varied colors—sometimes azure blue, or turquoise, or gray or, at the time of storms, black-gray with towering, crushing waves whose crests foamed white as they thundered into the isolated sandy cove Said used as their launching base. As the colors of the ocean were varied, so were the weather conditions and the surface of the sea. In the first two weeks of the training the elements had been ideal. The Mediterranean rolled with a calm surface under blue skies sometimes dotted with lumpy white cumulus clouds. The winds were light and the temperature in the middle sixties, excellent conditions under which to introduce three men, all skilled swimmers, to the demanding challenges of underwater living, where preparation, safety checks, top-notch equipment, and rigid maintenance can provide the difference between a safe operation and death; and where the margin for disaster by error is minimal when handling sophisticated explosives and their delicate electronic trips.

When, however, the winter winds and storms produced a cold and heavy sea condition, Said canceled further underwater training, explaining to his students that the place where they were going to carry out the operation never had below-freezing temperatures or high waves. There was no need to expose themselves to unnecessary risks.

No one argued with his decision. For that matter, none of the trio ever argued with Said. Intelligent and well educated, all three had quickly taken stock of the man who had selected them from more than two hundred applicants. Each knew that when he was with Said he was in the company of a man he would naturally follow. Said, whom they guessed to be in his early thirties, while they themselves ranged from twenty-two to twenty-five years of age, had an impressive range of experience and knowledge of the fields and he quickly won their total confidence and respect. They had speculated about where he came from, his background; but he gave them no clues, and they accepted him for what he was—headstrong, intelligent, articulate; and quick witted, inventive, and impatient with anyone who could not understand what he thought was a clearly explained, easily comprehensible proposition.

Said was in excellent physical condition. He had to be, in order to lead them in rigorous calisthenics or take them into and under the sea for long periods. And his dedication to the revolutionary cause of the liberation of the Palestinian nation, its recognition by the world powers and the return of its land, was absolutely and totally unswerving—as was his dedication to carrying out the plan that he fully believed would fulfill the dreams and gain all the objectives of the PLO for the liberation of the Palestinian Arab people.

As the small boat carried them silently through the early morning Beirut mist to begin the first phase of their operation, his three companions knew little more about Said's background than they did when they first met him. He was an enigma. The only hint they received had come when Said was in an unguarded and relaxed mood as they sat around their campfire after supper one night. There had been much talk about many things—families, the future of Palestine, the inequities of the past, and women. None of them was married. Said would not have chosen a married man to be on his team. During the conversation that evening, friendly arguments flared over Maan's provocative opinions. Said had remained silent until Hassan spoke of his university life in the United States and how much living in the midst of rich Americans had changed his outlook. He had been shocked by their wanton wastefulness and by the way they looked upon the rest of the world, especially Arabs and Blacks, as grossly inferior and unintelligent. Hassan's story had struck a responsive chord with Said, who acknowledged that he had found similar attitudes in England while attending the London School of Economics. His three companions were able to take from what he had said no more than the fact that he had been a student at the university. There was nothing about the nature of his studies or whether he had a degree. No one dared ask questions.

One question they longed to ask concerned Said's appearance. His burnt brown Arabic face, enhanced by a heavy black mustache, bushy eyebrows, jet-black, wavy hair already flecked with gray, framed a pair of stunningly incongruous eyes that set him apart from his Palestinian brothers. For those eyes were blue—not an ordinary shade of blue but clear and bright, sometimes like the color of the daytime sky, sometimes like the crystal turquoise of Arctic ice. They were eyes transplanted from some northern race, perhaps Scandinavian, maybe English. Could they be Russian? About their origin, Hassan, Ahmed, and Maan had speculated countless times after they had first been exposed to them. That had happened the first time Said had removed his protective sunglasses in order to put on his scuba diving face mask. Said knew that they had been startled by what they had seen. He expected they would be. It was customary. But he had said nothing to them about it nor did he to anyone, ever. Nor did anyone ever ask.

Said's eyes were his father's. He knew his father well, respected him, loved and admired him. As a child he had spent several summers with him at his home in another seaport far to the north in a land where towering white-capped mountains, a forest of tall evergreen trees, snow, ice, rock and long, sinuous, cliff-edged estuaries leading to the bordering sea were the pattern of the terrain. It was a hard country which produced hardy, tough, intelligent, industrious people, people with blue eyes, turquoise like the brilliant ice off their winter shores.

Notwithstanding the Nordic strain, Said was a Palestinian through and through. His Arab inheritance was nurtured by the experience of being raised in the poverty and deprivation of a Palestinian refugee camp. He was immersed in the life, language, culture and society of his mother and her parents, whose tent they had shared from the time of Said's first memories. He used his mother's surname, Kassem. In that atmosphere his growing mind had been filled with the bitter rantings and invectives of a subjugated and forgotten race, in a camp teeming with unproductive people whose only thoughts were for the injustices heaped upon them, who yearned for freedom, and for the restoration of their lands and their dignity.

Thus Said was a Palestinian Arab. And yet he also carried an unusual genetic strain of which his blue eyes were the manifestation. It was this combination that set him apart and provided for him the special initiatives. He thought as did his Arab fellows but unlike them he did not rant, rave and merely talk. He could act. It was because of his inborn reticence, combined with a compulsive need to perform, to do, to execute, that Said was in that boat being rowed, to nowhere it seemed, his eyes and mind now focused on the huge brown face of Ahmed, bathed in the yellow light of the cupped flame as the big man lit his cigarette. Then the flame was gone and Ahmed's face was a dark blurred background for the glowing tip of the sucked cigarette.

Ahmed will be as a rock, Said reflected. I only wish he didn't smoke those damned cigarettes. Such poison. Even so, like me he is nervous, and there is nothing wrong with that. If we get into difficulty, if there is shooting or something goes wrong underwater, if something happens to me—and of course nothing ever will—it will be Ahmed who will remain calm, will think things out. He is the cool one, perhaps even more than I. I envy him his strength. And Maan, the puppy dog, bright, funny. But he has just a slight tendency to panic if things aren't going right. Like the time when his oxygen flow was cut off. It was a good thing we were only about twenty feet down and I was there with him, watching. I made sure he got it fixed all right and quickly. But the wild thrashing about and the popping eyes behind the mask: he panicked. So I'll have to keep an eye on him. Apart from that he is good. Very good. And I guess being a schoolteacher helps you to learn. In fact he's almost as bright as Hassan.

Said's eyes shifted from the dim countenance of Maan to the back of Hassan's head, visible over the right shoulder of the pumping oarsman. He has to have one of the finest brains I've ever run across, thought Said. He contemplated the tall, thin, athletic body, which he sometimes thought resembled an elongated crab, particularly when Hassan was working underwater, huge flippers on his feet thrusting and propelling him through the sea. If we have any kind of a problem I'm certain Hassan can cope. He doesn't panic. No problem with him. He isn't physically as strong as the rest of us but he shouldn't have any problem handling what we have to do when we get there. He really pressed me last night to tell them the plan—where we're going, what we're going to do when we get there. I could tell he was annoyed when I refused. Do they have a right to know? Hassan thinks they do and I think they do too. But Yassir thinks not. He is the chief and so that's it. We have such a long way to sail; many things could go wrong. If one of them fell into the hands of unfriendly interrogators, the whole operation might be blown. I can't quarrel too much with Arafat's thinking. Not knowing the plan just makes it that much more difficult for my team. Anyway they'll know soon enough.

Said's train of thought was interrupted when the boatman leaned on his oars, turning his head round to the right so he could look forward and past Said. He was searching the mist for the anchored ship. It should not be too much farther. The light was improving rapidly and with it the mist was dissipating.

"There she is, dead ahead!" he announced triumphantly. All eyes in the rowboat squinted as they peered at the vessel waiting to receive them. She was about a hundred yards away, her bow pointing out to sea, meeting the incoming roll of the waves.

Across her stern, just below the deck level, her name was emblazoned in flaked, dirt-streaked white against rust-pocked black paint that had long ago been slapped over her

300-foot-long hull. She was the *Mecca*. The word appeared in both English and Arabic script, as was appropriate for a homeless coaster that traveled the length and breadth of the Mediterranean, putting into small ports and large, serving particularly the fishing villages and shallow harbors denied the larger freighters.

When briefed about his team's travel arrangements, and the supply of its weapons and equipment, Said was informed that arrangements had been made with the Beirut owners of the *Mecca*—all of them dedicated Palestinian Arabs except for a convenient Egyptian partner. The old vessel would pick up a full cargo at Piraeus, the bustling major Greek port near Athens. Her cargo was to be a mix of foodstuffs, bagged grain, six four-wheel-drive motor vehicles, oil exploration equipment, and ten large wood-crated compressors for a natural gas installation being built in Kuwait.

The *Mecca*'s first stop out of Piraeus would be Beirut where she would put ashore two of the motor vehicles, using her own crane to off-load them into lightering craft as she stood at anchor offshore. She would then take on board four large wooden crates which would be stacked for convenience next to the German manufactured compressors.

She would arrive off Beirut at about three in the afternoon of March 8 and complete her unloading. Her captain would go ashore to complete his paper work with the port authorities and check in with the Lloyd's of London agent to confirm his voyage intentions. Then he would get back to his ship as quickly as possible.

In the old days, Captain Rashid loved Beirut. He would go hundreds of miles out of his way to get his anchor into the waters off the craggy shore so he could spend the night at the fabulous gambling casino that sat at cliff's edge overlooking the Mediterranean, just a few miles north of the city. He swore that the Beirut casino presented the most spectacular floor shows in the entire world, with the most beautiful of all European women, long legged and bare breasted, on the stage. Back in those days he would take a shower before he went ashore because, more often than not, he was able to make arrangements for a little after-the-

show association with one of the casino's gorgeous creatures
—he being a regular and recognized customer, well able to
afford the substantial fee.

But those days were long gone. Now Beirut was completely ravaged from within. Its religious factions were still
fighting and killing each other. To be in a place where
shooting was going on was not in the least attractive to
Captain Rashid, a man who placed the highest value on his
own hide. Furthermore, the glamorous casino, like the
center of the city of which it was a satellite, was dead. Its
slot machines and games rooms stood silent, its choice,
high-stepping European beauties long since back in Ham-
burg and Paris and London. It was all very sad.

Thus Captain Rashid was on board his ship rather
than bedded in Beirut when the rowboat carrying the four
black-robed men and their hand luggage pulled alongside
the *Mecca*'s battered hull shortly after 7:20 on the morning
of March 8. Indeed, the captain was on deck waiting for his
passengers. He had climbed out of his large bed shortly
after six. After a leisurely breakfast, he completed his
morning ablutions which concluded with a careful
combing of his short beard, a gray and white one as befitted
a man with sixty-five lustily lived years. In the scratched
mahogany paneled bedroom of the master's cabin, which
ran almost the width of the vessel under its bridge, he had
dressed in his usual gear: a dirty rolled-neck wool pullover;
heavy, navy-blue, unpressed trousers and jacket of the same
material. The last thing on was his scruffy captain's flat
cap, its peak sporting tattered, salt-tarnished gold braid.
The cap sat squarely on a head of thinning white hair
trimmed at collar level. Captain Rashid was pleased with
what he saw in the mirror. He fluffed the underside of his
beard with the back of his hand. Smiling at himself with
gold-mottled teeth, he smoothed back the strands of hair
pushed down and out by the cap in front of his ears.
Satisfied, he stepped out the cabin door to stand at the top
of the gangway on the starboard side of the craft, moments
before Said's boat bumped to a halt against the gangway's
landing platform.

At the railing, Rashid watched the movement of the

boat some ten feet below. He uttered no greeting as he looked down in the morning light into the strange faces peering up at him. He would watch to see who moved first or gave an order. That man would be the leader of the group. No order was given.

The boatman reached out from his seat to grab and hang on to the gangway platform, steadying the small craft against it. Without a word, Said lifted himself up from the seat in the bow and picked up his dunnage bag from the boards at his feet. Effortlessly he flung it over his left shoulder and stepped lightly past the oarsman's horizontal right arm, up and over it and onto the platform. With a nod of appreciation to the boatman, he lifted the hem of his robe to avoid tripping as he took the gangway steps three at a time.

At the deck he was greeted with a welcoming smile by Captain Rashid.

"God be with you."

"And with you, captain. I am . . ."

"Yes, I know. You are Said. You are the leader." It was a statement, not a question. The two men shook hands briefly as the captain went on.

"Welcome to my ship. I hope you and your companions enjoy the trip. You will be with us . . ."

Said nodded. "Yes, we'll be with you for a long time. Too long, I'm afraid."

Out of the corner of his eye he could see the rowboat pulling away and could feel the weight of his three colleagues on the gangway behind him. Stepping aside to allow them to go by, he introduced each man as he stepped onto the deck. The greetings out of the way, the captain walked aft, beckoning the group to follow him.

"I have accommodation for you on the poop in the crew area just up there on the second deck." He pointed upward toward the stern of the craft.

On the deck level on which they were standing there were hatches leading to the cargo hold. To each side of those hatches, both fore and aft of the bridge, ten huge crates with German markings on them were lashed to the deck. Those would be the compressors. Six were between the bridge and the crew's quarters. The other four were between the bridge and the fo'c'sle. Four smaller wooden crates, brought on board the day before, were also lashed on the afterdeck in the space between the compressor cargo and the bridge. This was as planned. Said was pleased to note that, so far, everything was in accordance with the arrangements. As he understood it, Captain Rashid had not been informed of the true contents of the crates boarded at Beirut. According to the bill of lading, they each contained one hundred subsoil very high frequency [VHF] electronic transmitter-receivers. The papers declared that, like the compressors next to them, the electronic devices had been manufactured in and were shipped from West Germany. It also showed that, having been picked up at Naples, they had arrived at Beirut one week earlier in another coaster for transfer to the *Mecca* and furtherance to their final destination, Kuwait. The consignee for the electronic communication devices was the same as for the compressors, the Kuwaiti National Oil Company.

Said was pleased. The positioning of the smaller cases was perfect for a quick transfer of their contents to the compressor boxes, if need be.

Captain Rashid spoke as he continued to walk along the cargo deck toward the steps up to the cabin deck.

"Unfortunately it is not possible to provide you with single cabin accommodation. There are only eight crew members other than myself and the first mate—his cabin is back here also—but this vessel was not built for people or comfort. The best I could do is to put you two to a cabin." He shrugged his shoulders and turned both his hands palms upwards in a gesture of regret.

"Where is the crew?" Ahmed asked. He had not seen a soul on the deck save the captain.

"The deck hands are still sleeping. They had a big night in Beirut—with permission of course, even though I personally avoid the place. They're sleeping it off. That includes the first mate. He has a—how should I put it?—a close friend in Beirut. He has an interest in her business.

You do understand. And whenever he's here,"—the captain's eyebrows arched and his mouth twisted slightly into a leer—"it is essential for the two of them to have a business conference."

Maan could not resist interjecting. "Which of course lasts all night?"

"But of course. And why not? As for Nabil, the first mate, you can be sure he's back on board. He arrived just a few minutes ahead of you. My two engine room men are down below getting ready for our departure."

"What time are you planning on leaving, captain?"

"We will up-anchor in an hour, at 8:30. That will be enough time to get my crew back on their feet."

At the ladder the captain appeared to shed his years. With the agility of an old sailor he hoisted himself up the near-vertical steps to the cabin deck.

Said stood at the bottom of the ladder and assessed the situation for a moment. It was almost impossible for him to raise his gown with one hand, balance his huge dunnage bag on his shoulder with the other, and get up those steps. He guessed there were perhaps ten or twelve. Without a word he eased the bag to the deck, undid the buttons down the front of his gown and pulled the garment away from his shoulders. With a quick movement he lowered it to his feet and stepped out, transforming himself instantly into a military figure. Under his gown he wore a light olive-green, short-sleeved shirt, open at the neck, with buttoned epaulets on each shoulder and trim, tight-fitting, light material trousers of the same color tucked into the tops of tan, calf-length combat boots. His shirt bore no markings or insignia of any kind. Nevertheless, with his headband holding the cloth piece on his head at a slight angle—as his chief always wore his—the trim, heavily muscled Said looked every inch a well-trained soldier, which indeed he was. Said's men followed their leader's example. In a few seconds their gowns were off, revealing that all of them were in the uniform of the Palestinian Liberation Organization.

Captain Rashid's bearded jaw sagged in surprise as he

watched the silent stripping on the deck below. He knew that the men coming on board were PLO soldiers. That had been made perfectly clear to him by the owners' agent in Piraeus. He had no problem accepting their presence because he was a Palestinian Arab himself but, fortunately for him, one who was already free from the shackles of refugee camps and out in the open world. Nevertheless Rashid was apprehensive about these men. Furthermore he detested the kind of reflecting sunglasses Said was wearing because you can't read the man's eyes, you can't see who he is or how he is reacting to what you're saying or doing. But there was no reason to believe that Said would be anything but friendly and cooperative. After all, they were in the same cause, Palestinian Arabs together in support of the PLO and freedom for the Palestinian people and the recapture of their lands. No . . . there was no reason to be alarmed.

Even so an alarm had sounded in Captain Rashid's head. He had often had to handle unusual, sometimes mysterious, passengers whom the owners had forced upon him; or for that matter whom he himself had secretly allowed on board in exchange for an appropriate package of money.

I'm sure I have nothing to fear from them, thought the captain as he watched the four lithe men bound up the ladder. But I must handle them with care. Yes, great care. Those packing cases that came on board yesterday. I wonder . . .

The captain led the group along the open starboard passageway to the door of the first cabin which he shoved open but did not enter. Walking straight on, he similarly opened a second door. Then he turned to face Said. "There you are." Rashid waved his left arm toward the two open doorways inviting entrance. "The best rooms in the house."

Said, his dunnage bag still on his left shoulder, stuck his head in the cabin door and took a quick look around the cramped compartment. He saw two bunks, each with a mattress but no sheets or pillows, a chair, two tables under the porthole, a light over each of the bunks, dirty gray-painted walls. On the floor was a filthy, once-green carpet. A pair of cockroaches scuttled across it. The place stank of a hundred bodies that had lived in that cubicle and the thousands of pungent Arabian cigarettes they had smoked. Said's first thought was that he would throw out the mattresses, hose the place down, disinfect it somehow.

He backed out into the passageway. Looking at the captain, he said in a subdued voice, "They'll do. We'll clean them out. We won't use the mattresses. Do you want to store them or should we just pitch them overboard?"

Rashid smiled and shook his head "No, young man. I make it a practice to keep everything I can . . ." he couldn't resist a slight twist, "even my patience with members of the PLO." He paused to wait for a reaction from Said but he was frustrated. He could not see the eyes behind the mirrored glasses. The face remained expressionless.

"You can take the mattresses and store them in the paint locker aft beside the heads. One of my men will show you where it is later." He made to move by Said and his men, saying, "Now, if you'll excuse me, I must get this ship under way." He started to move back down the companionway past the men, but Said stood firm. He did not step aside to let the ship's master pass. His voice was cold. His words were delivered in a monotone. "We are not on your ship to try your patience, captain. We are here because we have no choice. We have a mission to carry out in the revolutionary cause of the Palestinian people. The only way we can get to our objective is on this stinking, filthy ship. You have been well paid to carry us and that includes the price of your patience. Get your ship under way, captain, and I will see you in your cabin at ten o'clock. There are some things you and I must settle."

The captain was incensed. He drew himself up to his full height, his white beard quivering with rage. "You cannot give me orders on my own ship!"

"I'm not giving you an order, captain. Not yet, anyway. I will be at your cabin at ten o'clock."

Those words spoken, Said turned abruptly and went into the first cabin while his team stood aside, their backs against the railing, to allow the indignant captain to storm past toward the first mate's cabin on the port side of that same deck.

In the next half hour the ship came to life. The angry Rashid rooted Nabil, the still half-inebriated first mate, out of his bunk, shouting at him to get the ill-begotten crew on deck, and get the ship under way. Nabil, the nephew of the Egyptian partner in the *Mecca*, was a scrawny twenty-nine-year-old with bulging eyes and matted, unkempt black hair, a pencil-thin mustache, and huge ears which he was partly able to hide by covering them with greasy strands of hair. The captain was forced to accept him, like it or not. The slovenly young man at first scarcely knew the ship's stem from its stern, but in the past three months he had learned quickly under the shouting, snarling direction of the normally calm Rashid.

Shaken out of his drunken sleep by his irate captain, the first mate stumbled around his cabin dressing, struggling into his long-soiled clothes, trying to pull himself together before he half fell out the door. The brilliant light of the morning sun was a shock to his bloodshot eyes. Steadying himself, he made his way aft to the heads, the communal toilets. Having relieved himself, he staggered along the starboard passageway, making for the ladder that Said and his men had ascended just a short time before. Nabil was startled and puzzled to find four bareheaded, bare-chested, and shoeless strangers in scruffy blue jeans, spraying high-velocity water from the starboard firehose into one cabin, and in another using scrub brushes on the walls, ceiling, and floor.

The first mate's eyes bugged even more than normally when they ran over the size of the enormous man handling the hose. Ahmed, the nozzle in his two hands, stood with feet planted wide apart just outside the second cabin door. His face was split by an ear-to-ear grin of enjoyment as the powerful jet of water screamed from the nozzle, hammering against the layers of dirt on the grime-encrusted walls. Just to make sure his comrades were doing their share of the work, he had let all three of them have an accidental short burst on the backsides as they scrubbed away in the water-soaked first cabin. Roaring with laughter, they cursed and shook their fists at him. Within a dozen paces of this wild scene, the first mate quickly sized up the situation and made the right decision. Back aft he went to scuttle across toward the deck ladder on the port side and down. Suddenly he remembered what the captain had ordered him to do before he went to the bridge. In two minutes he had opened every cabin door, shouting at the besotted deckhands to report to their assigned departure stations immediately.

Half an hour later, Captain Rashid, standing on the starboard flying wing of his bridge, shouted the order to the three weaving deck hands assembled on the fo'c'sle deck, "Up anchor!" Turning to his left he growled at the first mate standing in the center of the bridgehouse by the wheelsman, "Slow ahead to take the slack off the anchor chain."

"Aye, aye, sir." The first mate moved the engine telegraph levers to slow ahead. He knew that in the bowels of the engine room aft, the so-called chief engineer would hear the signal bell and move the throttles of the two diesels to the slow ahead position. Then he would wait for the stop signal to come. This was the usual pattern in lifting anchor. A relatively simple one in a calm sea, much more difficult in heavy weather.

On the fo'c'sle, the three deck hands, still debilitated by the previous night's carousing, gritted their teeth and leaned into the arms of the capstan to begin the rounds that drew up the anchor chain like a gigantic bobbin taking up thread.

As soon as the ship's propeller began to bite into the sea, moving the craft slowly forward, the captain ordered, "Stop engines." Power off, the *Mecca* coasted toward the anchor while the laboring deck hands ran their capstan arms in a wide circle, picking up the chain slack as quickly as they could; they slowed as the ship's bow passed over the anchor and the taut chain picked up its full weight from the rocky bottom a hundred feet below. Fifteen minutes later, after countless back-wrenching revolutions of the capstan, the *Mecca*'s anchor was up and on the fo'c'sle.

As soon as he was satisfied that it was securely on board, the captain ordered, "Full speed ahead!" and the *Mecca* was under way out of Beirut. Her hoary diesels thundered in the hot, fume-filled engine room cavern, while black smoke belched from the spindly stack that pierced the center of the crew's quarters. With the smoke began the reassuring thumping of the drive shaft and the huge single screw that pushed the *Mecca* through the waveless blue waters of the eastern Mediterranean under a cloudless sky.

When Said had decided to scour the cabins, he and his men had made a fast change from their olive-green uniforms into well-worn blue jeans. Ahmed found the firehose and Maan discovered four long-unused scrub brushes and one serviceable mop, complete with bucket and some soap, stored in the corner of the paintless paint locker. Those weapons of cleanliness had been out of favor for years on the *Mecca*. The use of them involved work which any right-minded crew member of a decrepit Middle Eastern coastal freighter would avoid like the worst kind of plague.

By ten o'clock they had finished their cleaning chore. The soiled, foul-smelling mattresses had been shoved into the paint locker. Every inch of the small cubicles had been hosed and scrubbed with brushes and soap, then hosed again. The wooden bunks, tables, and chairs received the same treatment. Cleansed, they were placed along the forward edge of the cabin deck to dry in the lifting sun and light breeze that flowed along the *Mecca*'s decks. Their four dunnage bags had been left on the open passageway, well away from the flow of the cleansing stream of water from the firehose.

Said and his men changed back into their olive-green uniforms, Arab headdresses, and combat boots. Said had decided that he would be properly dressed for his confrontation with the old man. He intended to take a soft-line approach to Rashid, at least until the first part of their mission had been completed. That should be in two weeks and a day, Allah being with them.

Said had given much thought to his upcoming meeting with the captain, in his own way a rather intimidating man. It would not do to appear in scruffy work pants for this first formal discussion when an understanding would have to be reached between the two of them as equals. And equals they would have to be, whether the captain liked it or not, notwithstanding the substantial age difference between them. Said had years ago perceived that the social structure of each country of the world, whatever its politics or race, had as its skeleton a sharply-defined pecking order, pervasive even in its lowest extremities. And that in all business, governmental, diplomatic, academic, and other institutionalized relationships, certain outward manifestations were necessary to mark, sometimes dramatically, sometimes subliminally, the station of the person in that pecking order. Of these manifestations, the manner and style of dress was of the utmost importance. This was particularly so during the opening engagement, the initial sparring round with a stranger with whom business had to be done, negotiations undertaken, and arrangements made on a level of equality.

Equality was especially difficult to achieve when the youthfulness, and therefore apparent inexperience, of a younger person was enhanced by the older person's lack of knowledge of the younger's background and credentials, his authority, or his intelligence. It was in this kind of encounter that Said recognized he was naturally disadvantaged at the outset. That impediment would be increased if he failed to present himself to the captain in his PLO garb. The uniform of the PLO army clothed him with dignity and prestige, made him a recognizable symbol of the power and authority of the PLO army, its chief and the Palestinian people.

Said shaved before he changed into his uniform. There was no sink in the cabins assigned to them so he had to do his shaving in the heads on the cabin deck, aft near the stern. Like the rest of the ship, the place was filthy and stinking. They would have to hose it down too. Barely able to breathe the stench, he shaved as quickly as his heavy black stubble would permit. When he returned to his nearly dry cabin he changed into his uniform. He was ready for Captain Rashid. As he walked to the steps to the cargo deck and the captain's cabin, he gave instructions to his three companions. Following his orders, they dispersed as Said went gingerly down the still-unfamiliar steep steps.

Rashid was standing on the starboard wing of his bridge, watching him. There was no way the captain would be waiting in his cabin at ten o'clock. That would have been an acknowledgment of Said's authority. No, he would watch for him, then leave his bridge to go down to the cabin when Said arrived at its door.

"Keep her steady as she goes." With a perfunctory, unnecessary order to the suffering first mate whose red, bulging eyes could barely focus on the bow of the *Mecca*, thumping steadily along at its cruising speed of twelve knots, Rashid went to his cabin down steps leading directly into it from the bridge.

As he opened the door to allow Said to enter he noted that the young man was freshly shaved and carefully dressed. Motioning him in with a cordial smile, he offered Said a seat at the long, pock-marked table that doubled as a desk and an eating place. Papers, maps, and charts were stacked untidily at each end but the working space in the middle was clear except for a pot of Arabian coffee and two cups brought in by the ship's cook just a few minutes before. The cups were small, the coffee thick and strong. The captain sat in his own chair opposite Said, offered the coffee, which was accepted, then a cigarette, which was declined. When his cigarette was lit, the captain took off his ever-present cap and threw it on the closest pile of papers, picked up his cup and leaned back in his high-backed, threadbare upholstered chair. He was ready.

"Well now, what am I permitted to call you?"

"Said."

"And no military rank?"

Said shook his head.

"But I was informed that you were a lieutenant-colonel in the PLO army." He wanted the young man to believe that he knew quite a bit about him, although, in fact, he knew almost nothing.

"My rank is not important. On this ship I simply want to be known as Said."

The captain shrugged. "Very well. Now, you wanted to talk with me."

"I'm not sure how much you have been told about us."

"Not very much. Simply that the four of you are members of the PLO army and that I'm to take you to Kuwait. Beyond that I know nothing except that having you on board has its risks."

Said did not believe that this was all the captain knew. But he was certain that he had no knowledge of the operation to be carried out and in which the *Mecca*, its captain, and its crew would have a part. "What risks? We are signed on as part of the ship's crew. Our papers are in order. What risks could there be?"

Rashid took a deep drag on his cigarette and a sip of the powerful coffee. "You know as well as I do, Said, that in Egypt—and we have to go through the Suez Canal—in Egypt the PLO is as welcome as a snake in a whore's bed. And in Aden, well, maybe not so much there, but in Kuwait, it's the same as Egypt. They're scared to death of the PLO. After all, most of the population is Palestinian, brought in to do the work. To the Kuwaiti, you PLO people, particularly the revolutionary wing, *you* people are unwanted enemies of the state . . . even though they support the right of all Palestinians to have their own land. So I can tell you, as far as I'm concerned, having you on board involves risks. The last thing I want is to have my ship impounded or get into any kind of trouble with the port authorities. As it is, I'm well received wherever this ship goes."

"I assure you the last thing I want to do is cause any trouble for you. We want to get to Kuwait just as badly as you want to avoid any trouble. So I'm here to tell you, captain, that my group and I are prepared to cooperate with you in every way. We're supposed to be part of the crew."

Rashid leaned forward, his face and eyes showing the hardness of his voice. "Then you'd better start by understanding that I am the captain of this ship, not you; that you and your people are signed on as deck hands and you'd better start behaving like deck hands. I told my crew you are deck hands. And what do you do as soon as you get on board? You strip down to your uniforms for all the world to see. Fortunately I was the only one on deck at the time, but here you are again. You just let my whole crew see you in this regalia. Maybe they won't know what the uniform is, but I can tell you, Said, it won't be long before they start asking questions."

No reaction from Said.

"I don't want to see those uniforms again. Before you leave this cabin I'll have one of your men bring your work clothes so you can change." The captain did not wait for Said's agreement. "What about weapons, guns, knives? I assume you've got those things in your bags?"

Said shifted in his chair to pick up the coffee pot. He would not wait for the captain to pour for him. Rashid had said all that Said had expected he would. Now it was time to respond.

"You worry unduly about uniforms, captain. So far as I'm concerned it could not matter less who sees us in our uniforms. There are how many people on this ship other than yourself? Nine?"

Rashid nodded his agreement.

"I would expect that out of that nine, you personally would trust not one. Correct?"

The captain snorted. "Correct."

Said hesitated. "The point is this, captain: you don't trust your crew. I certainly don't trust them. I don't even know them. Furthermore I have no reason to trust you, either. I'm quite sure that if you thought it was to your advantage you would sell us to the highest bidder."

The captain made as if to protest but Said waved him down. "Don't be insulted. Please. In my profession, if I am to survive, I can trust no one except my own people. You ask about guns, weapons. Sure we have them. You wouldn't expect us to come aboard your vessel unarmed. As a matter of fact, at this very moment one of my men is on your bridge and another is standing beside the cabin door." His right hand lifted to point to the entrance to the captain's cabin through which he had walked just a few minutes before, "and the third man is on the cabin deck where he can see any of your crew members moving to or from that area. My people are in uniform, captain, whether you like it or not. Furthermore, they're armed to the teeth. Each man has an automatic weapon that he can fire with great skill. And each man has a pistol that he can use with equal skill. They also all carry knives, which they can throw into your heart from thirty feet."

Captain Rashid's face was white with shock. His vein-laced hands gripped the arms of his chair. His lips blurted out the word "Hijack!"

Said's head shook once again. "No, no, captain, I'm not hijacking your ship. Not at all. What I'm doing—how should I put it?—is for security purposes and to ensure the ultimate success of our operation. In fact, for the safety of your own crew, we're going to impose military—perhaps you would call it naval—discipline." He made a conciliatory gesture with the hint of a smile. "But not over you."

Rashid's voice was filled with sarcasm. "That's extremely decent of you."

"This is your ship, captain. You know how to run it, navigate it, handle it . . ."

"And I know how to handle my crew."

"With kid gloves. Obviously you have about as much control over them as an old dog over a pack of thirsty camels. Letting them carouse all night in Beirut . . . And the condition of this ship. It's filthy. And it's badly maintained."

The PLO leader nudged his mirror sunglasses, pushing them back on the ridge of his nose. For one second, Rashid thought he was going to take them off. Finally he would be able to see those hidden eyes. Said had no such intention. He went on: "From now on my men and I are in charge of this ship. I want that understood clearly. On the other hand, so long as I know you are sailing it competently and in accordance with your instructions from the owners, I will not interfere with its operation. I want life on the ship to go on normally. But I want the crew to understand without a doubt that they are responsible to both of us. Any orders I give them will have to do with how they handle themselves when we're in a port and when we get to Kuwait. The ship will load and unload its cargo. You will do your business and we will sail as quickly as possible. As soon as you and I are finished here I will confiscate all the weapons you and your crew have. And when that's done I want everybody on the afterdeck. Everybody. That includes the people in the engine room. I want to talk to them and tell them what's going on."

As Said was speaking the wily old captain was assessing his own situation and that of his ship. He could not have cared less about the crew. To a man, they were a soulless lot, the dregs of Mediterranean ports. They had no loyalty to him nor he to them. The only thing that mattered was that he and his ship had to survive. The *Mecca* was his life. He could not quarrel with the young Palestinian's description of it. Maybe Said and his people could force some work out of the lazy crew members. While he was running those thoughts through his mind he was paying close attention to everything Said was saying.

"I want to stress this, captain. I wish in no way to interfere with the operation of your ship. On the other hand, there may be some way I can help you. That's up to you. But our objective is far more important than this putrid ship or its crew."

"Including me?"

"Yes, including you and, for that matter, including me."

The old man stubbed out his cigarette. "If you're looking for my cooperation you're certainly going about it the wrong way." He did not wait for a response from Said. "What about those packing cases?"

"What do you mean?" Said sounded puzzled.

"They came on board last evening. They're sitting on

the deck. You saw them. The smaller ones. There are four. I'm sure you saw them."

"What does the bill of lading say? You've got the papers. How should I know?"

The captain leaned forward and to his right to leaf through the pile of papers on the table. He pulled one out and placed it down in front of him. He read aloud, "Cargo—four packing cases each containing fifty subsoil electronic transmitter-receivers. The consignor is a company in Germany. I can't pronounce the name. The consignee is the Kuwait National Oil Company.

Said added, "The same consignee as the big crates on the deck. The compressors."

"How did you know that?" He was startled.

The Palestinian smiled. "It is printed on the side of the crates—and I happen to be fluent in German."

The document was thrown back on the pile from which it had come. The captain persisted, "Do you mean to tell me you don't know what's in those cases?"

Said ignored the note of incredulity. "Look, if you really want to find out what's in them why don't you open them up and take a look."

That produced a reaction he had not expected.

"Perhaps I don't want to know after all."

"Why not?"

The captain pulled out another cigarette and lit it quickly, blowing a cloud toward the ceiling of the cabin. "You can't or won't tell me. Either way I will leave it at that. As to opening them up to take a look—really I can't do that."

"Why not?"

"Well, the customs people, particularly at Port Said, have eyes like hawks. If goods are traveling in bond as these are,"—his right hand waved vaguely at the bill of lading back on the pile—"and if there is any evidence that the crate has been opened, they will be sure to catch it. Then the trouble begins. They will insist on opening it themselves to make sure that the contents do in fact match the manifest. And if they were to find what I think they might find, then I am in very serious difficulty, my friend. My ship can be impounded, I can be fined, even imprisoned—again if those crates contain what I think they might contain."

He shrugged, puffed on the cigarette, and continued to talk. "On the other hand, if those crates are untouched, and if for whatever reason the customs people decide to open them for inspection, then I have a complete defense. I know only what the bill of lading, the manifest, tells me." He butted his cigarette in a small tin ashtray. "So I think not, Said, I think not. You don't want to tell me what's in those crates. Perhaps you don't know. That's fine. But open them? Never. You were asking about my cooperation. Before I answer, let me ask you a question. It's a question I ask often. What's in it for me? You do understand, young man?"

Between the two Palestinian Arabs, whose ancestors from time immemorial had been traders, the meaning of the question was perfectly clear. Said had anticipated it. He would indeed make it worth Captain Rashid's while to cooperate. The worth was in cash, half of which Said produced then and there. The remainder would be handed to the captain when the *Mecca* next anchored off Beirut, whenever that might be.

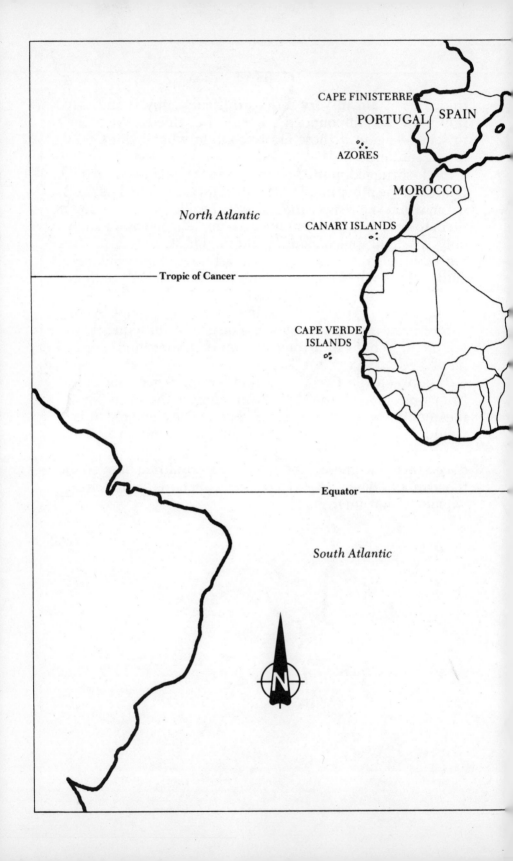

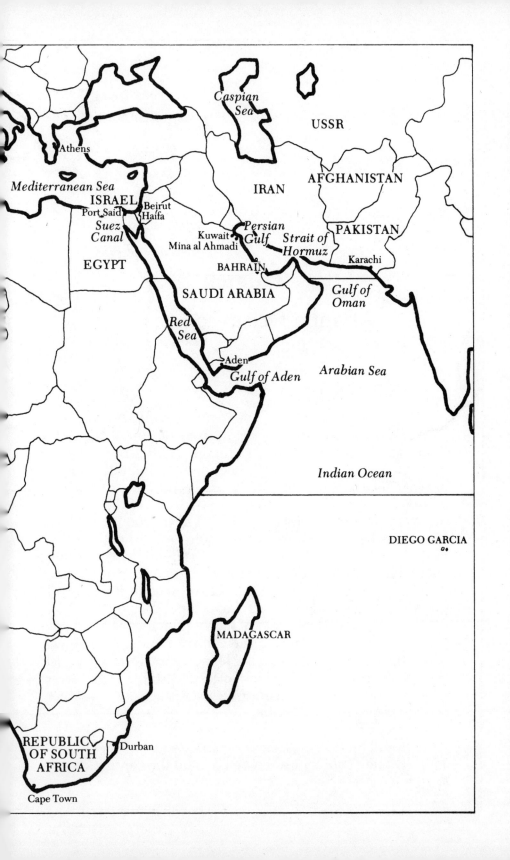

2

9 March

Atlantic Ocean, off Spain

"Up search periscope," the captain called.

When the eye pieces were in front of him at the right level, he said, "Stop." The periscope shaft halted. Commander Marcus Leach, RN, snapped the handles down, put his face to the eye pieces, and, slowly turning the periscope, searched across the rolling surface of the Atlantic eastward in the evening darkness for the familiar Cape Finisterre light. Some day he would go to Spain to see Finisterre, to go up the steep circular steps to the top of that ancient lighthouse. He would touch the tall cone of circling glass that blasted out its coded light across countless miles of the Atlantic. Outside, the sea was whipped up by winds of fifteen knots laced by squalls of heavy rain under low, black scudding clouds. But inside the control room of the Royal Navy fleet submarine, the nuclear-powered attack vessel H.M.S. *Splendid*, riding rock-solid and stable, her tower fifty feet below the churning water surface, the weather above was merely a statistic.

"Stand by bearings."

"Stand by bearings, sir." The messenger of the watch, Able Seaman Tom Smith, moved behind the captain, ready to read off the bearing from the periscope compass ring on the shaft above Leach's hatless head.

Leach kept turning the periscope slowly, intently searching through the dark night, concentrating on the area due east to the port of *Splendid*. She was cruising southbound out of her home base of Faslane in the Firth of Clyde. According to the navigating officer, they were abeam the Finisterre light and 26.2 miles due west of it. There was no real need to use the periscope to check on the Finisterre light, because with the submarine's vast array of computers and electronic gear and her inertial navigation system—the same device that guided jet aircraft from continent to continent with perfect precision—the navigating officer, Pilot as he was traditionally called, knew the exact location of his ship.

It had been six months since the most senior of the fleet submarine captains had been to sea, except for the working up trials of *Splendid*, so Leach was keen to get hands on his above-surface eye, the only visual contact with the upper world that the ship would have for the eight weeks—perhaps longer—she would remain submerged.

His orders were to take *Splendid* south in the Atlantic past the Tropic of Cancer, the self-imposed southern boundary of the North Atlantic Treaty Organization's jurisdiction, under the sea lanes of the huge supertankers running between the Persian Gulf and Western Europe past Cape Town and the Cape of Good Hope at the southern tip of Africa. Then north up the Indian Ocean to the east of the Island of Madagascar, north beyond the Seychelles into the Arabian Sea to join the British Second Flotilla cruising those waters in a joint show of strength with the American Fifth Fleet. *Splendid* would have to sail for 12,000 miles just to get to her station. It would take her sixteen days.

A flicker of light in the distant darkness. Leach steadied the periscope "Bearing is . . ."

"Zero-eight-nine, sir," Smith read off the compass ring.

"Just where you said it would be, Pilot."

The navigating officer was pleased. "Yes, sir."

Leach stepped back from the eye piece and snapped the handles up, ordering, "Down search." The device began to move silently down into its well. "Keep two hundred feet." The planesman responded as he pushed forward on the ship's control wheel, easing it toward the ordered depth.

Leach stood for a moment looking around his control room, bathed in its dull red night lights. The navigation officer was busy at his chart table. Peter Pritchard, the torpedo and sonar officer and officer of the watch, was perched in his chair behind the two-man team steering the submarine with control wheels that looked as if they had been taken from an aircraft. When the wheel was pushed forward or pulled back, it would cause the hydroplanes at the stern and those forward near the nose to move, pitching the vessel down or up. A roll of the wheel would cause the submarine to bank into a turn. In front of the two control positions the "blind flying panel" with its instruments and electronic inertial attitude displays was being carefully watched. The radar watchkeeper was in his place. Everything appeared to be in order and functioning smoothly.

A few steps took the captain into the small sonar room which opened off the control room. At the far end of the room sat the sonar's huge electronic screen, on which white blips of light showed the reflections of the sounds produced in the waters for several miles around the submarine, creating patterns that provided an image not unlike a map. At the center of the screen was a bright dot, *Splendid*'s position as it moved down the Spanish coast at a comfortable rate of thirty knots.

As the captain poked his head in the door, he nodded to his communications officer, Lieutenant Peter Pritchard, but asked his question of the sonar watchkeeper, Petty Officer Pratt: "Any joy?"

"Yes, sir. I was just going to report. You can see it on the edge of the screen."

Yes, there it was, a blip at the top right-hand edge of the screen.

"Green four – zero, range 11,000 yards. Sound signature

on the computer says she's a single-screw tanker, a super-tanker judging by the cavitation noise." A computer check had been made against the noise created by the engines of the craft and the sound caused by drops of water falling off its screw—the cavitation noise. While *Splendid*'s computer did not contain the sound signatures of the world's mercantile fleet, it had in its brain every class of warship in every navy. Of these, the most important were accurate readings on all classes of vessels in the American, Soviet, and British fleets.

"I had a look at the NATO log this afternoon," the captain told the sonar watchkeeper. "The Soviets have an unusual number of submarines in the Atlantic at this time. It's put the wind up for the people at NATO headquarters. But it's the usual Russian pattern when there's a world crisis on like the one at the moment. It seems there are over a hundred bandits at sea out of the Kola Peninsula and the Baltic. They're of all classes—everything they have, the SSBNs to the SSs."

In naval jargon the SSBNs were nuclear-powered submarines of the ballistic missile class, while the SSs were patrol submarines, diesel powered. The NATO log had also confirmed that the operational strength of the Red Navy's submarine fleet was an astounding 426, with ten abuilding. The log contained a series of signals that set out the Admiralty's estimates of the location and numbers of the Soviet warships around the world. In the area of interest to Leach, the Atlantic and the Indian Oceans, over two hundred ships were listed, including two aircraft carriers, the *Kiev* and the *Minsk*. There were two helicopter cruisers, the *Moskva* and the *Leningrad*. A substantial number of these ships were deployed in the Arabian Sea, where *Splendid* had been ordered to join the small British flotilla made up of the helicopter cruiser H. M. S. *Tiger*; the Rothesay class, antisubmarine frigate H. M. S. *Rhyl*; and their supporting provisioning vessels.

The NATO log cursorily assessed the strategic military situation as it was developing in the Middle East. The Soviets were continuing to build up their ground forces in

Afghanistan and had been observed by satellite to be massing at least ten divisions of troops, tanks, artillery and their supporting tactical air squadrons at several marshalling points along the mountainous, thousand-mile northern border of Iran, both to the west and east of the Caspian Sea.

The Soviets had planned to conduct their five-yearly, Moscow coordinated and controlled naval and air exercise, code-named OKEAN, commencing April 1. It would last for one month, with attack and defense naval forces deployed in the Atlantic, Indian, and Pacific Oceans. The plans for OKEAN had long been in preparation.

The captain explained none of those factors to the sonar watchkeeper. He was simply alerting him. "You'll have to keep a sharp watch, unusually sharp. Not only are the Russian submarines out in force, the Americans have almost every one of their Atlantic attack submarines, everything that's serviceable, at sea."

"How many do you estimate that to be, sir?"

"In the Atlantic, it has to be fifty-five."

The young petty officer's head had moved incredulously from side to side as he muttered, "Christ!"

Turning his head toward Pritchard, who was standing just in front of the sonar screen and watching it, but listening to the conversation, the captain said, "So, Peter, I want you to have all your watchkeepers on alert. I don't want any goddamn Russian, or any American for that matter, up our ass on the sneak!"

3

9 March   Evening
Mediterranean Sea, off Haifa

Said stood by the railing outside the galley where he and his men had just finished their first evening meal on board the *Mecca*. He was watching the far distant shore to the east on the horizon edge, the land where he and all Palestinian Arabs yearned to be, their land, now called Israel. Was that Haifa? He could barely see, in the far distance, the hills and tall buildings of the city of his birth, the place to which he was dedicated to return. His mind could picture the house of his grandparents where he had been born, the house that had been stolen from them by the Israelis. He had only seen photographs of it, but one day the Palestinian Liberation army would win the battle, and Haifa would again be theirs.

As he was contemplating, picking scraps of fish from between his brilliant white teeth, his eyes caught sight of a slash of white foam made by a fast-moving boat cutting through the calm, darkening sea. The sun was still above the cloudless horizon behind him in the west. Squinting to focus, assessing what he was seeing, Said quickly confirmed his first suspicion. Shouting to his team, who were chatting just a few feet aft of him, Ahmed having his after-dinner cigarette, Said pointed toward the oncoming craft.

"It's an Israeli patrol boat. Get to your stations!" The sharp bow of the patrol ship was clearly visible. She was about three miles off, closing rapidly, doing about twenty-five knots. As he sprinted toward the bridge to warn the captain, Said sized up the approaching warship. About eighty feet long, with two torpedo tubes plus two missile launchers. He could not yet see a gun. Most likely she carried two twenty-millimeter cannons, a brace of .5-inch machine guns and some depth charges. The speeding craft was still too far away for him to see any of the crew on deck, or behind the glass of the wheelhouse or the canvas of the flying bridge. Said took the steps to the *Mecca*'s bridge two at a time. There he found the captain, binoculars in his hands, calmly watching the fast-approaching Israeli gunboat.

Rashid saw Said out of the corner of his eye. Without a word, the captain lifted the powerful binoculars over his head, and handed them to Said, saying, "This often happens."

Momentarily turning his back to Rashid, Said slipped off his sunglasses and put the binoculars to his eyes. "But why? We're in international waters."

"Not as far as the Israelis are concerned. They think they own this part of the Mediterranean and to hell with boundary lines. They're afraid of commando attacks from you people."

The point was acknowledged with a curt nod by Said.

"And they will confiscate any armaments, weapons, shells, rockets, vehicles being shipped to a destination country that they think might be capable of using the stuff against them."

"That's piracy," Said objected.

"Not according to Israel's rules. They're at war with the entire Arab world—except Egypt. And Allah only knows how long that peace will last. In the rules of war, you're entitled to capture, seize—whatever you want to call it—the enemy's supplies."

The Israeli warship was less than a mile away and still closing rapidly. The captain thought of calling Nabil to the bridge. The Egyptian was off watch and sleeping. Rashid decided to leave him be.

Through the powerful glasses, Said could see every detail of the low-lying, lethal warship: the twin 17.7-inch torpedo tubes straddling the wheelhouse; the gray bulk of the surface-to-surface rocket launcher on the foredeck near the bow. Just ahead of the glinting glass of the wheelhouse, twin twenty-millimeter cannons, manned by two white-uniformed sailors, were pointed directly at the *Mecca*'s bridge. He still could not see inside the glass-enclosed wheelhouse, but above it and behind the shield of canvas on the flying bridge, he could see half a dozen white-capped men. The one with binoculars trained back on him had gold braid on the peak of his hat. As Said watched, two crew members moved smartly to their stations next to the torpedo tubes on each side of the vessel. She was at full attack readiness.

His head turned away so that his unprotected eyes could not be seen, Said handed the binoculars back to the captain and put his sunglasses back on.

Rashid slipped the strap around his neck but did not use the glasses. His eyes were riveted on the sleek, gray ship as she corrected her converging heading to run parallel to the *Mecca*, abreast of her a hundred yards to port. The thundering roar of the warship's engines, clearly audible on the larger ship, suddenly abated. Her speed dropped to match the ten-knot progress of the weatherbeaten, ancient freighter.

Without looking at Said, the captain told him, "I think you should get off the bridge. They'll be suspicious, wondering what you're doing up here. At least you're not wearing those damn uniforms. Where are your men?"

"One is up near the bow. One is just under the bridge, and one is at the stern. Like all good deck hands, they're leaning on the railing watching what's going on."

"They're not armed?"

"Of course not."

"What have you done with your weapons, the stuff you brought on board?"

"We've hidden them under the junk in the paint locker."

The captain was satisfied. He had last taken a look in the paint locker about six weeks before and was appalled by what was piled in that small cubicle—mops, brushes, cans of paint, rope, buckets, heavy sea gear, and soiled rags. It was a mess. He had left it that way. If the PLO people stashed their weapons in there, an Israeli search party would never find them.

But Said lied. After he had had his meeting with the captain, Said and his team talked to the crew members one at a time. All four of them clustered around each intimidated sailor while Said explained that they were members of the PLO army; that they were on a special mission; that they would be serving as deck hands with the other members of the crew; that they didn't want any trouble; that they would take care of anybody who gave them trouble or tipped off port authorities that they were on board. A direct threat to each man was essential. It was the only code those riffraff sailors would understand. In his own way, each told Said not to worry about him.

That job done, the PLO men had changed from their uniforms into faded blue denim working clothes and set about making a thorough inspection of the ship from one grime-covered, stinking end of it to the other. Said wanted to find out whether, in the fo'c'sle or under the cabin level aft, there was a compartment that they could clean out and use as a secure workshop for the last two days of the voyage when the final preparations for their operation had to be made. Said had not asked the captain for permission to take a look around his ship, or whether there was a suitable space available. He intended to find out himself.

There was no space in the fo'c'sle. The entire cargo area had been filled with some sort of bagged commodity. But in the engineer's compartment Maan had discovered a spacious area where the engineer kept his tools, machinery, and other equipment necessary to repair and maintain the humping, ancient diesel engines that drove the *Mecca*. The compartment was just forward of the engine room on the lower deck level, where the noise from the laboring engines was only slightly dampened by a heavy separating bulkhead. A door led to the engine room. A second door opened onto the passageway and steps led up to the cabin deck level. The ten- by twenty-foot space had two portholes almost at ceiling level. Left open, those two windows in the wall of the ship vented part of the overpowering heat and fumes from the *Mecca*'s engine room. Said was well pleased with Maan's find. He would make a deal with the chief engineer at the right time.

During their inspection, they had also been looking for places on the upper deck where they could hide their automatic weapons, but at the same time get at them easily. They had to have three such locations. Each would become a fighting station in the event of an emergency. Ahmed would be aft, Maan amidship on the port side, and Hassan in the fo'c'sle. With their hidden automatic weapons a step away, within seconds the three men could be armed and able to sweep the ship's deck with a withering crossfire. They could take on an attacking boarding party or any craft within reasonable range. In the bow, Hassan's weapon was on the deck covered by a heavy coil of rope. Amidships on the port side, the corner of the canvas covering the aft cargo hold concealed Maan's gun. The starboard lifeboat on the cabin deck received Ahmed's automatic weapon under its protective tarpaulin. Said's instructions were that if the threat came from the port side, then Ahmed would move his gun to the port lifeboat. If it came from the starboard, Maan would move with his weapon across to that side.

As the Israeli gunboat cut its speed to run parallel to the *Mecca*, Said shoved his automatic pistol between his flat stomach and his trouser belt under the tails of his untucked blue denim shirt. He stood at the port rail with Maan. Ahmed was aft by the port lifeboat. Hassan was on the fo'c'sle. At their assigned stations, all four PLO soldiers looked for all the world like simple, slovenly, lazy, harmless Arab deck hands.

The gold braid on the peak of his white cap sparkling

in the evening sun, the Israeli captain moved to the starboard side of his bridge. Lifting a bullhorn to his mouth, he shouted up to the bridge of the plodding, old rust bucket, speaking in English, "Where are you bound, *Mecca*?"

Having been through this routine before, Rashid was ready with his own bullhorn. "Port Said and Kuwait."

"What do you have in those crates?"

"The big ones have natural gas compressors, and the smaller ones have transmitters—some kind of electronic devices."

Rashid's explanation did not satisfy the Israeli captain, who could be seen in discussion with one of the other men on his flying bridge. The bullhorn went up to his face again. His words were distinct. They were clearly understood by Said and Hassan, the only two of the PLO team who could understand English. The amplified words put an extra charge of adrenalin through Said's body.

"Heave to, *Mecca*! Stand by to receive a boarding party!"

From the port wing of his bridge, Rashid responded, "I'll lower the gangway on the starboard side. You can come alongside there." Turning to Nabil, he quietly ordered, "Full stop." The Egyptian promptly moved the telegraph lever back to the stop position. The unexpected ringing of the order bells startled the chief engineer in the bowels of the engine room. He immediately complied, then called the bridge on the ship's loudspeaker system to ask what was going on. Nabil's brief explanation was sufficient.

The warship's captain declined the offer to come alongside. To put his ship next to an unknown ship would be courting disaster. He would be vulnerable, totally open to attack from the deck above.

Even so, the old decrepit coastal freighter looked harmless enough. For a moment, the Israeli pondered the situation. He wanted to get back to Haifa as quickly as possible. He had a date with a woman he had been eyeing for weeks, Rachel, a gorgeous creature, the secretary of the harbormaster at Haifa. The captain's wife was in Tel Aviv visiting her parents. He was to meet Rachel at eight at her apartment for a drink and then they would go to dinner. With luck they would go back to her apartment. He was sure he would score that night. She had given him such a come-on during his last visit to the harbormaster's office. He looked at his watch: 6:35. If he got this boarding over with quickly, he could be back in Haifa just in time to be at Rachel's at eight. Maybe five or ten minutes late. But if he put his boarding party on board the *Mecca* in his boat's small dinghy, he would be the better part of an hour late, and she might not wait. The decision was made. He would throw caution to the winds and save time. He would take his vessel alongside and do the boarding himself. He could feel Rachel's large, firm young breasts under his hands.

Over his left shoulder, the Israeli captain ordered his helmsman, "Hard aport and half power. Take her around the freighter's stern to the starboard side. We'll see what his gangway looks like when we get there." As his twin diesels roared to half power, he turned back to the *Mecca* and raised the bullhorn: "Lower your gangway, *Mecca*. We will come alongside. Have your papers ready for inspection!"

Said turned to Maan standing to his left. "Walk slowly with me back to our cabin and don't ask any questions. Just do as I tell you." A once-in-a-lifetime opportunity was being handed to Said. He had to seize it.

The Israeli patrol boat turned abruptly to the left, swinging in a tight, white-foamed arc behind the *Mecca*, still moving slowly. At quarter power, the chine of her bow did not lift out of the water.

Said judged it would take the gunboat about four minutes to get to the landing platform of the *Mecca's* lowered gangway. Maan, who could not understand what was being said by the Israeli captain, was startled by Said's unexpected order, but immediately complied. The two of them ambled aft up the steps to the cabin deck, Said leading. The patrol boat had rounded the stern of the *Mecca* and passed out of their line of sight when they reached the cabin deck. With Maan following, Said raced down the port passageway, swinging left into the cross-ship corridor where the crowded paint locker was located. When he reached its door, Said hauled it open.

"Scuba gear and make it fast," he shouted to Maan.

Maan flicked on the weak light and fiercely shoved aside the mix of brooms, buckets, cans, and brushes. In a few seconds he had his hands on two flippers, an oxygen bottle with its shoulder and belly straps and its tubes to mouthpiece and face mask in place. He thrust the gear out through the door to Said, who spoke quickly.

"I'll get this on while you find the limpet." Again, Maan routed under the pile of junk. In short order his sensitive hands felt the smooth surface of the white, molded plastic package. It contained a radio-operated, explosive-packed limpet mine. Said had intended to use it as a practice device to maintain their standard of training during this long three-week voyage to their first destination.

Said pulled off his shirt and shoved his mirror sunglasses into his trouser pocket. By the time Maan had pulled the mine out from under the junk and turned to step outside the door, Said had strapped the oxygen bottle on his back and pulled on his face mask. His penetrating, cold blue eyes leaped through the glass of his face mask as he barked at Maan. "Take it out of the packing case and set it to frequency 3."

Bending over, Maan set the white package on the deck. It was about a foot square and nine inches deep. Gingerly, he lifted off the top section of the plastic container. Lodged in the protection of the white styrofoam, like an oyster snug in a safe, sandy seabed, sat a shiny, gray, thick, circular metal device. In its center was a dial with the numbers 1 through 10 stamped on its face like those on a combination lock. Maan's nimble fingers turned the dial setting until the 3 lay against the red line. Before he lifted the limpet device out of its protective package, he looked up at Said. "What about arming it?"

Said shook his head. "I'll do it when I'm in the water."

Closing the door on the paint locker, the two men dashed down the corridor to the port side of the ship. At the railing they glanced quickly around; then Said pulled on his flippers and swung his legs over the side, planting his feet on the outside edge of the deck. Hanging on to the railing with his left hand, he activated his oxygen bottle with his right. Then he shoved the mouthpiece between his teeth and nodded to Maan, who carefully handed him the deadly magnetic mine. Clutching it to his breast with all the strength of his powerful arms, Said jumped. Thirty feet below the deck he hit the surface cleanly. The impact from that height tore his mouthpiece away, but as soon as the cushioning water stopped his downward descent, he stuffed it back into his mouth. The buoyant salt water lessened the weight of the mine but still he clutched it tightly. Orienting himself, he looked up through the pale blue water. The bottom side of the stern of the old *Mecca*, its propeller stopped, sat in the water like a barnacle-covered black whale. Kicking his flippered feet, Said swam to the rounded edge of the freighter's hull, just forward of the propeller shaft, then down under the sharp edge of the keel to the ship's starboard side. There above him, nestled against the ponderous bulk of the *Mecca*, sat the Israeli patrol boat, its shiny twin propellers turning ever so slowly. Said could hear its engines quietly rumbling at idle and the popping of the exhaust from the pipes at the stern of the powerful craft.

His target area was the stern plate near the surface. It would have to be metal for the limpet mine's magnetic clamp mechanism to hold fast to the hull. The stern plate was ideal because it was out of the main pull of the flow of the sea water. On the underside of a hull, moving at twenty-five to thirty miles an hour, the force of the surging water might rip the explosive device away from the ship's surface, even though the mine was contoured to lie flush like a leech against the body of a boat.

To avoid detection by one of the warship's crew who might see the bubbles from his oxygen system, Said swam quickly out from under the hull of the freighter to a position about ten feet directly under the idling propellers of the Israeli vessel. There his bubbles would mix with the turbulence caused by the propellers and the burbling exhaust pipes. At that point, he paused to assess the situation before beginning his contact maneuver.

On the *Mecca*'s cargo deck, thirty feet above him, the

youthful Israeli patrol boat captain, a lieutenant-commander by rank, stood beside one of the large packing cases containing, as its manifest papers stated, a natural gas compressor. Behind him as he faced aft were two of his seamen, dressed like their captain in spotless white from their caps to their shoes. Each carried a stubby automatic weapon at the ready, its safety catch off. Standing at the top of the gangway, one of the strapping young Israeli sailors stood scanning the deck of the forward part of the ship, watching for any suspicious or hostile movement.

On the bridge above him, he could see a gaunt Arab face under an officer's cap, peering down but making no move. On the fo'c'sle, sitting on the capstan, was a deck hand—an Arab, judging by his unkempt clothing and his *khafia* headdress. There was no one else to be seen. The other Israeli soldier covered his captain, the *Mecca*'s cargo, and cabin deck aft. At that level, he could see a huge, dirty-looking—weren't they all?—Arab deck hand casually leaning against the starboard lifeboat puffing on a cigarette. He looked harmless enough. Between the bridge and the smaller crates immediately aft of it, he could see another Arab sailor squatting on the deck. His back was to the railing, arms folded, apparently trying to keep out of the way while watching what was going on.

In his hand, the Israeli captain held the sheaf of bills of lading that Rashid handed to him as soon as he stepped on board. The top bills covered the natural gas compressors consigned to Kuwait. With an expert eye, the Israeli checked the information on the document against the markings stenciled on the crate. He was satisfied that they tallied. He then flipped through the papers to the bills for the smaller crates. Again the information stenciled on them was satisfactory. Nevertheless, it was his responsibility to open one of the crates to confirm the contents by visual inspection. Rashid's experienced eyes watched the patrol boat captain carefully. He knew that a look-inside examination was part of the routine. What would be found in the smaller crates, the *Mecca*'s captain did not know. But he expected the worst.

As the Israeli moved toward the closest small crate on the starboard side, Ahmed at his vantage point aft flicked his cigarette overboard. He moved casually to the lifeboat where his automatic gun was stowed. He knew he could have it in his hand within seconds. In the fo'c'sle, Hassan slipped off the capstan to sit on the large coil of rope on the deck. He was ready to reach for the gun concealed under it, close to his right hand. Amidships Maan remained where he was. The activity on the far side of the vessel was out of his line of vision. Any move that he might make could cause suspicion. So he just sat, his eyes on Hassan.

The patrol boat captain, still checking the markings on the small crate, turned to Rashid. "A crowbar, captain."

Without a word, Rashid walked past the Israeli and his two guards toward the forward side of the bridge, where crowbars and other deck handling tools were stowed. As he did so, the gunboat officer's left wrist twisted so that he could see his watch.

"Never mind, I haven't got enough time." Rachel was at the front of his mind. If he opened this crate he would lose another ten minutes, and he was going to be late enough as it was. Anyway, the bills of lading and the information on the crates cross-checked. The motor vehicles lashed down on the deck were obviously nonmilitary.

Relieved, Rashid stopped and turned back to face the Israeli, who asked, "What's below in the holds?"

"Bagged stuff, grain and cement. You have the manifests. If you'd like to take a look . . ?"

The Israeli shook his head. It was clear that he wanted to get off the *Mecca* and get going. "No, that won't be necessary." He thrust the wad of papers into Rashid's hands, declaring, "You are cleared to go, captain."

He threw Rashid a hasty salute, which the startled Rashid returned. The Israeli trio scrambled down the gangway into their waiting craft, its engines still rumbling at the idle. Climbing the ladder to his bridge, the Israeli captain shouted his orders to cast off. Immediately the lines were clear, the warship's engines thundered to full power, driving the craft rapidly away from the *Mecca*, a billowing rooster-tail plume of white foam and spray in its trail. Its sharp bow lifted out of the water, its hull planing along the smooth Mediterranean surface at high speed toward Haifa and the waiting arms and—the expectant Israeli captain hoped—the waiting breasts and open thighs of Rachel.

As soon as the Israelis left the deck of the *Mecca*, Maan seized the length of rope he had brought from the paint locker when he returned to his station after Said had leaped into the sea. He tied one end of it securely to the railing and threw the other over the side into the water. Peering down over the railing, he was relieved to see Said's masked head surface just a few yards aft. Spitting out his mouthpiece, his face split in a wide grin of triumph, Said lifted both arms out of the water, his fists clenched, the thumb of each pointing rigidly up. He had done it!

Swimming easily to the rope, Said quickly hand-hauled himself up to the level of the deck where Ahmed, flanked by Maan and Hassan, reached over the railing to lift him by the armpits. They shouted with joy as the big man lifted their leader as lightly as a small child and set him gently on the deck. There was much back-slapping, laughing, and hooting as Said, still too excited himself to think of slipping off the oxygen bottle, let alone getting out of the flippers and face mask, explained every last detail of what he had done. The limpet mine, fully armed, was securely attached to the Israeli patrol boat's stern plate just above the rudder, about two feet below the water line. The mine's telescopic radio antenna was fully extended, waiting only for the detonation signal.

Caught up in the euphoria of the moment, none of them noticed the *Mecca* get under way almost at the same time that Ahmed was lifting Said over the railing. They did notice, however, when the booming voice of an incredulous Captain Rashid came down upon them from the bridge immediately over their heads.

"Said!"

At the sound of the captain's commanding voice, all four faces turned up to look at the bridge. For a moment Rashid was speechless, for at that instant he saw Said's unguarded, crystal-blue eyes shining at him through the glass of the diving mask. No Arab could have eyes like that! Yet, no one was more an Arab than this young man.

"Said! What in the name of Allah is going on?"

From the look of astonishment on the captain's face, Said realized that the old man had seen his eyes. Slowly and deliberately, Said removed his face mask and reached into the pocket of his wet trousers for his mirror sunglasses, which he wiped dry on Ahmed's shirttail and put on. He looked up again at Rashid, who inexplicably felt relieved that he did not have to look into those astounding blue eyes again.

"My dear captain, we have been undertaking some operational practice. That's all, just some operational practice." The three heads surrounding him, faces at full grin, vigorously nodded their agreement.

The captain could not contain his curiosity any longer, but he did not want any member of his crew to hear the explanation if, indeed, he was to get one. His face disappeared from the bridge opening. They could hear him noisily clambering down the metal steps. In a moment, breathless, he was standing nose to nose with Said. By this time the PLO leader had unbuckled the oxygen canister which Ahmed tucked protectively under his muscular arm.

"What have you been doing?" Rashid demanded. "I'm the captain of this ship, and I have a right to know."

The smile disappeared from Said's face. It was replaced by a look of grim satisfaction. "The Israeli patrol boat . . ."

"Yes, what about it?"

"Attached to its ass-end, clamped on like a bloodsucker, is a beautiful metal mechanism, packed, my dear captain, with enough high-power explosive to blast it and anything close to it to a million pieces."

The old man's teeth sucked air. "A mine!"

"A mine."

Rashid's eyes opened wide with astonishment mixed with fear. "You fool. When that thing goes off, the Israelis will be out after us like a pack of bloodhounds."

"They will not. I can assure you, captain, they will not. If I had thought otherwise, I wouldn't have done it. I don't want to foul up our main mission—or this boat."

The captain was adamant. His right arm lifted to point over Said's shoulder toward Haifa. "I tell you, if that damn thing goes off between here and Haifa, we'll have the whole Israeli navy after us!"

"There's no way it can go off between here and Haifa. It can't explode unless I set it off myself."

"And how can you do that?" There was a tone of disbelief in the captain's voice.

"By radio signal."

The nonplussed Rashid contemplated the consequences of that information until its significance dawned on him. His voice rose in a hiss of protest, "You are not going to . . . You can't. In the name of Allah, no!"

"I not only can, but I will. They'll never know what hit them. Don't worry. There won't be any evidence to tie this old rust bucket with what's going to happen."

Hassan, the radio expert, added, "Because it's going to happen right in the harbor at Haifa." He repeated what Said had said. "They'll never know what hit them."

"And," Said went on, "with any luck we'll destroy any other ships close to it."

That was the end of the explanation. It was time to get on with the business of finishing the first operational exercise. Said bent down to take off his flippers. As he stood up, he asked the shocked captain, "Give me your best estimate on how long it will take them to get back into port at Haifa and tie up. And remember, captain, it's in your best interest as well as mine to have them in the port, well inside it."

Rashid looked at his watch. "I checked our position on the chart just before they came on board. We have just gotten under way. We're about thirty-six miles off Haifa, and it's ten to seven now. They should be in the harbor by five after eight, ten after, at the outside."

Said turned to Hassan, "Get the transmitter out. Test to make sure it's working properly. We go at quarter past eight."

The captain protested, "But the crew will still be on board."

If Rashid could have seen Said's eyes through the sunglasses, he would have caught the cold determination that filled them. "Precisely. The destruction must be maximum. The Israelis are our enemies to the death."

The conversation with Rashid was at an end. Telling Maan and Hassan to bring his gear, Said walked aft, his bare feet padding against the metal deck, his mind rejoicing with his success, yet impatient for the next step. Would the mine go off in response to the radio signal? Detonating the deadly device on the tail of the Israeli patrol boat would be crucial to the chance of success in the big operation to come.

By eight o'clock, Hassan had completed his meticulous testing of the radio transmitter-receiver. He was satisfied. The portable, battery-operated unit was a compact high-powered HF (high frequency) radio with a designed transmission range of up to 4,000 miles. Ingenious Japanese miniaturization had produced a radio that weighed less than three pounds, a black box of the most sophisticated type. Hassan was confident that it would not fail.

He had set up the radio on a wooden table that Ahmed had appropriated from the galley of the protesting cook and placed on the open passageway on the port side of the *Mecca*. That position provided a clear line of sight to the area where they estimated Haifa, now well over the horizon, to be. The sea was still calm, but with a gentle roll from the west to which the ship responded as it plowed on. The table on which the radio rested was solid and stable, a good base for the testing equipment as well as Hassan's tool kit. Now all they could do was wait in the gathering darkness. The sun had gone down at 7:15. By eight the darkness was virtually complete. The sky was crystal clear. A rising half-moon split the horizon to the southeast. The running lights of the *Mecca* were not matched by those of any other ship as the old freighter thumped along its lonely course to Port Said, drawing farther and farther away from the menace of Haifa.

At ten past eight, all four PLO soldiers were near the precious radio. Ahmed and Maan squatted a few feet forward of it in the passageway, talking as Ahmed sucked on a cigarette. Hassan sat at the table on a chair he had brought from his cabin. He wore earphones as he twisted the radio's receiver dial in the futile hope that he might pick up some message from the Israeli patrol boat as it approached and entered Haifa harbor. It was doubly futile in that, had he been lucky enough to pick up their operating frequency, he did not understand the language. Even so, there was an off-chance.

At two minutes past eight the Israeli boat was in the entrance of Haifa harbor, moving fast past Bat Galim. The twinkling lights of the city glittered close by on the starboard side, rising up in the distance to the heights of central Carmel, some 600 feet above the sea. At half speed, the warship moved past the long pier that stretches eastward for almost a mile from Bat Galim and protects the main harbor from the onslaughts of the Mediterranean. The anxious Israeli captain picked his way slowly through the ships anchored in the main harbor at the agonizing speed of eight knots, steering for the pier lights that mark the narrow entrance to the inner Kishon harbor, where his craft and the six others of the patrol squadron were berthed.

At 8:10 he cut his speed back even further in the darkness. With his searchlight on, the commander ordered hard to starboard to round the northern end of the western jetty forming the Kishon harbor. Ahead he could see the long forms of the other five patrol boats of his squadron crowded along the U-shaped dock. His boat's berth was in the middle, right at the bottom of the U. Towering floodlights bathed the area with glaring white light. In a few minutes he would be docked. Then he would turn over the ship to his second-in-command to secure for the night. The filing of his report on the boarding of the *Mecca* could wait until the morning. At 8:12 the starboard side of the patrol boat touched gently against the protective rubber bumpers lining the pier wall. Reversed engines brought the craft to a full stop. He gave instructions to his first lieutenant as hands secured the mooring lines fore and aft. He tried to control his impatience, but the need to get to Rachel was compelling. He was already ten minutes late. By the time he got into his car at the end of the pier, it would be another fifteen minutes before he was at her apartment in the Kiryat Hatechnion area of the city to the south.

At 8:15, the captain of the patrol boat stepped from the gangplank to the pier. He took one quick step southward toward his car, looking to his left with pleasure and pride at his magnificent boat. At that instant, the Israeli captain, his splendid craft and crew, were no more. They dissolved, totally disintegrating in the vortex of the thundering, flaming blast as its devastating shock waves hammered out in all directions, filling the air. A rolling mass of fire and smoke, torn, shredded, broken bits of metal, plastic, glass and human flesh burst up and out in a black, red, and white ball mixed with steaming harbor water sucked from the spot where the patrol boat had sat only a second before.

Within the trapped confines of the small naval basin, the reverberating waves rammed out against the fetid salt water, shoving it over the confining piers and lifting the five other patrol boats into the air with the outward thrust of the blast. They shattered like toys as they smashed against the unbending concrete of the dock. Secondary explosions burst from their splitting fuel tanks as they opened to spill thousands of volatile gallons of diesel fuel into the already raging inferno.

Far out to sea, to the southwest, on a weatherbeaten, derelict old freighter, four young Arabs clustered in the darkness watching in silent awe as the tip of a gigantic, orange fireball lifted above the eastern horizon like a new sun. The pressure of Hassan's index finger on the radio's detonate button, orange and circular like the fireball it had created, was all it had taken to cause death and destruction in the harbor of Said's birthplace.

The four uttered no sounds of jubilation, made no signs of the lifting emotions of victory. Rather, it was a moment of sober assessment of the scale of the power that was in their hands. It was a mammoth power. Brutal. Instantaneous. A power of mass destruction that could annihilate a target-object a hundred, hundreds, or even thousands of miles distant. All that was needed was the pressure of a single finger on the small orange button on a black box.

In Haifa the woman named Rachel would never know that she had influenced the course of events that would soon turn the direction of the world.

4

9 March   10:00 A.M.

Cabinet Room, the White House

"To sum up the main points of the briefing, Mr. President . . ."

John Hansen, the forty-first president of the United States of America, moved his eyes away from the Pentagon briefing officer standing at the lectern on his right at the end of the cabinet room conference table. He looked across the table at his secretary of defense, Robert Levy. On Levy's right was the chairman of the Joint Chiefs of Staff, a five-star air force general, Glen Young. To the president's immediate left was his secretary of state, John Eaton; on his right, Vice-President Mark James; and immediately beyond him, his National Security Council special adviser, Walter Kruger. This group comprised the executive committee of the National Security Council. It was this team the new president would rely upon for assistance and advice in dealing with foreign crises.

Before his installation two months before, Senator John Hansen, as he then was, did not have a full appreciation of the amount of time and attention the president must give to foreign affairs. It seemed to him he was spending at least half his waking hours considering how to deal with problems in South America, how to handle Cuba, and the intrusions of the Cubans in Africa with their mentors the Soviets, how to cope with the sensitive Western Europeans, and the problems in NATO, the North Atlantic Treaty Organization. Then there was the subject matter of this meeting on the morning of March 9—the buildup of Soviet forces, not only in Afghanistan, but also along the Soviet-Iran border both east and west of the Caspian Sea.

The briefing was almost finished: "Six new infantry divisions and two armored have been identified along the Soviet-Iran border. In Afghanistan, indications are that another 20,000 troops with supporting equipment have been deployed with concentrations in the area of Herat, a major Afghanistan city in the northwest sector of the country, near the border with Iran. The estimated number of Soviet troops in Afghanistan now is 130,000, supported by tanks and aircraft. All the increases in strength in Afghanistan and along the Soviet-Iran border have occurred in the last seven days and are significant in terms of a potential Soviet move against Iran. That is the end of the briefing, sir."

The president looked to the other men around the table and at the one man he had not appointed, General Glen Young. He wasn't sure about Young. In the meetings they'd had in the two months since Hansen took office, he had had difficulty in drawing the general out. Perhaps it was that, having been appointed by Hansen's predecessor, a man quite different from Hansen and of another party, Young simply did not like the president and his politics. In Young, Hansen found a degree of truculence as well as condescension. He was no expert in military matters; the general had made that very clear several times in the patronizing way he answered the president's questions. It was quite obvious that General Young considered himself to be superior, even perhaps to the president himself.

Hansen spoke to the heavyset air force general. "What do you and your people make of this?"

Young was ready with his reply. "We think they're

about to make a move on Iran, Mr. President. We don't know when it's going to come. It could be within the next week or ten days. Or they may wait until the weather is better, say the beginning of May. That's what we think they'll do, wait for good weather. The highway net into Iran from the north is good. They'd have a straight run in unless the Iranians were able to mount a defense. The Iranian army is in a shambles, as is the country. Their defense is nonexistent. As we see it, the Russian troops in Afghanistan would have difficulty crossing the mountain range on the east side of Iran, but we think they would try it, at the same time the main force was moving down from the north."

Secretary of State John Eaton asked, "What about Pakistan?"

The general nodded: "We think that when the Russians move against Iran, they'll also go for Pakistan. They invaded Afghanistan for the weak reason that they wanted to protect their influence there. They have a far more compelling reason to invade Pakistan: they want the warm water port at Karachi for the Red Navy."

"I'm interested in compelling reasons." The president turned to his Secretary of State. "John, if you were Grigori Romanov in the Kremlin, what would be your compelling reason to move into Iran?"

Eaton opened the leather file folder he had placed on the conference table in front of him at the beginning of the meeting. He ruffled through the papers and found the one he wanted. He scanned it for a moment, then lifted his head to reply.

"There's more than one compelling reason, Mr. President. The first is an oil shortage. As you know, at the end of the seventies the Soviets were net exporters of crude oil, about one million barrels a day. Today, we estimate they have a shortfall of half a million barrels a day and their shortages are escalating rapidly. In fact, we may be conservative in our estimates, but that's the best number I have at the moment. The fact is that the Soviets desperately need oil. They haven't had any big finds of their own in recent years. The place to make up that shortfall is Iran, which is capable of producing about four-and-a-half million barrels a day, even though recently they've only been producing one-and-a-half and that's falling. All of their production equipment is American and since our hassle over the hostages with the Ayatollah Khomaini, it's a wonder they're producing anything. So that's compelling reason number one."

The secretary checked his notes.

"The second is to maintain the Soviet Union's fulfillment of the ideological doctrine of world domination. You may not think that's compelling, Mr. President, but it is. Iran is in a shambles, in virtual anarchy. With the counter-revolutionary activity that has been going on, it's in a state of civil war. If the call for help came from one side or the other in Iran, that would be the pretext for the Soviets to enter to stabilize the country. The same justification was used for the first incursions into Afghanistan, long before they went in in the last days of 1979. In keeping with the Marxist-Leninist ideology of world domination, Iran is an ideal objective.

"The third compelling reason is the one General Young has outlined. It goes along with the taking of Iran. The Russians desperately need that warm water port in the Indian Ocean, one they can put money and equipment into and know they're not going to lose it, as they lost the Port of Berbera in Somalia. If they had Karachi, no one would take it away from them. While the invasion of Pakistan is not the same as an invasion of Iran—which is your question, Mr. President—I agree with General Young. The two things would be done together."

The president went back to the chairman of the Joint Chiefs of Staff, "What can we do if we have to stop them, General Young?"

"In Iran or Pakistan, Mr. President?"

The president thought his question was perfectly plain. He was tempted to answer, "In the whole of the Persian Gulf," but said instead, "Both—Iran and Pakistan."

The general examined his fingernails, then looked up at the president.

"Not as much as I'd like to," he said finally. "You're

aware of these things, Mr. President, from the briefings we've given you over the last two months."

That was designed to put me in place, the president thought.

"I'll review the situation for you. In the whole of the Persian Gulf area, the Arabian Sea, and the Indian Ocean we have only one base available to us. That's Diego Garcia.

"Diego Garcia is a British island, one thousand nautical miles south of the tip of India. We made a deal with the Brits back in the middle seventies and took the island over. It has a good anchorage. We've put in everything that's needed for a complete support base for a full fleet. There's a runway 12,000 feet long which can handle anything we put in the area, even a C-5. The Soviets countered us by doing a deal recently with the Maldivian government—the Maldive Islands are about 450 miles north of Diego Garcia. They've taken over abandoned British military installations, airport, harbor, the whole works.

"The only other place where we can use facilities is Bahrain in the Persian Gulf. We can do bunkering and reprovisioning there. They have one of the biggest dry docks in the world. Beyond those two places, Mr. President, we have nothing. As you know, the previous administration was negotiating with Oman for the use of their facilities at Muscat and Masirah Island; with Somalia for Mogadishu and Berbera. The Russians had Berbera for quite a while and put in excellent facilities, but got kicked out when they sided with Ethiopia in its war with Somalia. And there have been negotiations for Mombasa in Kenya. But negotiations are negotiations, Mr. President. Nothing's been finalized yet in any of those places."

The president acknowledged, "I'm aware of that. State," he nodded to the left toward Eaton, "has been instructed to carry on with those negotiations with the highest priority and urgency." He paused to let Young continue.

"That's all we have, Mr. President. We're in an extremely weak position. The only operating base we can use is Diego Garcia."

"What about Pakistan?" Vice-President James asked.

"You didn't mention that. We've been in negotiation with their new president since he took over ten days ago."

General Young was startled, "I knew that Zia had been ousted by a coup of his own generals, but I haven't heard about any negotiations with the new man—what's his name?"

"General Mujeeb-Ul-Rehman," James replied. "In all fairness, you didn't know this, but immediately after the coup that put Mujeeb in power, President Hansen instructed the secretary of state and me to open negotiations with Mujeeb for the use of the port and airfield at Karachi. We've been dealing with the Pakistani ambassador here. With things so unsettled after the coup, we haven't made much progress. And from what you and the briefing have told us this morning, it appears that the Soviets are building up their forces to take Iran or Pakistan or both. In other words, we're heading for a direct confrontation with the Soviets, but with no foothold in the area we're virtually powerless to stop them."

General Young agreed. "The best we could do would be to get in by air the 82nd Airborne Regiment and perhaps two marine battalions. We could do that within two weeks. That would be 20,000 men and a handful of reconnaissance tanks and helicopters. With aircraft from the Fifth Fleet and with what the British have in the area at the moment . . ."

"But the Russians could take the whole of the Persian Gulf in two weeks, long before you got there. Right?"

The general glumly nodded in agreement, as the vice-president went on, "It seems to me, Mr. President, that we should expand the scope of our negotiations with the Pakistanis for not simply Karachi and the airport there, but for a full-scale positioning of our troops, equipment, and aircraft in Pakistan. In other words, a matching force to what the Russians have in Afghanistan: 120,000 men, fully equipped, tanks, fighter attack aircraft, the whole thing. After all, we have an obligation. There's a 1959 security accord between the United States and Pakistan. What do you think, general?"

The president broke in, "I'll answer that question. I think it's one hell of a suggestion, and I think we ought to do something about it right now." To the group at large he put the question, "What do we know about General Mujeeb?"

It was his National Security Council adviser, Walter Kruger, who responded. "I have a complete file on him, Mr. President. I'm sure State does too." Eaton nodded that he had. "Believe it or not, he is very pro-American. He took his helicopter training in Key West. He's more likely to accept an offer from us than General Zia was. You may remember that Zia turned down President Carter's offer of 400 million dollars back in 1980, saying it was 'peanuts'."

The others around the table nodded.

Eaton added, "Mujeeb says that he will have free elections within the year, but then Zia had been saying that for years. As you know, Mr. President, the generals are still in tight control of the government of the country."

"I know that. In this particular instance, it might be good because in a dictatorship the head man can make a decision on the spot. In a democracy like ours, I have to get permission from Congress practically every time I want to go to the john."

Smiles appeared all around, but disappeared quickly when General Young spoke up.

"I'm sorry, Mr. President, but from a military point of view, from a logistics point of view, a 13,000-mile line of supply, highly vulnerable to submarines and surface ships . . . Well, I just don't have the resources. I haven't got the ships, haven't got the budget, haven't got the men."

Hansen's voice had the hard edge of determination. "We'll find you the ships, we'll find you the money, we'll find you the men, we'll call up the reserves."

The general shook his head. "Even if I had everything I needed, from a military point of view lugging 120,000 Americans to some godforsaken place like Pakistan where the full weight of the Soviet army and air force can be thrown at us from their home ground, would be disastrous, Mr. President. I'm sorry, I have some real reservations about this. Maybe we can do it. Yes, we can do it if you give me the men and the ships and the money, but I say from a military point of view, it's dangerous. And the logistics are next to impossible."

Hansen did not answer immediately. He was angry, but hid his emotions. "But from my perspective, from my viewpoint, general, I must take into consideration not only the military, but all the other factors in deciding whether we do or do not act in the presence of obvious Soviet initiatives. I must take into account the grand strategies of the Soviet Union—their economic strategies, their geopolitical strategies, their goal of world domination by peaceful means if they can achieve it that way. And God knows they've been successful since World War II in doing just that. What I have to do is to develop strategies to counterbalance the ever increasing Soviet aggression. I'm talking about economic and political as well as military aggression. Soviet agression in the Persian Gulf is a threat to the lifestyle of the United States and the free world. If they interfere with our oil supplies it could mean the end of our way of life. I have to take your objections into account. But I cannot allow the military point of view to be the only consideration. If I took your advice and yours alone then I would probably decide against going to Pakistan."

John Hansen was not going to let that caustic bastard off the hook yet. "You may be surprised to know, general, that I not only have sympathy with the deplorable state of the American military, I also understand something about it. I know that since 1968 our military manpower has declined by more than one-and-a-half million men. Right now it's about 600,000 below the pre-Vietnam level. Just look at our navy. In 1968, the navy had 976 ships, now it's down to 472. Whereas the Red Navy, in the days of the Kennedy-Khrushchev confrontation, was nothing more than a coastal offense and interdiction force, now it is the strongest, most formidable blue-water navy in the world.

"Since 1960, Soviet military manpower has grown from approximately three million to 4.5 million, more than twice the size of our military organization. In every class of military hardware, even helicopters, the Russians are producing far more than we are. In ground forces equipment, their output ratio is about six to one, particularly in tanks. They're producing fighter aircraft at rates that exceed ours by a factor of four. The CIA tells me that the Soviets outspend us on defense by about forty-five percent in dollar equivalence. A pretty bad scenario, general. It reflects, I think, the military turn-off of the American people that flowed out of Vietnam. That also comes from our not being a militaristic people. The fact is, the Russian military machine has it all over ours like a tent. Just look at that submarine fleet of theirs, almost 400 in service. What do we have? One hundred and forty."

Although Hansen was directing his remarks to Young, the general sat with his hands clasped, his eyes looking down at the table. He did not like being lectured to by a politician on the state of America's military, a matter about which he was the most knowledgeable of all Americans. Furthermore, going into Pakistan with a task force, however big it was, was military madness.

"I'll tell you this, general, if I can work a deal with Pakistan, I'll guarantee you the men, the money, and the equipment to do the job."

Jim Crane, the president's chief of staff, came into the meeting. Before sitting down next to Levy, he handed a note to Secretary Eaton. As he read its contents, Eaton's eyebrows lifted and he shook his head. Hansen stopped and asked, "Anything important, John?"

"Nothing of earth-shattering consequence. Perhaps that's a bad way of putting it. Six Israeli ships have been blown up in the harbor at Haifa. Fifty people killed. Probably a PLO raid."

Eaton was right. The item was not earth-shattering, but it was a link in the chain of events that would follow the decisions that were being taken around the Cabinet conference table that morning.

Hansen had made up his mind what he wanted to do. "Gentlemen, it's obvious to me that we're getting down to the short strokes with the Russians in the Middle East. Under no circumstances can the United States afford to lose Persian Gulf oil, and for Western Europe the situation is even more critical. It is apparent to me that it is vital to the interests of the United States and the Western world that we get forces into the Middle East to counterbalance the Soviets. There is only one place we can do that—Pakistan. The vice-president is right on. We should expand our negotiations. We should go for putting in as many troops as you, General Young, and your staff might advise: *a*, that are needed to produce an effective balancing force—it might be 120,000 more or less, that's up to you to advise on, general; and *b*, a force that we can afford to take out of our existing troop and equipment resources, having in mind all our commitments around the world. To put such a force in place, will we have to call up the reserves? These are questions you'll have to answer, General Young. What I want you to do is to put together immediately a Pakistan Task Force Plan. I want that draft plan by Monday noon, two or three pages with all the meat in it. You can expand it later on. I want to know how many troops for Pakistan, how we'll get them there, your best estimate on an arrival date. I know this is Saturday, general, and a bad day to try to collect people, but I have to move quickly." The president was pleased to see that the general himself was taking notes.

"As to Pakistan and General Mujeeb, it is imperative that we make a maximum effort to negotiate an agreement that will let our forces into Pakistan and in strength. Furthermore, it is of the utmost urgency that the agreement be negotiated forthwith. There is only one person in the United States of America who can do the negotiating." The President broke his line of thought. He turned to Crane. "Jim, ask the energy secretary to have his people produce an aide memoire for me, or maybe it should be some economist in the General Accounting Office. Yes, I think you better ask GAO. I want something on the economic and other ramifications for the United States if the Persian Gulf oil is cut off. Do the same for Western Europe. And I want a second aide memoire covering both the United

States and Western Europe: what happens if *all* the OPEC oil is cut off?"

"Do you mean *all*, sir?" Crane asked in astonishment. The other faces around the table reflected the same emotion.

The president was emphatic. "I sure as hell do!"

General Young wanted to quarrel with that request. "That just couldn't happen, Mr. President. Anyway, we're only dealing here with the Middle East, the Persian Gulf, not with Malaysia or Venezuela or Mexico."

Hansen, who was six-foot five when he stood up, looked down across the table at the chairman of the Joint Chiefs of Staff. "General Young, such a study may not be relevant to the military mind, but it sure as hell is to mine."

5

10 March   6:00 P.M.

Port Said, Egypt

The coastal approach to Egypt's ancient, timeless Port Said must be navigated with considerable care. On each side of the constantly dredged channel, which weaves inward from the Mediterranean past the port's protective western pier into the harbor basin, lurks a shallow, muddy bottom. The harbor of Port Said is the northern gateway to the Suez Canal, a hundred-mile-long finger of lockless water that can take ships of up to 45,000 tons, small vessels in comparison to the mammoth crude-oil tankers that range up to half a million tons. Those tankers must round the southern tip of Africa to deliver their cargos from the Persian Gulf to Western Europe and America.

On the west bank of the 570-acre harbor sits a tumble of docks and warehouses through which the goods of Egyptian trade and commerce have moved over the centuries. Beyond the dock area, to the west, lies the city in which over a quarter of a million Egyptians live and work, their existence tied to the fortunes of the port and the Suez Canal.

On the eastern side of the harbor are antiquated shipbuilding and repair yards, which look more like cemeteries for the rusted hulls and skeletons of ships that litter the channel-webbed, flat landscape. In the prolific smuggling trade, goods of all kinds, including opium, cocaine, and marijuana, pass over the labyrinth of waterways of the east bank.

At Port Said, all loading and discharging of freighters is done by lighters, small craft which carry cargos to and from shore. Vessels are prohibited from coming alongside the quays. Fuel, water, and provisions are readily available.

Whenever he went south through the Suez Canal, it was Captain Rashid's practice to make sure that his bunker fuel and water tanks were topped up, and that he had ample food supplies on board. To satisfy his taste for good wine, illegal in many of the Muslim ports he visited, he would also indulge himself by buying several cases of acceptable French white and red wines. These he would store in a secret compartment in the ship's hold beneath his quarters. So expertly had the compartment and its hidden entrance been built that even the most skilful customs inspectors had not found them. A curious inspector would only see, at the forward end of the aft cargo hold, a solid stress-carrying bulkhead. Conversely, when he entered the forward cargo hold, he would perceive, at the aft end of it, the other side of the bulkhead he had seen in the first compartment. The only entrance to the covert compartment was located in the captain's bathroom at the port end of his suite. In order to gain access to the trap door on the bathroom floor, a concealed lever allowed the entire shower stall to swing away from the wall. Under it was the ladder down into the hold.

Only Rashid knew of the existence of the secret compartment. To have shared that knowledge with any of his itinerant first officers or crew would have been to share it with the world. The customs people in every port he called at would have known that the innocent-looking old *Mecca* had a clandestine hot spot. They would investigate it as a matter of routine.

There were severe limitations to what the captain

could do with his smuggling hold. He could only put cargo in it that he could load himself without the assistance of any of his crew. If he was carrying armaments, weapons, marijuana, opium, whatever the contraband goods, they had to be packaged so that one person could handle them. At the pick-up port, he would send his entire crew ashore for a night on the town, as he had at Beirut. It was usually during the period between the fall of darkness and midnight that a small craft, its running lights dark, would pull up to the lowered gangway platform. In short order its cargo would be deposited on the floor of the captain's cabin, just inside the doorway.

Rashid would then go to work. The shower stall would be moved to one side, the hatch below it lifted. A heavy pulley would be screwed into a hole in the ceiling above the hatch. A rope would be fed through it and tied to a small cargo net, which Rashid would use to lower the goods through the hatch down to the deck of the compartment, or to lift the stuff out at its destination.

As old as he was, the captain was still in excellent condition. He was a powerful man, thick chested, carrying heavy muscular arms developed from a lifetime of hard physical work in the tough business of being a Mediterranean sailor. For survival, Rashid had to be strong. He had to be able to lift cargo or take on the world in a bar-room brawl. He prided himself on still being able to handle up to a hundred pounds, a lot less than he used to lift, but, at his age, not bad. In an hour, perhaps an hour-and-a-half, of work, he could get any incoming cargo neatly stowed below, the hatch back in place, the pulley out of the ceiling and the shower stall returned.

From time to time, Rashid took on board another kind of cargo. Human cargo. Many times he had been sought out in the favorite bars of sea captains in Alexandria, Piraeus, or Marseilles by some desperate soul seeking escape to another country. When the compartment had been built, its use as living quarters had been anticipated. A toilet and a sink were installed at the starboard end. Primitive and filthy, but practical. There were no bunks, chairs, furniture of any kind—not even a porthole for air.

On this voyage, the captain's special compartment had a cargo. It, too, had come on board at Beirut: a thousand pounds of opium for shipment to Kuwait. It was packaged in thirty-pound plastic bags enclosed in ordinary-looking burlap sacks. Rashid guessed that when it was off-loaded the stuff would find its way onto one of the tankers waiting to be loaded with crude oil. The white treasure would then be carried to Europe or North America. Where the opium came from he did not know and cared less. Probably Afghanistan or Pakistan. All that mattered was that he and the ship's owners were paid handsomely and in cash for carrying the contraband.

While the captain was satisfied that no customs inspector would be able to discover the existence of the compartment or the entrance to it, nevertheless he was always apprehensive when he was anchored in a harbor such as Port Said, which teemed with other freighters, tankers, customs boats, and prowling Egyptian naval vessels. There was always the chance that something could go wrong.

The *Mecca* had arrived at the entrance to Port Said just before ten o'clock on the evening of March 10. Since she was not on a tight schedule, the captain elected to wait until morning before proceeding into harbor. He picked out the familiar light of the Fairway buoy, the main channel marker outside the port's entrance. He then steamed two miles west of it, where he dropped anchor to spend the night. During that day, he had been following the news reports from Beirut, Cairo, and the BBC about the massive explosion in Haifa harbor that killed fifty-three naval personnel, destroyed six of the Israelis' best, most modern high-speed patrol boats, and leveled three warehouses. The Israelis were still uncertain about the cause of the blast, but officials believed it was the work of PLO terrorists. Did that mean that they suspected the *Mecca*? Rashid had agreed with Said that the Israeli officials would not be able to find any evidence to tie the two together. On the other hand, the patrol boat that had stopped them had been dispatched by staff at the Haifa naval control of shipping office. They would know that the *Mecca* had been stopped and boarded and that it was that particular patrol craft that had taken the full brunt of the blast.

So far Said was right in one respect. In the destruction, chaos, and ensuing panic, no one would think of chasing after the *Mecca*. Indeed, there would be nothing in Haifa to chase her with. A patrol boat could have been sent out from Tel Aviv to intercept her. It wasn't. But Rashid turned the situation over in his mind as he monitored the radio news reports. He was becoming convinced that, in the light of day, the Israelis might connect the boarding of the *Mecca* with the harbor explosion. Possibly it was only because by late morning after the blast his ship was not only well into international waters, but also well out of range, that she had not been pursued and brought back into an Israeli port to face investigation.

It was the six o'clock BBC evening news that jolted Rashid as he sat in his cabin eating his supper. It also disturbed Said, sitting in his cabin listening to the same newscast coming from Hassan's black box. In his droll English accent the BBC reporter added to the information about the explosion that had been repeated during the day:

"Israeli officials have now determined that the cause of the blast was a radio-activated Russian mine planted on the hull of one of their patrol boats in the harbor. As yet they are not certain how the mine was planted, but they are sure it was the work of PLO terrorists."

The captain immediately phoned up to the bridge, instructing Nabil to send for Said. "I want to see him immediately. Now!"

Rashid was certain Nabil had slept through the Israeli boarding and that none of the deck hands had seen Said climb back on board the ship after the mine planting. They were too busy gawking at the patrol boat on the other side of the *Mecca*'s packing-case-filled cargo deck. Undoubtedly Nabil and the rest of the crew had heard the news reports during the day about the explosion on Haifa, but would not connect them with their own ship.

In short order, bareheaded, barefooted, and dressed in his blue denim work clothes, Said was standing in front of the captain's table, looking down at the agitated old man puffing furiously on a mutilated cigarette.

"You wanted to see me?"

"Did you hear the BBC news report just now?"

With a curt nod of his head, the young Arab acknowledged that he had.

"A Russian mine. Is it true? Was it a Russian mine?"

There was no answer. The furious Rashid stubbed out his cigarette, leaned forward, the palms of his hands planted on the table, and growled at Said, "I want you to understand one thing, you young idiot. If what you planted on that Israeli boat was a Russian mine, and if what you've got in those ill-begotten packing cases out there," his right hand rose to point over Said's shoulder, "are Russian mines, and if you think I am going to take this ship into Port Said with those things sitting on my deck, you must be out of your mind!"

Still no response from the PLO leader.

"The Israelis and Egyptians are bedfellows now. Even the Egyptians hate the PLO. When we go in that harbor, the police, the navy, somebody will swarm all over this ship." The captain drew himself up to his full height. He had to be strong. "Those packing cases will have to go overboard."

With a slow, deliberate motion, Said removed his mirrored sunglasses. His crystal blue eyes were ice, as his voice hissed through clenched teeth. "Touch those crates and I'll kill you."

The cut of the words made the captain flinch inside. "But in the name of Allah, we can't go into the port with that stuff on deck—Russian mines!"

The sunglasses went back on again. Said was not about to admit what was in those crates. However, the captain had a point. As a matter of diplomatic courtesy, the Egyptians would have nothing to lose and much cooperation to gain by responding to an urgent Israeli request to go over the *Mecca* and her crew with a fine-tooth comb. He could not understand how the Israelis had found out that it was a

Russian-made mine or, for that matter, that it was a mine at all. Said had thought that the blast would wipe out any trace. He realized he ought to have known better. He had made a mistake. He recanted. "You're right. I've been through this ship from one end to the other looking for a place to . . ."

It was against Rashid's better judgment but . . . He held up the palm of his right hand and said, "I have the place for the stuff."

"And what about us?"

The beleaguered captain managed a weak smile. "And for the four of you, too."

He slumped back in his chair, waved Said into the chair opposite, pulled out a cigarette and lit it with a trembling match. Blowing out the first cloud of smoke he told Said, "This is what we'll do. I'll break out some Italian wine for the whole crew. By midnight, they'll all be drunk, and when this lot drinks, they're right out of it."

"Including Nabil?"

The captain guffawed, "Nabil? He'll be the first one under the table. Now this is what I want you and your people to do. We can start say at one o'clock, not any earlier . . ."

The *Mecca* arrived at her anchorage in the darkness at about 8:30 that evening. When the captain was satisfied that the anchor was down and the ship was secure, he announced over the loudspeaker system that because they had to stand offshore and couldn't get into port that night so the crew could get ashore, on behalf of the owners he was opening the wine locker at two liters per man, red or white. He could hear cheers from cabin deck. Both Nabil and the helmsman with him on the bridge gave the captain happy salutes and disappeared toward the galley. There the cook was already dispensing bottles and glasses amid laughter and the popping of corks. Among the nine crew members were two men with guitars who knew every foul song sung by Mediterranean sailors.

As predicted, by midnight all the wine was gone. Every man of the crew, all nine of them, had passed out.

Some had made it to their bunks, others just collapsed where they were. Their evening of revelry had taken place on the fantail of the ship, with singing, shouting, cursing, and one short fist fight which wound up with the participants amicably throwing their arms around each other after not a single drunken blow was landed.

At one o'clock, the captain made a tour of inspection of the cabin deck. As a precaution, he nudged or pushed each man with his foot, watching for a reaction. Not one of them responded.

Satisfied, he went to Said's darkened cabin, tapped on the door, opened it a crack and said, "Let's go."

The four PLO men were ready in their blue work clothes. This would be their job, not the captain's. Crowbars were removed from their stowed position, one for each man. In the dim light cast by the red, green, and white running lights, they began prying open the tops of the small crates, one at a time. When the first came off, Captain Rashid had no idea what to expect. Gray shining objects perhaps. Guns. He didn't know, but he was expecting the worst. He was disappointed when all he could see were the tops of what appeared to be styrofoam squares tightly packed together. Putting his crowbar down, Said lifted out the first white package. It was heavy, awkward to remove. The rest would be easier. He looked at the captain who turned, opened his cabin door, and led Said through to the washroom. There the shower stall had already been moved aside. The hatch was open and the pulley, rope, and net were in place.

Said asked, "Spread the net out for me, please." Rashid quickly flattened the net out on the floor, pulling the corners taut to make it square. Said put his heavy, white package in the center. It was quickly joined by three more, carried in by the team close behind. When eight were on the pile, Said decided that was enough weight for the first lift.

He ordered Ahmed, "You go down into the hold. We'll lower them down to you. Stack them . . ."

The captain broke in. "Stack them against the forward

bulkhead over toward the toilet. Just keep away from the sacks. I'll turn the light on."

"What's in the sacks?" Ahmed asked.

"Seed," was the partly true reply.

Satisfied, Ahmed lowered his enormous bulk gingerly down the vertical steps into the dimly lit compartment. When he reached the floor, his head almost touched the ceiling. To his left, about ten feet toward the bow of the boat, was a solid bulkhead that ran the width of the ship. To his right was an identical bulkhead about three feet away. At each end of the compartment were the steel ribs and curved plates of the hull. Ahmed was satisfied that there was plenty of room for their weapons and equipment, and, for that matter, themselves.

"It looks good," he whispered up the hatchway to Said. "Lower away whenever you're ready."

Standing outside the washroom, the captain watched as Said and Maan hauled on the rope, pulling up the four corners of the net. The square white packs were firmly in the pocket of the net which swung over the hatch as soon as it cleared the deck. Maan steadied the net as it swung back and forth like a pendulum. Gently, they lowered it through the hatch into the waiting hands of Ahmed, who guided it to the floor. Working quickly, he lifted each piece out, setting it down carefully. When the net was empty he called, "Take it up for the next load." Then he began stacking them against the forward bulkhead, keeping well clear of the sacks of seed which filled the room with a peculiar odor, almost a perfume. Ahmed didn't know what it was, but he could smell it when he first came down the steps.

Nine loads later, three of the packing cases had been cleared of their contents. It was the fourth one that caught Captain Rashid's imagination. From it, Said, Maan and Hassan extracted two forty-horsepower outboard motors and gasoline tanks; a pair of large, noiseless, electric outboard motors and their wet-cell batteries; two sets of plastic oars in sections; two large dunnage bags, each filled with a large rolled-up object; and four oxygen bottles, face masks and sets of flippers.

When those items were stowed, the next things to put into the compartment were the sleeping bags off their bunks, all their personal gear and sufficient canned food from the galley to last them a week. They expected to be confined for a much shorter period than that, but the captain had cautioned Said to be on the safe side.

Finally they broke up the wooden packing crates and threw the debris overboard. The one-and-one-half-knot current flowing across the entrance to Port Said would take the pieces of wood many miles to the east by dawn.

At seven the next morning the captain did a repeat of his Beirut wake-up rounds to get his crew and his ship going. He routed the still half-drunk Nabil out of his bunk, shouting at him to get the rest of the crew up and moving. The ship had to get under way as soon as possible.

The captain returned to his quarters and waited for about ten minutes until he heard footsteps on the bridge above. That was the signal that Nabil and the helmsman had finally pulled themselves together. When he heard the groaning chatter of the deck hands, moving forward to the fo'c'sle to bring up the anchor, he knew it was time to go up top.

As he stepped on the bridge, the brilliant rays of the early morning sun shining through the streaked forward glass of the wheelhouse made him squint. It would be another hot, humid, windless day.

Nabil's eyes were twitching from his hangover. Nevertheless, he was perceptive enough to realize that something was missing.

"What happened to the crates, the four small crates that came out of Beirut?"

The captain ignored him. He flicked the speaker switch to the engine room, shouting, "Engine room, are you ready to get under way?" There was a long pause as the wine-soaked chief engineer hauled himself within range of his speaker and summoned enough precision to find the transmitting switch.

"Engine room ready, sir."

"Slow ahead" was the order to Nabil.

It was only after the anchor was up, the fo'c'sle secured, and the order "full ahead" given, that the captain chose to answer.

"Our PLO friends disembarked last night and took the packing cases with them."

Nabil scratched his forehead, lifting the peak of his cap. "Last night? I didn't hear anything."

Rashid roared, "Hear anything! You were dead drunk. A lighter came by shortly after midnight and took them off. I was happy to see the last of them."

"They must have used the crane to get those crates off . . ."

"The big one, Ahmed, had the crane motor going in no time. Must be an expert. He had the crates on the lighter in ten minutes."

Shaking his head in bewilderment the Egyptian mused, "I wonder if they had anything to do with that big explosion in Haifa."

Busying himself with the navigation of the ship, the captain made no response. "Starboard ninety" was his order to the helmsman, as the Mecca passed the Fairway buoy. The captain's next order was to bring the ship directly into the channel line "Yaminak shwayya, starboard a bit." The new heading would take them straight into the harbor channel of Port Said. Half an hour later, the Mecca dropped anchor once again, this time at the south end of Port Said harbor, in the lee of a large luxury passenger ship. To the north of the freighter Mecca stood a crude oil tanker in ballast, to the south another freighter, and beyond it a second tanker. If he could get his port clearances finished in time, the Mecca would join those ships in the afternoon southbound convoy down the Suez Canal.

Because the procedures were complex, Captain Rashid normally went ashore to pay the canal transit dues. But he was uneasy about the Haifa incident. He had a feeling in his bones that something was going to happen, that he should stay on his ship. If the authorities came aboard while he was away and Nabil was in charge, only Allah knew what would happen. No, he would send Nabil ashore. Anyway, an Egyptian could deal best with an Egyptian. He thought of all Egyptians with condescending disdain and about Nabil with disdain without condescension. Furthermore, Nabil could use the experience and undoubtedly somewhere in the city he had a little woman he could spend a fast hour in bed with.

When the anchoring procedures were finished, Rashid turned to the sallow-faced young officer.

"Go and shave. Get cleaned up. I want you to go to the transit office for me and get our clearances. And I want you to look respectable when you go ashore." The captain added with a tone of sarcasm, "You might take a shower, even if it's the only one this trip. When you're ready to go, report back to my cabin. I'll give you some money and instructions as to what has to be done."

When Nabil reported to the captain half an hour later, Rashid was astonished. The first officer had indeed shaved and showered. His wet, black hair was plastered down and neatly combed. Instead of the usual scruffy brass-buttoned jacket and dirty gray turtleneck pullover he wore ashore, he had on a clean, neatly pressed uniform, two stripes of gold braid gleaming on the sleeve. A spotless white shirt sported a black tie. Even his shoes were polished and—the last straw—his fingernails were clean.

"Allah be praised! I should bring you to Port Said more often!" Rashid couldn't believe the transformation. "She must really be something."

The clean first officer smiled, his crooked, shiny white teeth showing his anticipated pleasure. "She's gorgeous." His hands made an arcing motion out in front at chest level. "She has the biggest, hardest . . ." Then his hands dropped to his crotch. "And the tightest, wettest black . . ." His bloodshot eyes rolled upward towards the ceiling as he ran his tongue back and forth across his mustached upper lip.

It was almost too much for the old seaman, "In the name of heaven get a grip on yourself, Nabil. She might not be at home."

"I have worthy alternatives, captain."

It was time to get down to business. "This is what I

want you to do. Go to the transit office. Here's the money for the transit dues and a list of the information you have to give, and here's the Suez Canal special tonnage certificate. Anything else?"

"What time do you want me back?"

Never, if I had my choice, the captain thought, but the words he spoke were "Twelve o'clock. That's noon today, Nabil, noon. It's coming up to nine now. Do you think you can get everything done and be back here by noon?"

There was a pleading look on the first officer's face. "One o'clock would be much better, much, much better."

"All right, one o'clock, but not one minute after. The convoy moves out of the harbor at three, and we have to move with it. Understand?"

Nabil was surprisingly deferential. "Yes, sir. One o'clock, sir. I'm very grateful, sir."

"Get going!" the captain growled. He wanted Nabil off the ship as quickly as possible. If there was going to be any trouble with the port police or the navy over the Haifa affair, the last person he wanted to have on board while inspection and interrogation was going on was Nabil. The Egyptian scuttled out of the captain's cabin, ran down the gangway steps and into the waiting, leaky lifeboat to be rowed by a sullen deck hand westward to the transit office dock. The deck hand was annoyed because the captain refused him permission to stay ashore to wait for the first officer's return. The ship's master knew better than to allow two of his crew ashore at Port Said when he needed both of them back in time for departure and at least one of them sober.

Rashid's plan for the rest of the morning was to keep his crew, other than the cook and the two engineers, busy on deck scraping and painting. It was time to start cleaning up the grimy old ship, reluctant as the crew might be. Furthermore, he wanted to be on deck himself or on the bridge to keep an eye open for any approaching official Egyptian craft. By nine o'clock he had organized all hands, including the one who had taken Nabil ashore. All five were busy scraping on the fo'c'sle, having started their chore by cleaning up the paint locker which in the last two days had received more attention than it had in years. All of the PLO team's gear had been removed during the darkness a few hours earlier. The captain calculated that if he had his men working at the bow of the ship, they would be out of the way in the event of a boarding. They would, of course, be available for questioning, but at least they wouldn't be immediately underfoot or within earshot. Having assigned each man a specific area of the deck for its scrape down preparatory to painting, Rashid called to the cook for coffee and went up to the bridge to escape the increasing morning heat.

When the coffee was brought to him on the bridge, he took a cigarette from the pocket of his open-necked, white, short-sleeved shirt on which he had put his captain's epaulets. He was in his best white tropical uniform. When he had awakened that morning he had decided he should be properly dressed to greet any boarding party that might appear. Puffing contentedly on his cigarette and sipping the thick coffee, he looked out, past the work party at the bow, toward the city's docks and buildings to the west. As his eyes scanned, he noticed the gray, rakish, swept-back bow of a small vessel as it moved out from a hidden jetty in the area where he knew the customs offices to be. The craft, however, was no customs boat. Rather it was another of those cursed naval patrol boats. This time, however, it was Egyptian and not nearly so heavily armed as the Israelis'. She carried torpedo tubes but no surface-to-surface missile launchers. A pair of machine guns was mounted on the forward deck, unmanned as she turned the jetty corner heading out into the harbor. What would she do? It was unusual to see a naval patrol boat in the Port Said harbor. And since it was putting out from the customs docks, most peculiar.

Rashid kept his eyes fixed on her as he alternately sipped his coffee and pulled on his cigarette. Across the water came the booming roar of her engines as they were thrust up to full power, driving the bow of the whippet-like vessel up out of the water and then down as it gained high

speed on the smooth harbor surface. Rashid was relieved
when she turned north toward the harbor mouth, disappearing behind the huge bulk of the passenger ship lying
between the *Mecca* and the western edge of the port.
Moments later his heart sank when she reemerged heading
east and close in behind the cruise ship. The boat was no
more than a hundred yards to the north of the *Mecca*. It
was then that he could see that all the faces of the sailors on
board the patrol craft were looking at his ship, at him.
There were eight white-uniformed men in the wheelhouse.
All of them were armed. At least four of them had stubby
automatic rifles. Wherever they were going, they meant
business—and trouble. Perhaps they were headed for the
labyrinth of channels of the eastern side of the harbor,
smugglers' haven. The captain's wishful hope was not to be.

As the Egyptian gunboat passed a point just a few
yards beyond the stern of the *Mecca* and still to the north of
her, it swung south in a tight arc to come in on the
freighter's starboard side from astern. They were coming
aboard.

The old captain's heart raced with apprehension as he
moved quickly down to the head of the gangway to receive
his unwanted visitors. Her engines cut to an idle, the war
boat was brought skilfully alongside and made fast. Rashid
read the boarding party leader's rank on his shoulders as he
mounted the gangway steps, followed by six armed sailors.
The peak of the man's cap and his epaulets told Rashid that
he was a commander in the Egyptian navy, an unusually
senior rank for an officer leading a boarding party, even
though he was assisted by a much younger lieutenant-
commander who followed immediately behind.

When the commander stepped on the *Mecca*'s deck,
the greeting formalities were quickly disposed of.

The naval commander, gray haired, had a narrow,
angular, and weather-creased face. He was a slim, erect
man but a head shorter than the *Mecca*'s captain. He
quickly got down to business as his people fanned out along
the ship's railing on each side of him.

"I am Commander Faher. I am in charge of the Port

Said naval district. I have been personally instructed by the president . . ." He paused, relishing the importance of being able to drop that exalted name, "by the president himself to do a thorough inspection of this . . ." He looked up and down the length of the unkempt vessel with disdain, "this ship."

Rashid began his side of the game. "Why does the president so honor the *Mecca*?"

Commander Faher gave a hint that he was an impatient man, particularly when dealing with inferiors. "Come now, captain. Surely you heard on the news about the big explosion at Haifa. Six patrol boats destroyed and over fifty people killed?"

The captain shrugged, "Yes, but what's that got to do with me?"

"You were boarded by an Israeli gunboat two days ago?"

"Yes. Off Haifa and in international waters. I intend to file a protest."

Commander Faher was sympathetic. Even though there was a peace between their countries, the hatred of the individual Egyptian for the Israelis continued unabated. Here he was acting as agent for the Israeli navy. It was a matter of extreme distaste for the commander. Had it not been for the direct order of his beloved president . . .

"Typical of the Israelis. They think they own the world," he sniffed. "What the Israelis say is that there is a possibility that while their boarding party was on your ship, someone somehow planted a mine on their patrol boat."

Rashid protested. "That's ridiculous. They were on board ten, maybe fifteen minutes. We were minding our own business, making for Port Said when they stopped us. How in heaven's name could anybody plant a mine in that kind of a situation? We had no notice. And furthermore, you can talk to my crew. There isn't one of them who would know what a mine looks like."

The naval commander folded his arms in front of him. "Come now, captain. You had four PLO soldiers on board." The Egyptian was smug, knowing that the information would catch the *Mecca*'s captain by surprise. He watched Rashid's face carefully for a reaction that did not come. He would try again. "They left your ship last night when you were anchored outside the harbor."

Outwardly Rashid gave no indication of surprise, but inwardly he was taken aback. Clever little bastard, the commander. "Where did you get that information?"

Again a smug look on the commander's face. "We've been watching your ship since dawn. When your first officer came ashore, we intercepted him. He and I had a nice chat over coffee. Being a true and loyal Egyptian, he wanted to get about his business as quickly as possible, so he told me everything he knew. Four PLO soldiers led by a man called Said who wears sunglasses night and day. They got on board at Beirut. Also four packing cases came on board there. When it was apparent that the Israelis were going to board you, the PLO man warned the crew that his team would kill all of them if they tipped off the Israelis. When the Israelis were on board, the PLO men were located in the bow, amidships and at the stern. But your man Nabil could not account for their leader."

"He was off watch, in his cabin at the time."

"Yes. He said that. But the crewmen on deck at the time told him they didn't see the leader. So, perhaps he got overboard and planted a mine."

The captain shook his head. "Impossible!"

"Maybe." The commander shrugged. "My instructions are to search this ship thoroughly. Your first officer didn't see the PLO men get off last night and he didn't see the packing cases being transferred to a lighter. If they're still on board this ship, I intend to find them." He paused, seeming to be uncomfortable about his actions. "You must understand, captain. I am under the personal instructions of the president. I am not an Israeli sympathizer."

Captain Rashid thought he might like this little man. "When you have finished your search, commander, I will have coffee ready for you in my cabin."

Within twenty minutes, Commander Faher and his

men had been through every part of the *Mecca* from the engine room and the cabins and lockers at the stern to the hold under the fo'c'sle. They had been into both the forward and aft cargo holds. The four motor vehicles lashed in the forward deck had been carefully scrutinized. The tops had been pried off all six of the huge compressor packing cases, their contents checked out and the lids nailed back again. Faher was satisfied that there was not a square foot of the boat which had not been accounted for.

When the inspection was finished, the commander accepted the captain's invitation to coffee. The two men chatted politely about ships and politics. When it was time to leave, the commander asked permission to use the captain's washroom. The apprehensive Rashid could only agree. It seemed to him that Faher was secluded in that room for an inordinate length of time, even though it was perhaps no more than four minutes. The Egyptian finally emerged. He picked up his hat to leave. Holding out his hand to Captain Rashid, Commander Faher said, "It would have gone well on my record to have found what I was looking for. But I must tell you, captain, as an Arab and an Egyptian and as a naval officer, I was delighted with what happened at Haifa. And so I would have been most unhappy, most disappointed if I had found the PLO men. Frankly, I have the fullest sympathy for the Palestinian people. So, captain, I am pleased to have failed. By the way, the latch that moves your shower stall away from the hatch should be oiled. It is a little sticky."

Rashid was caught by surprise and showed it. His jaw fell open with astonishment as the sprightly commander stepped out of the cabin and disappeared with his men down the gangway steps.

6

11 March   6:00 P.M.

Atlantic Ocean

By 1800 hours on the evening of March 11, H.M.S. *Splendid*, holding at 500 feet, was midway between the island of Santa Maria, at the eastern end of the Azores, and Madeira, coming up on its port side. From the time it had passed the Finisterre light, the moving panorama of the sonar screen picked up the blips of forty surface vessels. As the plot record showed, all but seven were tankers carrying their precious crude oil, without which Western Europe could not survive, north to waiting ports, or steaming south in ballast toward the Cape of Good Hope still some 6,000 miles ahead. There they would gradually turn eastward and then north up the Indian Ocean toward the Strait of Hormuz and the Persian Gulf or, as it was known by the Arabs of the area, the Arabian Gulf.

The captain was in his cabin on number one deck, just forward of the control room. He had chosen to have supper by himself in his tiny cubicle, cramped by its bunk, desk, cupboards, lockers, a pair of chairs, and a wash basin. On the desk was a telephone and above it shelves holding official publications, charts, and a clutch of the newest paperback books to come out of London. Above the shelves was a depth gauge and beside it a clock and barometer, the most basic of all nautical instruments.

He had eaten in a leisurely fashion. The dish was curried shrimp which the senior of the wardroom's two stewards, Petty Officer Robert Joyce, a squat, short, kindly Glaswegian, had served with dexterity after covering the desk with a stiff linen tablecloth and setting out shiny new silverware, each piece bearing the name *Splendid* along its handle. His final touch was a sparkling silver tankard into which, before the food was served, Joyce had poured a pint of lager beer.

"Is there something significant about having Indian curry?" Leach had jokingly asked Joyce.

The reply came with almost a giggle, "After all, sir, we are going to the . . ."

"Yes. I know, the Indian Ocean."

The telephone, stark black against the white tablecloth, rang sharply.

"Pritchard in the control room, sir. I have a sonar contact. Looks like a bogey."

Brushing past his startled steward, the captain was in the sonar department in a few rapid strides. Pritchard was there, standing behind Petty Officer Pratt and his assistant, both seated and wearing earphones. All eyes were glued on the sonar screen.

Their heads turned momentarily as the captain entered the tiny space, asking, "Where is it?"

Pritchard pointed to the right-hand bottom corner of the screen. "There it is, abeam of us and closing on a parallel course about a mile to starboard."

The captain was astonished. "Closing? Cor' crikey. We're going thirty knots and she's closing?"

"Yes, sir." Petty Officer Pratt checked at the red numbers coming up in his computer readout faces. "At ten knots."

"What depth?"

"Eight hundred feet. Range 9,500 yards."

She had to be either an American or a Russian. With

that speed she had to be an attack vessel like *Splendid* herself.

The sonar watchkeeper's voice was calm. "I'll have the answer on her signature in a minute, sir. It's in the computer now."

The identification came up in red digits against the black face of the computer glass, in the large electronic machine sitting against the aft bulkhead of the sonar room. It was one word: *Alfa*.

Leach knew the Alfa class Soviet submarines. There were only four of them in service. A downstream generation of the Novembers of the early sixties and later the Victors, her ship's complement was only fifty against that of his twelve officers and eighty-five men. Smaller than the *Splendid*, the Alfa was 260 feet against the *Splendid*'s 272. Her displacement was 3,300 tons deadweight against the 4,500 of Leach's boat. Her advertised speed was thirty-two knots plus, against the *Splendid*'s thirty. With her lesser weight and bulk, she had much greater power, 24,000 shaft horsepower from her nuclear reactor and steam turbine as against the 15,000 of *Splendid*. No wonder she was overtaking at ten knots.

"Has she got us? Has she been pinging?"

If the answer was yes, that meant that the "bogey" (now transformed through its Soviet identity to a "bandit") was on active sonar, sending out enormous belts of energy into the surrounding waters to bounce back from any object coursing through the depths of the ocean. On passive sonar, the huge hydrophones of the boat's sonar system sent out no energy pulse but would simply take in and record the noises it picked up.

Earphones in place but able to hear the words from the captain as well as the electronic sounds, Pratt, his eyes moving from his control panel to the huge screen, nodded vigorously. "Aye, sir. No doubt about it. She started pinging just as she came on the screen."

"We've got her and she's got us," Pritchard added.

"But she'll soon be long gone unless she wants to play silly bugger with us."

Suddenly the huge gray map of the sonar screen flickered, interference lines running up and down its face like a television set.

"What in hell is that?" the captain half shouted.

"Damned if I know, sir," Pritchard replied. "I've never seen anything like that before and it's not in any of the textbooks."

For a moment, the full sweeping image of the screen was restored. With it came another shock. Marcus Leach could scarcely believe what he saw. "Hell's teeth. There's another bloody sub."

There on the screen, about a mile behind the first bandit but slightly off to port, steering exactly the same course, was the blip of the second submarine. Was it another Alfa? Or was it a shadowing American?

"What's the second one?" Leach's voice had a note of urgency.

Pratt was furiously punching buttons on his console, trying to capture the signature and feed it into the computer, when the screen again lost its image and showed only horizontal rolling lines.

More furious button punching, switch flicking, dial twisting by the sonar watchkeeper. Suddenly he took the phones away from his ears. He turned to his right, handing the earphones past Pritchard to the captain. "Listen to that, sir. Gorblimey, I've never heard anything like that in my bleedin' life."

Leach clamped one of the phones to his left ear. What he heard was an undulating signal, a sound curiously similar to the range of white noise in the relatively narrow band of frequencies emitted by the engines, machinery and propellers of submarines but at a much higher, more penetrating volume.

"What do you think it is, sir?" Pratt had swiveled around in his seat to watch the captain as he listened to the peculiar sound.

Leach kept the phone to his ear for a few more seconds before saying, "I haven't a clue. I've never heard anything like that before either."

He handed the head set back to the petty officer and spoke to Pritchard. "There may be something wrong with our own sonar gear. Better check it out, chop, chop. I'll take over the watch while you're doing it."

"Aye, aye, sir."

Back in the control room, Leach dispatched the messenger of the watch, Smith, to fetch the first lieutenant. As he waited for Lieutenant-Commander Paul Tait to appear, he settled into the chair between the two watchkeepers on the steering and hydroplane controls, his eyes expertly reading the instruments in front of them.

When his tall, ungainly first lieutenant burst into the control room, sandals flapping, Leach told him to go into the sonar room, take a look at the screen and listen to the sound on the earphones. Tait promptly disappeared.

In a few minutes he was back, the forehead below his long, stringy, brown hair furrowed.

"What do you make of it, Paul?"

Tait's puzzled eyes contemplated the deck, unseeing, as he puzzled over what he had heard. Then they lifted to look at Leach. "I really don't know, sir. It's a new one on me. There's probably something wrong in our own gear."

A clue crossed Leach's mind. He got up and stepped forward through the doorway to stick his head in the sonar room again, where Pritchard and the two watchkeepers were busy running through the standard test checks.

"Is that Alfa still pinging us?"

"No, sir," Petty Officer Pratt replied, the earphones back on his head. "They stopped just after the big sound started, just before I gave the earphones to you."

"But you could hear the pinging over the big sound. It didn't blank out the pinging."

"That's right, sir."

"What about our back-up sonar?"

Pritchard shrugged. "We've tried it, sir. We get the same thing. The big noise, as Pratt calls it."

Back again in the control room the captain leaned against the periscope shaft as he turned this new information over in his mind. Either there was something wrong with their own sonar gear or there was some strong external force out there producing an overpowering, overriding noise on the white sound frequencies. His memory told him that he had seen an intelligence report some months back. How did it go? The Soviets had been trying out some sort of a noise-generating device in their "race track" testing area in the Barents Sea north of the Kola Peninsula. Intelligence had made no judgment on what the device was for. Just that the defensive hydrophone chain across the Iceland Gap to Norway had picked up short bursts of its sound.

Whether the interference was from an internal fault in the boat's gear or an external source, way below periscope depth, which was also radar depth, *Splendid* was blind. Then what about the ship's inertial navigation system?

"Pilot, is SINS functioning all right?"

The navigation officer appeared startled by the question, even though he had heard the commotion going on about the sonar. "No problem, sir."

So the navigation system was not affected. But without the sonar, *Splendid* was not only blind but, as an attack vessel, useless. With its sonar eyes in operation, the attack submarine could do many things. It could act unsupported against surface ships. It was complementary to aircraft and antisubmarine operations in that the long range patrol aircraft "located" the enemy ship, the ship-borne helicopter "pinpointed" and the submarine "destroyed." By itself the attack submarine was also an extremely good antisubmarine vessel, greatly aided by its ability to carry the biggest and best sonar—because of its size, its powerful nuclear reactor, and its ability to stay submerged for weeks on end. It was capable of firing a variety of weapons from its torpedo tubes in support of a task force such as the flotilla that *Splendid* was on its way to join in the Arabian Sea. But without the sonar, she could perform none of the functions for which she was built.

Pritchard appeared in the door behind the captain. "Sir, we've completed all the checks."

Leach was certain of what his sonar officer was going to tell him. "And?"

"There's nothing wrong with the main sonar or the back-up. We're getting interference from an outside source."

"That's probably why the Alfa stopped pinging at us. She's undoubtedly getting the same big noise. It would blanket her active sonar reception."

"That's right, sir," Pritchard agreed.

"Have your watchkeepers let me know the minute that damn noise disappears—if it does, that is—or if there's any other change in the situation. You can take back the watch."

"Aye, aye, sir."

To his first lieutenant, the captain extended an invitation, "Buy you a beer." Without waiting for Tait's acceptance, Leach went down the passageway toward the front of the ship to the cramped but comfortable wardroom. It was empty. All the officers not standing watch were down on the deck below in the Junior Ranks' Mess watching a movie from the ship's ample library of first-run films. The steward, Joyce, was hovering as soon as they entered his domain. He took their order and immediately produced two lagers. Leach slumped in the corner of the settee that ran along the curve of the ship's hull. His first lieutenant perched on a small padded chair, his long legs and big feet propped up on another.

"Well, what do you make of it, Paul?" Leach asked.

"Blessed if I know. It must be some diabolical device the Russkis dreamt up."

"Or the Americans, or for that matter our own research people."

Tait smiled, "Perhaps. What do you propose to do, sir?" There was no first-name familiarity permitted the first lieutenant. The captain was far senior to Tait. They had never served together in equal ranks and Leach never gave the first name invitation, nor would he.

"I think we should either surface or go to periscope depth, and I think we should do it immediately." The captain had come to that conclusion before they left the control

room, but he wanted to try it on for size with the first
lieutenant, out of earshot of the rest of the crew.

Tait was alarmed. "But, sir, going to the surface at
night in one of the busiest sea lanes in the world and with
no sonar. The chance of collision . . ."

The captain finished the sentence: "Is very high, I
agree. But there's a chance of collision down here, too.
Maybe not as great. We know that there were two subs.
The other's probably an Alfa too, about six miles behind us
and closing when the sonar went off. Right now, they're
probably just as blind as we are and they can be right up
our jaxy. As long as we're below periscope depth we have a
collision risk. Sure, it may be small, but it's there. On the
other hand, if we run close to the surface, we'll be able to
use our eyes and our radar. The risk of collision will be
practically nil."

"Except when we're on our way up."

"That's right," Leach acknowledged, "Furthermore, I
want to make a signal to Admiralty as soon as possible, telling them what's happened and asking for instructions."
Leach could not transmit while *Splendid* was completely
submerged. He could only do so if he surfaced or was running at periscope depth with his aerial exposed.

The first lieutenant was still not convinced. "Shouldn't
you wait until first light, sir?"

"I think not." The captain had made up his mind. He
had had only one sip of beer. He put his glass down,
reached over his head to the switch on the speaker on the
forward bulkhead immediately above him. Turning his
face toward the speaker, he pulled down on the switch, saying, "Pilot, this is the captain."

From the control room, the navigating officer's voice
crackled through the box, "Pilot here, go ahead, sir."

"What are the surface conditions?"

All ears in the control room listened with curiosity.
Why was the old man asking about surface conditions?

"The latest weather report, sir, at 16:00 Zulu [Green-
wich mean time]: We're in a high pressure area. Winds five

to six knots from 085 degrees. No cloud cover reported. Sea rolling, almost calm."

"What's the temperature?"

"Seventy-eight degrees, sir."

As he stood up to leave the wardroom, Leach turned to Tait and said, "Good show. It's a pleasant night up top, Paul. Let's hope there aren't any great goddamn tankers up there."

He was followed into the control room by the first lieutenant. Leach picked up the broadcast microphone and clicked the button twice to test it. He heard the clicking echo throughout the ship, alerting the entire crew that something was coming. Even those who were sleeping wakened, their ears sensitive to the signs of an imminent announcement.

"This is the captain speaking. We will be going to periscope depth in a few minutes and I want to tell you why. Our sonar is unserviceable. It has experienced a most unusual interference from outside the ship in the form of a big noise on the range of frequencies that it's designed to operate in. The result is that our boat is now blind in the water. By not hearing we can't see a thing." He thought he put that fairly well.

He then explained his line of reasoning, as he had to the first lieutenant in the wardroom.

"Everyone should realize there is a risk of collision when we go up blind, at least until we get up to periscope level. At fifty feet, we can take a look around to make sure no bloody tanker is bearing down on us. Most tankers don't have a draft of fifty feet, so they would pass over us. But these days some of the loaded big ones reach down ninety feet and more. If we have trouble, it will be from one of those. But I'm quite certain nothing's going to happen. I'm sure that when we get the periscope up I won't find a ship anywhere. So we're going to go to periscope depth so we can take a look around and use our radar for anticollision purposes. As soon as the sonar interference is cleared, we'll dive and go back to normal running procedures." He concluded by giving them a report on the weather up top. "That's all. Carry on please."

He put the microphone back on its storage holder.

Splendid was still running at 500 feet.

"Keep 150 feet."

"One hundred and fifty feet, sir," the planesman reported the order pulling gently back on his wheel. The cant of the deck tilted upwards while the blowing of the ballast tanks began. *Splendid* was headed for the surface.

At the systems console, the first lieutenant, who had taken over from Pritchard, gave a flow of running orders to the watchkeeper controlling the blowing, flooding, and topping of the trim tanks and the blowing of the main ballast tank.

Splendid was rising rapidly.

Leach sat in his chair, listening to the chatter of orders and responses around the control room.

"Two hundred feet, sir."

His eyes confirmed the figure on the depth gauges.

Slightly nervous, he got up to stand beside the periscope. Time to cut back the speed. If they were going to hit another ship, no sense doing it at full bore. "Half ahead."

"Half ahead, sir."

He could feel the propellers and the ship itself slowing down.

"One hundred and fifty feet, sir. Keeping 150 feet, sir."

He would keep it there for a few moments, making sure that the first lieutenant had the trim and was able to keep her level close to the hard-to-achieve neutral point of buoyancy that would allow her to sit at the desired periscope level so the ship would not pop out of the water. He wanted the glass eye at the top of the periscope to emerge cleanly and stop just about a foot above the surface. In the red glow of the control room, darkened to allow the captain to maximize his night vision, he called, "Keep fifty feet!"

"Keep fifty feet, sir." A gentle easing back on the control wheel. A shade of ballast blowing.

"Up search periscope!"

Instantly, the thick shaft standing vertical in the middle of the control room responded. Oil pressure rams forced down the unseen wire pulleys that silently moved the binocular and bifocal, high-powered periscope, able to see and search for many miles, upward in a shaft until its eye pieces stopped in front of the waiting face of the captain.

"One hundred feet, sir."

Leach moved the periscope handles out and down from their stored position. A question went through his mind. Would it be best to stop engines so that *Splendid* had no forward motion? Would that minimize damage in the event of a collision? He had thought of those questions before and decided against stopping. He reasoned that if his boat was making way at, say, fifteen knots when the periscope first cut the surface of the water, and some great bloody monster of a tanker was bearing down on him, his hydroplanes at fifteen knots would have sufficient bite to bunt the *Splendid* down the additional fifty feet to get under the biggest tanker's hull. He would stay with the fifteen knots option.

"Seventy-five feet, sir."

Leach grabbed the periscope handles turning the shaft until it pointed dead ahead. Then his face clamped into the eye piece.

His voice ranged out through the control room, "Be prepared for emergency dive. If I give the order to dive, just shove the goddamn wheel right through the front!"

"Aye, aye, sir!" came the sharp response from the planesman.

Through the flat, glass eye of the extended periscope, Leach could see nothing but smooth blackness.

"Coming up to fifty feet, sir."

"Up radar."

There it was, just a slight tone change in the blackness.

A streak of white foam, and phosphorescence, then a new, lighter blackness. The periscope had surfaced, cutting cleanly.

Dead ahead—nothing. A fast turn of the periscope to starboard, sweeping the horizon to ninety degrees. There in the distance, green and white twinkling running lights. No problem.

A quick wheel back to begin a sweep of the port side. He had moved the periscope no more than twenty degrees to port off the bow when he caught the first blazing running light. It was red and close. A swing further to port. A green light!

"Christ, she's coming right at us!" The words ripped through Leach's brain. Range? In the darkness and in a split second guess maybe 300 yards.

Leach could hear himself screaming, "Dive! Dive! Dive!"

He felt the boat lurch forward as he slammed up the periscope handle, shouting, "Down periscope! Down radar! Full speed ahead!"

By this time the submarine was approaching the maximum downward dive angle that the riding control systems would permit. In the stern, *Splendid*'s propeller spun furiously, pushing her faster and faster. The periscope slammed down into its well.

All that could be done was to wait. Wait.

"Sixty feet, sir." Yes, he knew it was sixty feet. His eyes were glued on the depth gauges, as they moved slower than he had ever seen them before. Seconds clicked by. Sixty-five feet. More seconds. Seventy feet. More seconds. Eighty feet.

He could hear the thumping of the churning screw of the gargantuan tanker, its booming noise reverberating through the hull of the plunging *Splendid*. Closer and louder came the petrifying, ominous pounding.

More seconds.

Ninety feet. The crescendo of deafening propeller noise shook *Splendid* from stem to stern. Its thumping beat was the signal of death and disaster for every man of the *Splendid*'s crew. At the peak of the devastating noise, a long screaming sound could be heard above like the screech of reluctant chalk drawn across a blackboard. That penetrating din lasted for two seconds. Then as quickly as it had started it was gone. Immediately the deafening thunder of the tanker's engine and screw began to diminish. Slowly, then more rapidly, their throbbing noise disappeared to the north as the distance between the two vessels rapidly increased.

Splendid's crew, many of them buffeted about by the harsh handling of their boat, knew what had happened, what the brutal noise immediately above them meant, and in fear of their own lives began pulling themselves together. The captain, steadying himself and gathering his wits after that closest of calls, ordered in a calm business-like voice, "Keep 125 feet!"

"Keep 125 feet, sir."

As the boat's descent stopped and she leveled off, Commander Leach picked up the broadcast microphone once again. After his usual testing and alerting clicks on the speak button, he said into it, "This is the captain. I think it is obvious to everybody that we've just had a narrow escape."

He heard the words muttered from the planesman, "By a bleeding snatch hair!"

"What I plan to do is this. The area to the west is clear. I checked it first just before I caught the tanker coming in on top of us. We'll sail west for ten minutes, then surface. There may have been some damage. However, I'm quite certain there are no ships in the area where we're going to surface next."

He released the microphone button, shouting forward toward the sonar room, "Any joy on the sonar yet, Pritchard?"

The young officer's head popped around the doorway. "No, sir, it's still duff."

Back into the microphone, "There's still no joy on the

sonar, so we're going to run on the surface as I earlier advised. Carry on please."

Ten minutes later, Leach brought his vessel to periscope level. Up went the search periscope. The horizon was clean and clear except for the port and aft running lights of the retreating tanker that had almost killed them.

To the first lieutenant went the order, "Clear. Take her up. Down periscope. Telegraph to stop. Wheel amidships. Planes amidships!"

Splendid was sitting comfortably on the surface of the South Atlantic, rolling gently with the swell. Orders were given to raise and drain the snort mast, to open the lower hatch of the tower and switch on the power and lighting. Before he climbed the rungs of the ladder into the tower, Leach planted his gold-braided hat squarely on his head, telling the messenger of the watch to get him a flashlight. There was something he would have to inspect in the darkness of the tiny bridge, high up the top of the tower. Young Smith was back within twenty seconds.

"Stick it in your shirt and follow me up the ladder."

The young lad, no more than seventeen, was thrilled to have the privilege of following his captain and to be the first one after him to be up on the bridge. "Aye, aye, sir."

The call came, "Lights switched on in the tower, sir."

"How's the pressure in the boat?"

"No pressure in the boat, sir."

Smith followed him up the ladder to the top.

"Shine the torch up here, lad."

In the wavering, strong light Leach took out the two upper hatch hooks and undid both. The hatch swung upward and back easily under the pressure of his right hand.

The captain hauled himself quickly up onto the deck of the small bridge. The steel of the vessel glistened as the sea water ran off through the perforated lattice work of the deck. Leach strained to adjust his eyes to the total darkness, moving rapidly in a 360-degree turn to scan the ebony sea for running lights. There were none except those of their near nemesis, now some miles to the north, its stern superstructure and port lights showing themselves to the master of *Splendid*.

Leaning down, Leach gave a hand to the young seaman scrambling up behind with the much-needed torch. Behind Smith, whose unsure feet were now solidly on the tower deck, came the first lieutenant with the portable voice pipe and the broadcast extension. Both communications instruments were essential to the sailing of the ship on the surface.

Leach stepped to the rear of the bridge, waiting until Tait was on the deck. He stood in darkness illuminated only by the internal tower lights shining up through the open hatch.

Ordinarily, the captain would have called for running lights by that time, but he was so preoccupied with the urgent need to examine the top side of the boat that the routine order had gone out of his mind.

When the first lieutenant was at his side at the aft end of the bridge, Leach looked back toward the stern. The cylindrical shape of the boat's black hull was outlined in phosphorescent foam where it met the lapping sea water. Leach switched on the torch, directing its penetrating beam along the flat top side of the tower to the point some twenty feet aft through which the attack and search periscopes and radar mast emerged. As Leach shone his torch across that section of the tower, he could see that the tops of all the retracted instruments were flush with the surface and undamaged.

The tower's topside should have been gunmetal gray in color, dull with its protective coats of heavily leaded paint. Instead, the entire surface shone with the bright glint of unpainted steel. There were no gouging lines, just the smooth, bare metal surface, gleaming as if newly polished. Wheeling to his right, Leach shone the torch beam along the port edge of the bridge, following its shining lip to the middle of the curve that formed the front of the tower. The paintless surface stopped abruptly in a line that ran roughly twenty degrees off the ship's bow to port. That demarcation line appeared again under Leach's torch on the starboard side of the tower's surface aft the bridge and on a reciprocal line 160 degrees off the ship's bow.

The captain involuntarily sucked air through his teeth as the full impact of what he had seen hit him. His first lieutenant gasped in astonishment, "Christ, the keel of that goddamn tanker . . ."

Leach, incredulous but happy to be alive, couldn't resist, "Almost polished us off."

His mind's eye saw the wide keel of the monster tanker gently contacting and screeching its way along the tower top, meeting *Splendid* almost head on and pushing the submarine down ever so slightly as the tanker's keel ran smoothly along the tower's surface from mid-bridge aft like a gigantic buffing tool.

"Another foot or two and she would have had us," Tait said.

The captain disagreed, "Try six inches."

Leach went to the portable voice pipe and shouted into it, "Control room, do you read me?"

The voice that came back was that of the ship's coxswain, Chief Petty Officer Richards. "You're a little muffled, but I can hear you all right, sir."

"Report telegraph when ready."

"Telegraph to stop, wheel's amidships, sir."

"Navigation lights on the bridge. Officer of the watch and lookouts on the bridge. Test raise and lower both periscopes and all masts and get an inspection party on deck with torches to take a look for any damage!"

The coxswain automatically responded, "Aye, aye, sir."

Leach watched the periscopes and masts go up and down. He was satisfied that they were functioning properly. The officer of the watch and two hands to serve as lookouts came up through the hatch to the bridge. The captain then clambered down the ladder rungs to the control room, followed by the first lieutenant and the messenger of the watch, who was still carrying the torch.

All faces in the rosy glow of the control room were turned expectantly toward the captain.

"Get her under way, Paul. As soon as the damage inspection party reports back, take her to periscope level. I'm sure they won't find anything. Pick up the same course we were following when we were so rudely interrupted. Have the watch on the bridge and the radar keep a sharp eye. I've got to start the bloody paper war."

In the event of any accident or incident it was mandatory that full written reports be made and recorded. Every detail would be scrutinized by the Admiralty. If the ship's captain was seen to be at fault, a court martial could follow. "But first I have to prepare my signal to the Admiralty. Tell Pots to stand by. It will take me about fifteen minutes to put it together." Petty officer telegraphists were now titled radio supervisors but the name "Pots" had survived for the senior rating in the ship's communications center.

At his desk in the privacy of his cabin, Commander Marcus Leach laboriously wrote out his reporting signal to the Admiralty in his strong vertical handwriting. He described the sonar interference situation, asking for an explanation and instructions if any. Then followed the preliminary report on the near miss with the tanker, the latitude and longitude of the spot where the incident occurred and a request that the identity of the ship be obtained and passed back to *Splendid*. Back at Faslane and then Whitehall the signal would send staff officers scurrying. The tanker's identity would easily be found, both from satellite photographs and from Lloyd's of London. Among other things, it would be interesting to know which ship almost did them in.

Within an hour after his signal was sent, the first of a series of responses arrived. The slip of paper was delivered by Pots to the captain, still at his desk writing the preliminary report on the tanker incident. The message read, "Your visitor was *Esso Atlantic*, owner Exxon Corporation. Built Japan 1977; deadweight tons 509,000, speed 15 knots; registry Liberia; length 1,334 feet, draft loaded 91 feet; sails mainly from Persian Gulf to Ports in northern Europe. Also lighters in Gulf of Mexico."

"Draft ninety-one feet!" Leach thought, "No bloody wonder I've got a polished tower top."

That was the first of two meetings between H.M.S. *Splendid* and the mighty Exxon Corporation's mammoth *Esso Atlantic*. The second would be more than a month and a half later on the first day of May, off Cape Town, South Africa.

7

11-13 March

Camp David   Diego Garcia

On Sunday, March 10, the presidential schedule for the following week was altered. The published version stated that John Hansen had canceled all appointments until next Friday to allow him four days of complete rest and seclusion at Camp David. He had long since decided that, while at the age of sixty-one he was in excellent health and quite capable of working eighteen hours a day, seven days a week, he had no intention of working himself to death. He recognized that his responsibilities were so heavy, covered such a broad range of domestic and international matters, that it was now an office that was too much for one man, that the overpowering pressure could kill, and that he, John Hansen, would not let that happen to him. So he had let it be widely known that from time to time he would retreat to the privacy of Camp David with minimum time notice to his staff and to the public and, for that matter, to his young wife, Judith Hansen.

The president and his wife arrived at Camp David shortly before five in the afternoon of Monday, March 11. Their arrival was duly noted by a covey of reporters and photographers. During the evening of the eleventh and on into the night, helicopters were heard banging their way in and out of Camp David. In all, four trips were made. Not an unusual number when the president was there. None of them had been the enormous Marine Corps chopper that usually carried the president. The helicopter that landed at two in the morning of March 12 was much smaller, a single-rotor, twin-engined aircraft. Precisely on time, it had picked up its four passengers: two secret service men, Judith Hansen, and the president. They carried no luggage. It was already on Air Force One waiting for them at Andrews Air Force Base.

At 4:01 A.M., Tuesday, March 12, the captain of the glistening Boeing 707, Air Force One, received his air traffic control clearance as he taxied to the end of the runway, navigation lights blazing, landing lights cutting the darkness ahead, the brilliant blips of strobe lights flashing from its wing tips. At 4:06, Air Force One was airborne, climbing steeply up from Andrews to turn east. The captain had punched into the inertial navigation system his ultimate destination over seventeen hours flying time away. Other adjustments were made in the aircraft's complex electronic navigation and control system. The president's aircraft would fly without the touch of the captain or his copilot on the controls during the entire 10,200 miles to its destination, a mere speck of an island in the Indian Ocean. On board were the president and his wife, Secretary of State Eaton, Secretary of Defense Robert Levy, the president's national security adviser, Walter Kruger, and President Hansen's chief of staff, Jim Crane. In addition, there were four secret service men, part of the highly trained Washington team whose principal function was to protect the president, the vice-president, and all those members of the administration who were by law entitled to security.

President Hansen spent the first hours of the flight with his cabinet members and Kruger. Judith was by his side listening to everything being said. From time to time she put in a question or a relevant comment. She was as much a part of her husband's team as were any of the men.

Crane sat within easy earshot of the conversation and took notes. The secret service quartet sat in the forward section of the aircraft near the flight deck, in a separate compartment. They chatted, read, played cards, and slept.

By the time Air Force One crossed the shores of northwest Africa, dinner had been served and the president and his lady had retired to their private quarters at the rear of the aircraft for some sleep. As it hurtled eastward in the clear, black, star-dotted night sky over Niger in central Africa, John Hansen, the president of the United States of America, lay naked on his side under silk sheets, his huge right hand cupping the firm breasts of his young wife, the skin of her back and round bottom tucked against his chest and his satisfied thighs.

At 07:10 local time on Wednesday morning, Air Force One gently touched down on Diego Garcia, a miniscule island in the Indian Ocean a thousand nautical miles south of the southern tip of India, and some 2,200 miles, five days' sail, away from the shores of Pakistan. Diego Garcia had no inhabitants except for the U.S. Navy personnel stationed there to operate the base, and a handful of British naval personnel who worked in a communications center which the Americans and British jointly ran.

Diego Garcia was part of the British Indian Ocean Territory (BIOT), created in 1965 to provide sites for joint U.K./U.S. military facilities. In the mid 1970s the U.S. government negotiated an agreement with the United Kingdom for the use of Diego Garcia as a permanent naval base. From that time, the U.S. Navy had continued to improve the naval and air facilities on the island. The original 8,000-foot runway on the west arm of the atoll was extended to 12,000 feet. The lagoon, which was twelve miles wide at its broadest point and twenty-four miles long, was dredged for anchorages that would accept the heaviest of the American aircraft carriers. Docks were built, fuel storage capacity was substantially increased, aircraft hangars and buildings for personnel accommodation were constructed. Marine maintenance shops were placed near the dry dock that was built in Japan in 1980 and installed inside Diego Garcia's lagoon just to the north of the air strip.

At President Hansen's request, the captain of Air Force One made a broad sweeping circle over the island before landing, so the president and his party could get a good look at the crystal clear water, and the multi-shaded coral reefs around the flat island's edge. That morning, as on most mornings on an island that received up to 145 inches annually, sheets of rain gusted across the atoll.

Hansen's spirits were lifted when he caught sight of the majestic flat-topped aircraft carrier, the *Dwight D. Eisenhower*, riding at anchor in the Diego Garcia lagoon, her vast gray bulk surrounded by a cluster of five destroyers and a cruiser. He was always thrilled by the raw power that huge warships exuded, particularly those of his own country. As he circled the remote island of Diego Garcia that morning, the president felt a strong surge of pride for his navy and his country. It was his responsibility to keep both of them strong.

On the rain-soaked ramp of the airstrip at Diego Garcia, the president and his wife, both dressed in their lightest white summer clothes, were received by the flag officer from the *Dwight D. Eisenhower*, followed by her captain, and the local base commander. The rain stopped momentarily as the president inspected the drenched honor guard of a hundred men from the *Eisenhower* before being lifted with his party by helicopters to the carrier's deck. As they stepped out of the helicopter onto the sunlit flight deck, Hansen could see a gray sheet of rain moving toward the ship across the airstrip. Fortunately the ceremony welcoming him on board was short. When it was over, he and Judith were escorted inside the towering superstructure of the *Eisenhower*, just as the next flood of rain enveloped the ship.

General Mujeeb-Ul-Rehman, the recently appointed president of Pakistan, had arrived at Diego Garcia in his own small jet aircraft forty-five minutes earlier and had been brought to the *Eisenhower*. With the two other Pakistani generals who had accompanied him, he had awaited President Hansen's arrival in the ship's aircrew briefing room. It was there that, amidst much formality, the two men met for the first time. When the captain of the *Eisenhower* and Judith left the conference room for a tour of the carrier, the two negotiating groups seated themselves opposite each other at the long table.

Hansen had not had much time to size up Mujeeb. Although he knew a great deal about him from the files that Kruger and State had produced, it was the actual presence of the man that had to be assessed. Mujeeb was of medium height, fifty years of age and looked it. His jet-black straight hair was combed directly back from a high forehead. His eyes were deepset, ringed with dark marks of fatigue. As did his colleagues, he sported a trimmed, black mustache. His even, unblemished teeth were often framed in a ready smile. His swarthy face was almost the same color as his light khaki, high-collared uniform. Mujeeb appeared affable enough, although he was obviously nervous in the presence of such power.

President Hansen opened the proceedings with an elaborate explanation of how the United States viewed the current buildup of the Soviet forces in Afghanistan and along the Soviet-Iran border. He stressed the growing probability of a Soviet move against Pakistan, Iran, and the Persian Gulf countries. He explained the American difficulty in not having an operating base from which it could quickly deploy forces to protect the Persian Gulf countries or to defend Pakistan under the terms of the 1959 agreement that obliged the United States to come to the aid of Pakistan against any attacker.

"I want to confirm to you, President Mujeeb, that the United States of America regards that 1959 agreement as still valid and binding."

Mujeeb smiled. "My government reciprocates, Mr. President. In fact we think that the existence of that agreement has been instrumental in deterring the Soviet Union from driving on into our country with its Afghanistan forces, at least to this date. But we share your concern. The buildup of Soviet forces in Afghanistan is—how shall I put it?—ominous indeed. We in Pakistan are virtually defenseless, as you well know. My predecessor never could bring himself to work out a deal with the United States for much-needed equipment."

"Perhaps he was afraid that if he made a deal with us he would incur the wrath of India, as well as the Soviet Union?" the President suggested.

"Perhaps," Mujeeb allowed. "I happen to know what was in his mind on those questions, but he is gone and the Soviets are threatening as never before. My country is in economic difficulty and we need help in defending ourselves. Nevertheless, Mr. President, I must not mislead you into thinking that we are so desperate that we are prepared to 'give the store away' as you might put it." Again Mujeeb smiled.

Hansen returned the smile, shaking his head in protest, "No, Mr. President, I don't think you're going to give us the store, nor would my government want you to."

One thing Hansen knew was that, like most Pakistanis, Mujeeb was a good haggler, a trader, a bargainer.

It was time for him to play his opening card. "As a matter of fact our price for what you want will be high, extremely high. That should be understood from the outset. Mind you, you haven't yet told me what it is you want of us. But I can guess that it's far more than just access to the Port of Karachi and the airport there."

"It is."

"Of course it must be, for the president of the United States himself to come this far to meet with a small, insignificant person such as myself."

Hansen was tempted to protest the Pakistani's self-demeaning remark, but resisted.

Mujeeb did not smile when he said, "My colleagues and I believe that you wish to put American troops and equipment on Pakistani soil; that is why you have come here. Is that correct, Mr. President?"

"Yes, it is."

"As I have said, the price will be high. Very high."

It was John Hansen's turn to smile. "If you're prepared to talk price, President Mujeeb, you're prepared to let us in. I'll tell you what we want. You tell me the price."

8

15 March   11:01 A.M.
Washington, D.C.

On Thursday, March 14, Air Force One had touched down at Andrews Air Force Base, where a small Marine helicopter sat waiting on the ramp for the trip to Camp David. Shortly after four that afternoon, the presidential limousine was bound for the White House. Ever mindful of the need for good relations with the press, the president stopped the car at the Camp David gate to get out and talk to the reporters and photographers waiting for him. Had the president had a good three-day rest? When did the president think that gas rationing would be lifted? Did he think that legislative steps should be taken to hold the price of gasoline at three dollars a gallon? Would the United States take any action as a result of the Soviet buildup on the Iran border?

The president parried all the questions with the expertise of a long-time politician. The experienced reporters quickly understood that any answer they got that day would have little meat. So when, after ten minutes of talk, he made to get back into the limousine, no one was pressing him with further questions.

At a presidential press conference in the East Room of the White House, there was never an empty seat. The president's decision to meet with the press the next day was made as soon as he arrived back at Camp David. The announcement did not specify the reason for the meeting with the nation's top journalists, a fact which piqued their curiosity. Hansen had considered asking for network time to speak to the people, but decided against it. The press coverage of the conference would be sufficient.

At the stroke of ten, on the morning of March 15, President John Hansen entered the packed East Room to stride briskly to the lectern. Everyone in the room stood up as he mounted the dais and looked down at the sea of faces.

"Good morning, ladies and gentlemen," he said, and then waited until everyone was again seated. "As you all know, my wife and I went to Camp David on Monday. My press secretary said that I was going because I needed a rest. Well, I needed a rest all right, but I didn't get one. Judith and I went to Camp David as advertised but we didn't stop there. We left by helicopter at two in the morning on Tuesday for Andrews Air Force Base where we collected the secretary of state, the secretary of defense, the national security adviser and Jim Crane, my chief of staff. From Andrews, which we left at four in the morning in Air Force One, we flew almost due east for seventeen hours to an island in the Indian Ocean called Diego Garcia."

The room buzzed as the press people asked each other. "Where the hell is Diego Garcia?" Some of the more knowledgeable, however, nodded as they took their notes. They knew where it was. But what the hell was the president of the United States doing at Diego Garcia?

"The reason for my trip was to meet in total secrecy with the president of a nation whose future is critical to the best interests of the United States. My meeting was with General Mujeeb-Ul-Rehman, the president of Pakistan."

As tape recorders and TV cameras recorded the scene and pens and pencils flew furiously, there was a buzz of side talk from his audience. A few faces looked up from their writing to stare at Hansen in astonishment. The room seemed to flow with tension as the minds of the top journalists from America instantly began to analyze what they were hearing. This was news, big news. Some wished they could bolt through the door to get to a telephone, but that was against the rules of presidential press conferences.

Hansen then listed the reasons why he was compelled to go. In the presence of the escalating Soviet military threat, it was imperative that a new understanding be reached with Pakistan and it had to be done quickly. It had to be done in secret and it had to be done head of state to head of state.

With the preamble out of the way, the president slipped on his bifocal glasses and read from his prepared text:

I am pleased to announce that at 10 A.M. local time yesterday at Diego Garcia, the President of Pakistan, General Mujeeb-Ul-Rehman, on behalf of his government, and I on behalf of the government of the United States, signed an agreement which will permit the entry into Pakistan of United States land, sea, and air forces in such numbers and on whatever scale the Government of the United States feels appropriate under the circumstances. The agreement does not permit the entry of any nuclear weapons. The American forces so deployed in Pakistan will be solely for the purpose of the defense of Pakistan against attack, although that limitation will not prevail in the event of any military action in the Middle East that might threaten the vital interests of the United States.

In consideration for the entry of U.S. forces to Pakistan, the United States will provide to the government of Pakistan up to two billion dollars' worth of fighter aircraft, tanks, surface-to-air missiles, and other weaponry designed to strengthen the ability of the Pakistan forces to defend their nation. The delivery of these armaments will begin on May the seventh, which is the day American forces will first be permitted to land. It will take that long to assemble our task force and transport it by ship to Pakistan. Furthermore, this agreement will require the ratification of Congress before it can be implemented. In this connection, I have been assured by the majority and minority leaders, both in the Senate and the House of Representatives, that they will support the accord with Pakistan. Therefore, I look for an early ratification by Congress.

In addition to the military aid package, the United States will provide Pakistan with four billion dollars in economic aid over the next three years. That money will be used for the purchase of food, the building of housing, the creation of new industry, and the general welfare of the Pakistani people. Almost all the foreign purchases to be made by Pakistan under this program will be from the United States. In addition, the United States will assist Pakistan in refinancing its extensive foreign debt.

The positioning of American forces in Pakistan will serve notice to the Soviet Union that it cannot have a free hand in the Middle East, that it cannot seize Pakistan or Iran as it took Afghanistan. It will serve notice to the Soviet Union that the United States intends to use its full might and power to preserve the integrity and sovereignty of the Arab and Persian nations upon which the Western world and Japan depend for their supplies of crude oil. Sixty-one percent of all the crude oil imported into Western Europe—ninety-six percent of its oil is imported—comes from the Persian Gulf. For Japan, which imports all of its oil, seventy-two percent is from the Persian Gulf. For the United States, which now imports forty-nine percent of the crude oil it consumes, some thirty-four percent of that quantity is from the Persian Gulf. Those supplies cannot be halted, they cannot be tampered with. The countries which provide them to us must be assured by the United States that they will not come under the heel of the Soviets.

The time has come when the United States must draw a line in the Middle East across which the Soviets shall not pass. Having drawn that line, we must be able to demonstrate that we can enforce it by having a military force in place on the ground, in the air, and on the sea, a force that can repel any Soviet incursion.

This agreement with Pakistan is a major step in achieving those objectives, all of which are designed to preserve world peace and stability.

The president left his text and slipped off his glasses. "That's the end of my formal statement for this morning, ladies and gentlemen. Are there any questions?"

Eleven people stood waving their hands for attention. The president selected the *New York Times* correspondent. The rest sat down. They would try again. Her question was, "Mr. President, what do you think the Soviet reaction will be to this agreement?"

"The Soviets are used to having a free hand in Africa and the Middle East. They are hypersensitive about the areas around their own borders. Therefore, I think we can expect a strong propaganda campaign to be mounted. Tass, *Pravda*, and *Izvestia* will undoubtedly be screaming about an American imperialist capitalist invasion of the Middle East. The Soviets will probably take action against us in the United Nations. So the answer is, I expect their reaction to be violent."

He turned to look across the audience. It was the signal that that answer was finished and he would accept another question. From the group who leaped to their feet he selected the correspondent from the *Chicago Tribune* whose question was, "Mr. President, do you think the Soviets would regard the entry of the United States into Pakistan as an act of aggression that they would go to war over?"

"In a word, no. They'll make threats. There's no question about that. But in the assessment of my advisors, they will not risk a direct shooting confrontation with us."

The next correspondent to ask a question was from the *Washington Post*. "Mr. President, there's been much speculation that Pakistan has developed a nuclear bomb.

India in particular is worried about that and about any strengthening of Pakistan, because she regards that country as a threat. Do you have any comment?"

Hansen nodded.

"It is part of the agreement with Pakistan that while we are in their country, they will not deploy or threaten to use or indeed use any nuclear weapon; and that any development of such a weapon—which they deny—will be stopped. They said that since they're not developing a nuclear weapon, they would not have any hesitation in agreeing to such a clause. As to India, I understand the concerns of their prime minister. They've always looked upon Pakistan as a threat and have complained every time weapons or aircraft have been provided to that country. However, our direct presence in Pakistan should provide a stabilizing atmosphere and ease India's concern. On the other hand, our 1959 Defense Pact with Pakistan, of which this new agreement is an extension, says that we will assist Pakistan no matter who attacks her. India was not happy about that agreement in 1959 and it won't be about this one."

The reporter from the *Wall Street Journal* asked, "Sir, have you had consultation with our NATO allies about this agreement or your intention to put troops into Pakistan?"

"No, I have not. There hasn't been time. Pakistan and the Persian Gulf are well outside the chosen jurisdiction of the North Atlantic Treaty Organization. The European NATO members don't want to get involved in the Middle East, although I have great difficulty in understanding why, because their interest in a continuing crude oil supply is far greater than ours. The fact is, they've chosen not to do so, except for the British. They've assigned a flotilla to work with our Fifth Fleet in the Arabian Sea, the approach to the Persian Gulf. In fact I talked to the prime minister late yesterday afternoon when I arrived back in Camp David. As to the rest of our NATO allies, no, I've had no consultation with them. This is a unilateral action on the part of the United States. If our NATO allies want to support us, they can do so by removing the boundary line at the Tropic of Cancer beyond which the NATO naval forces cannot operate, something I think they should have done years ago."

The next would be the final question. It was from the Associated Press. "This is slightly off the subject, Mr. President. The Soviets activated a sonar interference mechanism in the Atlantic on March eleventh. This is the first time it's been used. What is the purpose behind it?"

"Obviously, the sonar interference system is designed to make inoperative all the passive and active sonar systems that sit on the bed of the Atlantic Ocean. It also makes inoperative the sonar systems on all surface ships and submarines, whether they're ours or theirs. The best intelligence information indicates that the main purpose of the system is to prevent the hearing or tracking of their submarines when they move out of their bases in the Kola Peninsula or the Baltic or elsewhere. It also makes it impossible for us to know where their ballistic missile submarines are located in the Atlantic, and their numbers. However, we can tell how many submarines are at sea, because we do a regular satellite inventory of the Soviet submarine bases. Where they are when at sea can only be determined by sonar. Current satellite photographs show that there are an unusual number of submarines at sea, about a hundred out of the Soviet's 426-boat fleet. We are concerned about that, but we believe they've left to take part in the upcoming Soviet exercise. It's called OKEAN. If there was a mass movement of Soviet submarines out of port, that would be a significant danger signal to us. In fact we'd mobilize, go to a state of war readiness, if that happened. In any event, we're monitoring the sonar interference carefully. We don't know how long it's going to last. One of the devices has been found. It appears to be radio-activated and runs for a fixed period of time. We don't know how long that is. At this time we think they're just giving it a practice run. Whatever they're doing, it's very effective."

Hansen thought he'd take one more question. The man from Reuters: "Do you intend to talk to Chairman Romanov on the hot line about the Pakistan agreement, Mr. President?"

"We haven't had to use the hot line yet. The answer is, no, I don't intend to talk with him about it. But if he calls me, I'll be pleased to discuss it with him. One thing is certain, one way or the other, I'll hear from him, either by the hot line or by a formal note or letter."

9

17 March   8:50 A.M.
Moscow

The polished black ZIL limousine of Fleet Admiral of the Soviet Union Nikolai Ivanovich Smirnov, moved at high speed down the center lane of Kutozovsky Prospekt, slowing as it crossed the wet cobblestones of Red Square. It was ten minutes to nine on March 17. Smirnov reclined in the back seat, feeling splendid in his gold-embroidered admiral's uniform. His medals—Order of Lenin and Hero of the Soviet Union—gleamed on both sides of his chest. He had received the summons to the Kremlin in midafternoon the day before. Chairman Romanov himself had called, saying that a matter of the utmost importance had arisen upon which he required the admiral's advice.

As commander in chief of the Soviet navy and worthy successor to its principal creator, Admiral Gorshkov, under whom Smirnov had served as first deputy, he had found it annoying to be summoned without being told the nature of the meeting. On the other hand, he comforted himself by the fact that only two men in the Soviet Union, other than the chief of the General Staff, had the power to summon him. The chairman himself was the first. The second was the minister of defense. He had known them both for years. He had first met the new chairman of the Supreme Soviet Presidium when Grigori Romanov came to Moscow in September of 1970 as the Leningrad Oblast first secretary. Later he saw much more of him when Romanov became the youngest voting member of the Politburo in 1976. He had always liked the chairman. The younger man was courteous and amiable but could also be tough minded. He was a party man who enjoyed power and could make a show of it. Smirnov had been surprised when, on the demise of Brezhnev, the thirteen surviving members of the Politburo had elected the youngest member of their group to ascend to the pinnacle of power in the Soviet Union, the chairmanship of the Politburo and of the Supreme Soviet Presidium. He had been surprised because Romanov, not yet sixty, had been elected by a group of old men whose average age was at least seventy, men who did not like change and wished at all times to preserve the status quo, something that a younger man would not guarantee to do.

As to Marshal Ustinov, the minister of defense, he had been primarily responsible for the appointment of Smirnov first as Gorshkov's first deputy and then as commander in chief. Smirnov had a great affection for Ustinov. As matters stood, he, Smirnov, had a good chance, when the time came, of succeeding to the post of minister of defense. He had thought about that many times. And if he played his cards right . . .

He was speculating about why he had been summoned as he approached the door of the chairman's office at one minute to nine. He handed his cap to his aide and took from him his ever-present briefcase. The door was ceremoniously opened by the major of the Kremlin guard who had escorted Smirnov from his ZIL.

When the admiral stepped into Romanov's impressive office, it was immediately apparent to him that this was to be a meeting of the utmost importance. At the end of the long, green, baize-covered conference table with its eighteen leather chairs, which accommodated the executive membership of the Politburo when it was in full session, sat

Minister of Defense Ustinov, the perennial minister of foreign affairs, Andrei Gromyko, and army General Yu Andropov, like the others a voting member of the Central Committee of the Politburo and chairman of the Committee for State Security, the infamous KGB. One other man was seated at the table. He was Smirnov's immediate superior, the chief of the General Staff of the Armed Forces, Marshal of the Soviet Union Mikhail Kozlov. In the corner of the office to the right, Chairman Romanov sat at his working desk, speaking into one of the three white telephones that sat on a table at its side.

Smirnov was always impressed when he walked into this imposing room in which he had spent many long hours over the years, first when Leonid Brezhnev was its occupant and now under the forceful Romanov. The chairman's office, although big, was sparse in its furnishings. The off-white silk walls, their monotony broken by rectangular strips of mahogany molding, displayed two portraits, those of Karl Marx and Vladimir Lenin. At the end of the room opposite its main entrance were curtained double doors leading to a private study which the chairman used from time to time as a bedroom and dining room.

Smirnov made the ritual, punctilious, formal greetings to each of the men at the table. Although they knew each other well and most were on a first-name basis, it was the protocol that when in the office of the chairman and, in particular, when seated at the long Politburo conference table, formality was the order. The pecking order of position and seniority was strictly observed.

Smirnov seated himself at the conference table to the left of his superior, Marshal Kozlov. To Kozlov's right sat Ustinov. At the end of the table was the empty place that the chairman would occupy. Opposite the military trio sat Gromyko and, on his right, Andropov, their backs to the working desk of the chairman some thirty feet away.

When the chairman put down the receiver into which he had been speaking quietly and began to walk across the room to the conference table, Smirnov's eyes fastened on the younger man. Of medium height, heavy-set with a rounded Slavic face and pale-blue, Great Russian eyes and a full head of straight brown hair graying at the temples, Romanov looked much younger than his near sixty years. Like his predecessor, he was known as one of the best-dressed men in Russia, favoring finely cut dark suits and elegant shirts. Even though he had been installed in office for only a short period of time, he had already been recognized as an outstanding politician, a disciplined executive and a respected, if not feared, force in the quick-shifting sands of world power. He was seen as honest and straightforward in his dealings with the party, supportive of his political colleagues, conservative in his approach to policy making and, so far, resistant to any inclination toward purging among his associates. Like Brezhnev, he enjoyed widespread popularity among the countless Communist party bureaucrats who saw him as a centrist and an able administrator, to whom they willingly gave their all-important support. As with Brezhnev, his penchant for yachts, foreign cars, and luxurious living was both well-known and accepted. That penchant also enabled him to move comfortably not only among the leaders of the Warsaw Pact countries but among those of the North Atlantic Treaty Organization and, for that matter, the rest of the world.

Quite a man. An excellent choice for the old men of the Politburo to make, thought Smirnov as Romanov took his seat at the head of the conference table, apologizing for the delay.

"That was Kuznetsov." All knew he meant Vasili Kuznetsov, the Soviet ambassador to the United States. "I wanted to talk with him before we began this meeting. I had a couple of points to clarify about his conversation with President Hansen last night. As Comrade Gromyko knows, as soon as I learned yesterday that those fools, the Pakistanis, had agreed to let American troops enter the country, I instructed Kuznetsov to lodge a formal protest directly with the president. He saw Comrade Kuznetsov at ten o'clock."

"Did he deliver a note, sir?" Ustinov asked.

"Yes, a note. Comrade Gromyko and I put it together. It's short. I'll read it to you."

He opened the leather folder he had brought from his desk. Reading the note addressed to the president of the United States, he spoke slowly, his well-modulated, deep voice pronouncing each word carefully as was his practice:

The Soviet Union considers the agreement made between the United States and Pakistan for the movement of American military forces in strength into Pakistan as an explicit threat to the territorial integrity and the security of the Soviet Union. This threat to peace is a deliberately provocative and unjustified change in the status quo which the Soviet Union finds totally unacceptable.

Romanov looked up at the men sitting on each side of the table. "It is necessary for the Russian Bear to draw a line across which the American Eagle must neither step nor fly. In these words you will find the line." His eyes went back to the paper as he continued to read:

If the United States implements this despicable agreement either in whole or in part it will be regarded as an act of aggression which will require a full retaliatory response from the Soviet Union.

Gromyko, his face showing no emotion, added, "In the world of diplomacy the words 'full retaliatory response' leave us with all our options open."

"You mean economic . . ?" Andropov asked.

Gromyko nodded. "As well as military. Including nuclear if we have to go that far."

Romanov agreed. "If we have to go that far, and so far as I'm concerned, we will if the American imperialists push us there."

There was no voice of protest against that statement. Instead, the KGB head, Andropov, put a question. "Do you think the Americans understand we would be prepared to consider going nuclear?"

"We would be more than prepared, but the answer is no. They don't understand."

Gromyko, with his long experience in dealing with the Americans, silently nodded his agreement with the chairman's position.

"They cannot get it through their heads that our doctrine vigorously states that while we recognize that a nuclear war, an all-out nuclear war, would be extremely destructive to both sides, its outcome would not be mutual genocide . . . mutual suicide. The nation best prepared for it and with a superior strategy could win and survive with a functional society. The Americans cannot understand, cannot believe, that there would be a victor in a thermonuclear world war."

"Exactly," Gromyko agreed. "The Americans believe in the principle of mutual deterrent and have for decades. By themselves the words 'mutual deterrent' imply a reciprocal attitude on our part. They imply that we wouldn't be the first to strike and they certainly wouldn't be the first to strike. So neither side goes nuclear because both have the capability."

Andropov asked, "What was Hansen's reaction to the note?"

"Evidently he was taken aback. He said that if we were concerned about his action then we should take the matter to the United Nations."

"*Nyet*," Gromyko exclaimed.

"He said that we had no right to complain because we had invaded Afghanistan."

"Not true!" Gromyko spoke again.

"I know it's not true, Comrade Gromyko. We were invited in by the government of Afghanistan to stabilize a destabilized political and religious revolutionary situation. Hansen says that the United States too has been invited in by a country needing help, economic and military help. He claims that we and the Afghans are making incursions into Pakistan, that the Pakistanis are expecting a full-scale invasion from us."

"What did Kuznetsov say to that?"

"He said that that was a lie. The Soviet Union has no intention of moving against Pakistan—unless it commits an act of aggression against Afghanistan."

"That's a good answer."

Romanov smiled. "It's good enough for the moment."

The chairman decided to get to the point of the

meeting. "Gentlemen, the time has come for some hard decisions. The goal of the Soviet Union is world domination by the socialist order. We must continue to conduct a resolute struggle against American imperialism and to rebuff the evil designs and subversions of the American aggressors. We have drawn the line over which they may not cross. And now it is up to us to decide what retaliatory steps and what options are open to us if the Americans do, in fact, go into Pakistan on May 7. But even before that, we must decide what steps we can take to prevent them from moving into Pakistan.

"Before I ask you to give me your ideas, I must tell you that I think that whatever preventative action we take must be strong. It must be forceful. And because we have very little economic leverage, the kind of retaliatory pressure the Americans like to use on us whenever they can . . ."

Marshal Kozlov snorted his first entry into the discussion. "Like an Olympic boycott."

That brought laughter all around.

Romanov went on. "What we should look for is some sort of military or naval prophylactic action." Looking at Kozlov and Smirnov, the chairman said, "Which is why I have invited you gentlemen to this meeting and, of course, my colleague the minister of defense."

His left hand gently touched the sleeve of Marshal Ustinov's uniform.

It was the brilliant General Andropov, the head of the KGB, who made the initial response to Romanov's request for ideas. Looking more like a scholarly academic than the head of one of the world's most respected and feared security and intelligence agencies, he said, "Comrade Chairman, the KGB has been supporting the PLO in the mounting of a most unusual operation that I think will be of interest to you. It could be an excellent smokescreen for us."

The discussion at the end of the long green-baize conference table lasted another hour and twenty minutes. As Andropov outlined his proposal and a consensus appeared to be developing early in the meeting, Romanov realized he would need advice from the economic administration of the Politburo on two counts. The first had to do with the basic figures and statistics in the crude oil segment of the Soviet economy. All of them knew the shortages would soon become crippling. A full paper on that subject would be necessary immediately. The second was an immediate study on the ramifications for the Western world if the plan they were developing around the table was, in fact, carried out. While the others talked, he quietly sent for the man who would be responsible for the preparation of the required studies. This was Aliyev, a man only three years younger than Romanov. He had been appointed only recently to succeed Tikhonov as first deputy premier, and was responsible for economic administration and industry. Aliyev was immediately available.

When the matter was settled to the chairman's satisfaction, he concluded the session by saying, "Gentlemen, this has been most productive. Because of the scale and consequences of the course of action we have agreed upon and are driven to by the imperialist Americans in our own defense, I feel I must have the approval of a plenary meeting of the Politburo. However, with four members of the fourteen being here present and in support . . ." Gromyko, Andropov, and Ustinov nodded their heads in agreement. "I think our decision will be supported."

The plenary Politburo session that approved the Andropov Plan took place in Chairman Romanov's office on the morning of March 20. The chairman himself had laid out the proposal in detail, using as presentation aids, photographic slides of charts from the comprehensive report that Comrade Aliyev's staff had produced on the current, short-term and long-range shortages of domestic production of crude oil, the commodity central to the sustenance of the economies of the Soviet Union and her Eastern Bloc satellites. Aliyev's report was also covered by Romanov in his presentation. By itself, the report was sufficient to justify in the minds of all Politburo members the drastic plan of action in the Andropov proposal. Now was the time. All of the factors at play pointed in only one direction—action immediately if a drastic shortage of crude was to be avoided.

The second report that was to be prepared by Aliyev's

people had not yet been completed. It was a new region of research that would require much more than two days to prepare. Furthermore, it would involve much supposition and speculation. However, when the Politburo meeting was informed of its nature, told that it would be presented to them in due course, and when its terms of reference were described, each man was able to conjure up in his own mind an image of the economic and cultural state of the society of the Western world that would result if the last and ultimate phase of the Andropov Plan was put into effect.

After a lengthy discussion, during which many members raised serious reservations about the wisdom of "going that far," the persuasive chairman convinced them that the actions of the United States in entering Pakistan would, in fact, be equivalent to an act of aggression, indeed, virtually an act of war against the Mother Country. At the end of his monologue, Chairman Romanov had pounded the table saying, "*Mir, mir, i yeshche raz mir*; peace, peace, peace, that is all we want for our people, but the imperialist American aggressor wants war! We must be determined not to let him have it, not to let him have his war but, at the same time, we must demonstrate to him all the consequences to his nation of the war he wishes to start. We are at the point of a showdown between capitalism and communism. It is not a time to be vacillating or sentimental. On the contrary, we may be on the threshold of permanent peace through a communist victory. Remember what Lenin said about the issue between capitalism and communism: 'Until the final issue is decided, the state of awful war will continue . . . sentimentality is no less a crime than cowardice in war.' Gentlemen, I ask your support for the Andropov Plan."

There was no need for a vote. Clearly there was a consensus among the Politburo members as they sat silent after the chairman's urging flow of compelling rhetoric ceased.

The Andropov Plan was approved.

10

22 March   12:00 Noon
Atlantic Ocean, off Cape Town

On the morning of March 22, *Splendid* received a message from the Admiralty to all Royal Navy ships at sea:

Urgent nonstop investigation of source of sonar interference in all areas North and South Atlantic and Arctic Ocean resulted in discovery March 14 of the Soviet-made, seabed-stationed noise generator. The device functions on principle similar to that of active sonar making constant rather than pulsing emissions in a band of transmission frequencies covering a full spectrum of known ship machinery, propeller and cavitation noises. The sonar interference device (SONINT) has high-volume sonar-interrupting range of up to one hundred miles. It can be deployed by aircraft or ship.

First device retrieved yesterday by U.S. Navy bathysphere from ocean floor one hundred miles off Maine coast. It is an electronic transmitter equipped with power package capable of estimated one-year operation, contained in rigid pressure-resistant plastic ball, color white, approximately two feet diameter;

appropriate weights attached to deliver to desired depths.

As it descends SONINT automatically deploys a ball-shaped antenna buoy six inches diameter, positioned six feet below water surface with quarter-inch plastic aerial rod appearing above surface making radar pick-up almost impossible; antenna buoy is connected to SONINT by a small diameter conductor cable which carries activating message received via satellite.

Estimate deployment of SONINTs commenced approximately nine months ago carried out by all transportation modes including Soviet fishing fleets and merchant marine vessels augmented by aircraft.

Also believe that, once activated, all SONINTs programed to produce transmissions for a set period of time thus cannot be halted by electronic countermeasures. It appears that Soviet surface and submarine fleets' sonars are not immune to SONINT.

Intelligence opinion is that Soviet activation of SONINT this time associated with opening of Red Navy's OKEAN operation.

The message underscored in the mind of Commander Marcus Leach the urgent need to allow NATO naval forces to operate below the Tropic of Cancer. South of that imaginary line the politicians of NATO would not go, although their naval and military commander wanted to extend their area of jurisdiction not only into the South Atlantic but around the Cape of Good Hope into the Indian Ocean and the Arabian Sea, thereby straddling with strong naval protection the sea lanes along which moved the crude oil and petroleum products necessary to sustain the civilization and economy of Western Europe. In those same sea lanes a substantial part of the daily oil consumption of the United States and Canada was carried. However, their political masters in Western Europe were intimidated by the presence of the ever-threatening Russians. They were dedicated to maintaining détente at all costs.

Furthermore, they did not want to prejudice the rich flow of their manufactured goods across the Iron Curtain into Eastern Bloc countries and the Soviet Union itself. Consequently, Western Europe had vacillated and continually demurred at removing from NATO the naval boundary line of the Tropic of Cancer. They were fearful of disturbing the status quo, notwithstanding the real possibility that their failure to protect their vital crude oil sources in the Middle East, and the equally important tanker transportation system, might lead to an interdiction of both.

The Royal Navy's captains knew that NATO's widespread sonar arrays throughout the North Atlantic were particularly heavy through the Denmark Strait, the gap between Iceland and Norway, and across the Skagerrak exit to the North Sea from the Soviet naval strongholds in the Baltic. The main fixed system was known as SOSUS. Those concentrated nets of hydrophones which were connected by seabed cable to computer and communications centers ashore, were in place for the purpose of monitoring and detecting the movement of any Soviet submarines from their major bases in the Kola Peninsula, abutting Finland and Norway high in the Arctic, and from the Baltic. The sound of any submarine—except the most silent moving at no more than one or two knots to negate any cavitation noise—would be picked up by the huge hydrophones mounted on their vast tripods standing on the seabeds of the North Atlantic even in the Newfoundland and Labrador basins.

During World War II, bombers of the Allied air forces were able to baffle the German radar by dropping clouds of tiny strips of aluminum foil which threw off the scanning enemy radar, preventing it from giving direction to their night fighters and aircraft guns. If a similar method could be found to baffle those sonars, then the Soviets would have a cover under which they could move their entire submarine fleet out into the Atlantic. The ability of NATO to discover the location and tracks of the lethal Soviet underwater fleet would be nullified. NATO's military satellites in space could keep count of the Soviet submarines at their Baltic and other northern bases, but the whereabouts of the Red Navy's submarine fleet at sea would be unknown.

It was, therefore, apparent to all ship commanders of the Royal Navy that should the Soviets come up with an answer to North Atlantic sonar arrays, they would have won a tremendous tactical advantage, one that would be particularly valuable during a prehostility buildup and deployment of forces in any escalating crisis.

At 1200 hours GMT on March 22, a full eleven days after the sonar interference began and two hours after Leach received the Admiralty signal, the interference stopped. It did so abruptly, just as if someone had flicked a switch.

At that moment, *Splendid* was still just below the surface in the Atlantic, abeam of Cape Town. The news of the rebirth of their sonar brought hoots of joy throughout the boat. Leach immediately dived his ship down into the sanctuary of the deep, warm sea over the continental shelf of Africa.

As *Splendid* descended, Leach reflected on the Admiralty signal and on the sonar interference capability of the Soviets. That goddamn SONINT thing wasn't just a toy the Soviets would use in an exercise, in a month of war games. If SONINT was as effective as he knew it to be—it had almost cost him his brand new ship, let alone his life—why in hell would the Red Navy let the whole world know they had the damn thing by turning it on just so that they could use it at OKEAN? The isolated captain had little information with which to make an accurate judgment.

What he did know, however, was that the Americans and the Soviets were eyeball to eyeball over the Middle East. The Red Navy had more ships at sea than it had ever had at any one time. Sure, the Soviets were mounting OKEAN, but OKEAN wasn't sufficient reason to trigger the use of SONINT. No, those bastards were definitely up to something. He'd bet his last pound on it.

Commander Marcus Leach was right.

11

25 March   4:00 P.M.

The White House

Washington, D.C.

Across the polished, historic desk of the Oval Office over which so many decisions had been taken and upon which so many documents had been signed, President Hansen watched the lined, pitted face and red, watery eyes of Vasili Kuznetsov, the likeable old Soviet ambassador to the United States, a man who had represented his country on the Washington scene for over two decades. He had been summoned by the president through the office of the secretary of state, John Eaton, who sat next to Kuznetsov.

Kuznetsov spoke excellent English, but with a heavy Russian accent. At this morning meeting with the new president, he was clearly unhappy that events had taken a turn for the worse between the United States and his nation. He felt responsible for maintaining good relations between the two giants of the world and took it as a personal failure that things had gone awry.

On the desk in front of Hansen was an envelope bearing the presidential seal. In it was President Hansen's reply to Romanov's harsh note, which Ambassador Kuznetsov had handed to him on March 16, the day following the president's announcement of the Pakistan agreement. Next to that envelope was a duplicate addressed to Kuznetsov. The president knew Kuznotsov well, having met the ancient ambassador countless times at cocktail parties during most of the twenty years he had been in the Senate. Kuznetsov, the gregarious, friendly, round bear, as he used to be, was now thin and emaciated with the advent of his eightieth year. He was a man whose open personality invited his American friends to loosen their tongues over drinks on the cocktail party circuit. He would pick up snippets of information from this one and that one from which he would put together relatively accurate scenarios of what was going on behind closed government doors at the highest level. The one thing Hansen knew about the old man was that he was totally loyal, completely dedicated to the cause of his Mother Country and to the principles of hard-line, Marxist-Leninist communist ideology.

This meeting, however, was no cocktail party. For all their long acquaintance and affection for each other, Hansen and Kuznetsov represented the full power of their respective nations. Each country was angry with and suspicious of the other. They were like two ancient medieval warriors, shield on one arm, sword in the other hand, circling each other and looking for the opening to strike the first blow.

Kuznetsov had been in the Oval Office many times before, delivering or receiving official notes to or from his masters in the Kremlin. He had been there with Kennedy, Johnson, Nixon, Ford, Carter, and the man who followed him. None of them had been as tough as he knew Hansen would be. He had told Gromyko many times that Hansen was tough-minded, hard-nosed, ideologically certain, and ruthless enough to be a member of the Politburo. Sitting across from the big man in the president's chair and listening to his words, Kuznetsov was disconcerted by the accuracy of his description of Hansen, for the man was now much harder, much tougher than he had been before he took office. He was a leader with power whose attitude spoke to his firm intention to lead his nation through adversity. In fact, Kuznetsov thought, in dedication, determination of spirit, aggressiveness and the willingness to fight for what he believed to be right and in his country's interest, President Hansen was the equal of Chairman Romanov. In the old ambassador's judgment, so strong was each man, so determined, that at a critical moment when compromise might deflect them from a shooting war, neither would back off.

"Your Excellency, please be good enough to deliver this official note to Chairman Romanov." The diplomat reached out with shaking hands to accept the envelope addressed to Chairman Romanov.

Hansen then gave him the second one. "This envelope contains a copy for your eyes." Providing the ambassador with a duplicate would enable him to telephone the contents of the note to the Kremlin well in advance of the delivery of the unopened original by courier.

When Kuznetsov had the second envelope in his hands, President Hansen said, "Please tell Chairman Romanov I regret that it took so long to prepare the reply. On the other hand the strident and, indeed, belligerent tone of his note was such that I wished to be as prudent, conservative, and unemotional as I could be in phrasing my response." The lawyer-president chose his words carefully and spoke them formally. "In short, my note says," his long right index finger pointed toward the two envelopes, "that the United States will not back off. We are going to put a task force of 120,000 men into Pakistan in order to protect our vital interests in the Middle East. We believe that the Soviet Union is building up its forces in Afghanistan and on the Soviet-Iran border to mount a strike against Pakistan and Iran. When we enter Pakistan, it will not be an invasion as the entry of the Soviet Union into Afghanistan was, but rather one country helping another under a long-standing agreement. We will be coming to their aid militarily strictly for the purpose of defense and we will be providing them with massive economic aid.

"Please tell the chairman, Your Excellency, that this is a situation of the Soviet Union's own making. On the other hand, I want you to assure Chairman Romanov that I am not inflexible, that I would be prepared to consider any quid pro quo that might relieve me of the necessity of dispatching my task force to Pakistan."

Ambassador Kuznetsov's normally benign eyes narrowed to slits. "The nature of my instructions, Mr. President, is such that I can tell you that if any quid pro quo is offered by Chairman Romanov, it will be in the form of an ultimatum that you will find difficult to refuse." His face suddenly changed, eyes opening wide. He smiled, displaying his well-known silver-filled teeth. "On the other hand, Mr. President, we both know that my government wishes to continue our peaceful coexistence. Perhaps there can be compromise. Perhaps. But I daresay the answer largely depends on the contents and tone of your note." His finger tapped the envelope addressed to Romanov.

The emaciated ambassador leaned on his cane and began to struggle to his feet. Hansen and Eaton stood as the old man pulled himself erect. He looked up at the president with a gaze that showed his personal affection. "You should know, my friend, just before I came to your office I was notified by Comrade Gromyko that I was being recalled to Moscow—for consultations of course. That is the sure sign that the relations between our two countries are indeed precarious. Perhaps more so at this moment than at any time since World War II. And you should also know that our ambassador to the United Nations has been instructed today to seek support for a motion of censure against the United States." The ambassador lowered his head momentarily, shaking it slowly. "A pity that we should come to this point. It is rather reminiscent of the Khrushchev-Kennedy confrontation over Cuba."

"In which you played such an important part."

"Yes, in which I played a part."

Ambassador Kuznetsov held out his wavering hand to his friend, John Hansen, who took it as the old man spoke. "History repeats itself, Mr. President. Let us hope that it will do so and that this confrontation can also be resolved."

"It can be—if your chairman is prepared to compromise."

12

25 March   Midnight
Moscow

The reply of the president of the United States to the stiff note from Chairman Romanov of the Soviet Union was handed to Ambassador Kuznetsov on March 21. Intensive diplomatic preparations went into the development of the reply. It was essential to secure the support, or at least the acceptance, of America's principal allies for the action Hansen intended to take. Romanov and his Politburo colleagues had monitored the strong efforts of the Americans to secure support by keeping close watch on their diplomatic activities in the capitals of Western Europe and North America and Japan. This was done through the Soviet Union's normal channels of surveillance, their worldwide net of embassies and consulates in which KGB agents, both men and women, functioned as important cogs in the worldwide Russian espionage machine, operating under the protective blanket of diplomatic immunity.

Great Britain had leaped in to support Hansen from the outset. But West Germany and France were reluctant. They were concerned with maintaining the last vestiges of détente in order to protect their valuable flow of trade with the Soviet Union and its Eastern Bloc satellites. Romanov knew that, under pressure from him, both the West German and French governments would waiver. West Germany, in particular, would vacillate, and if the right leverage was applied, he might force the West Germans to withhold their support for the United States in its proposed entry into Pakistan. At best, he could pressure them into denouncing the move. The chairman understood well the West German government's weaknesses. Germany was divided. The Red Army occupied East Germany, its government under the Soviet heel. The position of Berlin was still insecure. The value of West Germany's exports to the Soviet Union was greater than American sales to the USSR.

At the same time the West Germans relied even more heavily on Persian Gulf oil than the United States. That they were not equally concerned and willing to act against the Soviet Union baffled the American administration. It failed to understand the priorities and attitudes of a European nation that lived next to and had close economic ties to the Soviet Union and its Eastern Bloc satellites.

On the other hand, Chairman Romanov understood those attitudes and economic ties very well. He watched them resurface immediately. The American president began his diplomatic campaign in Western Europe for support for his plan to enter Pakistan. Romanov and Gromyko used every diplomatic weapon in their arsenal to dissuade West Germany and France from backing the American initiative, knowing that if those two major countries withheld their endorsement, it would severely blunt the willingness of the United States to risk a unilateral war with the Soviet Union. At the same time, it would drive a wedge into the U.S./West German heart of the NATO alliance, a body which the Soviet leaders regarded as an offensive rather than a defensive organization.

As Romanov saw it, by taking the initiative without first consulting their allies—it was an historically common fault of all American presidents and administrations to act without consulting allies—the Americans had put themselves on the horns of a diplomatic dilemma: to go or not to go into Pakistan if they could not get the support of their principal West European NATO allies. Worse, if even one of those principal allies denounced the American initiative in Pakistan, what then?

Romanov was at his desk in the Kremlin when Kuznetsov called from Washington at midnight, immediately after being handed President Hansen's reply in midafternoon of March 25. When Kuznetsov finished reading the note to him, Romanov did not respond immediately but sat silently contemplating what he had heard. Alone in his vast office of power, Romanov spoke into the white telephone to his apprehensive ambassador to the imperialist aggressor enemy. "Just as I expected."

"What will you do next, Comrade Chairman?" The security-unscrambled voice sounded as if it were coming from the depths of a well.

"I'm not sure yet. We will have to talk about it here. But I think . . . As you know we are going to the United Nations. This time it will be the United States' turn to be censured. And pressure, Comrade Kuznetsov, pressure. We will throw in the full weight of our propaganda machine. Tass, *Pravda*, and *Izvestia* will mount a worldwide campaign. We will harass the Americans everywhere. We will really put pressure on Hansen between now and the seventh of May!"

"And if that doesn't work?"

Chairman Romanov smiled. "Then we will put the boots to him, heavy Russian combat boots right where it hurts the most!"

13

28-30 March

Mecca, Suez to Aden

It seemed to Said that he had been on board the *Mecca* for an eternity. It was almost three weeks since their narrow escape at Port Said. The long voyage on the plodding *Mecca* had seemed interminable.

Said and his men had been let out of their hidden sanctuary by the captain at about three the next morning, when he was satisfied that his first officer and all his deck hands were asleep and that he, Rashid, the helmsman, whose eyes were fixed on the lights of the ship ahead of him in the convoy, and the engineer below were the only people awake on the *Mecca*.

While the crew was startled to find the PLO team again with them the next morning, no one questioned where they had come from, although Nabil had hoped never to see them again. He, who had talked so freely to Commander Faher, was startled to see them emerge from their customary cabins for breakfast. How did they get back on board? Or is there a secret compartment on this old tub? These questions went through Nabil's mind. But being a fatalist and being able to do nothing about their presence on board, he promptly forgot about them and their strange reappearance. What did it matter anyway?

At the tail of the long afternoon convoy, the *Mecca* had serenely steamed down the Suez Canal, past the battered relics of guns and tanks resting on the eastern sandbanks of the old waterway, souvenirs of the 1973 Egyptian thrust that had caught the Israelis by surprise; past the tall, tan-colored main building of the all-watching Suez Canal authority at the west bank of the president of Egypt's favorite city of Ismailia; by Port Tewfik at the entrance to the Red Sea and a gathering of ships waiting to take their convoy turn northward; then on into the long, dull 1,700-mile stretch of the Red Sea, down to the Gulf of Aden and east into the Port of Aden to take on fuel and food. The crew would have their night on the port's town of Tawahi. There was no cargo to be either off-loaded or taken on.

They had stayed in Aden overnight, snug in a slip which provided them with bunkering, supplies, and fresh water. After clearing customs, completing his arrangements with the port authorities, checking with the local Lloyd's agent, the National Insurance and Reinsurance Company, Captain Rashid turned his crew loose for the night. Said volunteered that he and his team would remain on board to keep security watch on the ship. When the crew had gone ashore, Said relented to Maan's pleas and allowed his three colleagues to go ashore with strict orders: no bars, no fights, no women. His men left the ship at seven but were back and in their bunks by ten, all perfectly sober and delighted with having seen the town. On the other hand, the crew's behavior was completely consistent with past performances. They began appearing in ones and twos after midnight, staggering up the gangplank, operating on homing instinct alone. The last to return were the captain and his first officer. Both were roaring drunk, but still able to navigate. They had become good temporary friends during the course of the evening, a relationship which would terminate in the sober light of the next morning.

Another nine days of sailing in windy, stormy weather

and heavy, uncomfortable seas had taken them east-northeast along the coast of south Yemen, past Oman, north past Muscat into the Gulf of Oman where they first caught sight of the never-ending outbound line of loaded crude oil and petroleum tankers, the decks of their enormous hulls down almost to the level of the sea, moving one after the other like a parade of plodding elephants; and the inbound line funneling into the Gulf of Oman from Japan, Europe and North America, riding high in the water in ballast, making for their assigned loading ports at Saudi Arabia, Qatar, the United Arab Emirates, Bahrain, Iran, Iraq, and Kuwait.

Turning west into the Gulf of Oman, Rashid had gingerly crossed the lines of tankers to take up a course for the Strait of Hormuz. That position put the *Mecca* to the north of the main line of fast-moving tanker traffic. In ballast, without cargo, the mammoth ships traveled at a much greater speed than the old *Mecca* could muster. For safety's sake it was wise to be well out of their way.

Late in the afternoon of March 28, three weeks after they had departed Beirut, the *Mecca* sailed into the Strait of Hormuz, the most traveled strait in the world, a narrow gut of water twenty-four miles across, containing a navigable channel about twelve miles in width.

The rising burnt hills on each side served to accentuate the narrowness of the water passage through which hundreds of huge tankers passed each month. This was the strait that the PLO's leader Arafat had often talked of blocking in order to publicize the urgency of the plight of the Palestinian people. He had spoken of sinking some large ships, but in running his eyes over the crowded strait that afternoon, Said could not visualize how it could be done. The ships that would have to be sunk in one place to provide a barrier would have to number perhaps a hundred, maybe two. Impossible. Mines could be laid but they could be cleaned out quickly. No, the plan that he had presented and Arafat and the council had accepted was by far the best solution.

As the *Mecca* left the Strait of Hormuz astern and

night fell, Said joined the captain on the bridge to chat with the old man and watch the mammoth tankers go by: the Ultra Large Crude Carriers (ULCCs), anything over 300,000 tons; the Very Large Crude Carriers (VLCCs), those in the range of 200,000 to 300,000 tons, and several smaller tankers, all of them large in their own right and huge in comparison with the *Mecca*.

"When will we be at Kuwait?" Said asked.

"We'll be there in two days. We still have about five hundred miles to go."

"We should talk soon about a plan of action when we get there."

The captain looked toward Nabil—who had not missed a word of what was being said on the bridge—and at the wheelsman. It would not do to talk about plans in front of those two.

"In the morning, Said. In the morning. Come to my cabin, say at eight."

At that time the next day, Said appeared at Rashid's quarters. He was surprised to find the captain's table cleared of its piles of papers. There was the usual pot of coffee and waiting small cups sitting at the port end, but in the center and at the starboard end of the table, Rashid had spread out two charts. One was of the channel approaches to the city of Kuwait and Shuwaikh port at its northern edge. The second was of the oil terminal at Mina-al-Ahmadi, on the coast some fifty miles southeast of Kuwait city.

The two men stood shoulder to shoulder at the table as the captain, having poured the coffee and lit a cigarette, began. "Let me tell you what I have to do first and then you can tell me what you have in mind."

Said nodded his head in agreement.

"All of my cargo, everything—except the special cargo—you know the stuff I mean . . ."

Another nod from Said. Rashid meant the opium of course.

"Everything goes off at Shuwaikh. I want to enter the harbor in daylight. I've only been there once, so it's best not to go in at night. The approach is too tricky." With a finger he traced a line from out to sea, west into the harbor mouth. "We have to go in through a channel. It's marked by dolphins and buoys. It's about four and a half miles long. Wide enough, 500 feet. With all the building that's going on in Kuwait, this port is quite often badly congested, another reason I don't want to go in at night. I have no idea where the harbormaster will put us, but it will probably be at the northwest corner. There are quays up there that can handle a small ship like this very easily. When we go by Bahrain in the morning, I'll radio in to the harbormaster there and ask him to notify Shuwaikh of our arrival intentions. According to the book, I have to give him my estimated time of arrival, the draft of the ship, state that the Kuwait cargo is clear, that my ship's discharging gear is in order, and since I can do it with my own crane, that all my cargo can be handled by the ship's own gear. The point is, once I give them an estimated time of arrival, I have to stick to that. So when I find out from you what you want to do, we can settle on an ETA."

The PLO leader was thinking ahead. "What about fuel, water and provisions at Shuwaikh?"

"Obviously, bunker fuel oil is not a problem in Kuwait. If they put us alongside deep-water berths numbers one through seven, we can take on fuel through hoses that are right there. Otherwise we might have to move to pick it up, but fuel is not a problem. We can get fresh water. The Kuwaitis are well organized. All you need is money."

The captain shifted his weight, reached across in front of Said and pulled the Mina-al-Ahmadi chart across so that it sat in front of them on top of the Kuwait map.

"At Mina-al-Ahmadi, there are two loading piers and a sea terminal. The south pier here has six tanker berths and depth alongside up to fifty feet. The north pier has five tanker berths, and depth alongside to sixty feet. The sea terminal has seven berths. For the big tankers, the VLCCs and ULCCs, there is a special offshore terminal that has two berths with a depth alongside of ninety-five feet. It can take just about anything that floats. The Kuwaitis operate their big refinery here. It processes about 800,000 barrels of oil a day, refines it that is . . . That's out of an overall production in the country of about a million and a half a day. They've cut back their production recently because they think it's better to keep the oil in the ground.

"So when we get to Mina-al-Ahmadi, we'll undoubtedly find all the tanker berths filled, that's about twenty ships. They'll mostly be VLCCs and larger. We'll find another twenty anchored, waiting their turn. They'll be in this area." He pointed to an area two to three miles out to sea from the piers and sea terminal.

Rashid walked around to the far side of the table, opened its small drawer in front of his chair, pulled out a sheet of paper and went back to stand beside Said again.

"The instructions for my special cargo are . . ." He read from the piece of paper, "Rendezvous at midnight of first night after entry Shuwaikh. Rendezvous point: five miles northeast off north pier of Mina-al-Ahmadi. Torch code: three long, two short." He folded the paper and stuffed it in a trouser pocket, then jabbed his right index finger at the chart saying, "That's where I have to be, five miles northeast of the north pier and well away from the tanker waiting area. The Kuwaitis used to keep a fairly tight security patrol around the tankers, but I hear they're lax now. Anyway, we'll keep well away from them."

Said repeated, "At midnight of the first night."

"Correct. Now what do you want to do? What's your plan?"

To that very moment in the long voyage, Said had not discussed his operation with the captain, although by that time the older man had some idea of what their objective was. Even so, Rashid was not sure.

For a moment Said contemplated the chart. "Will you anchor her at that point?"

"Yes, I'd like to be there early some time between ten and eleven. Yes, we'll anchor."

"As we go by Mina-al-Ahmadi on our way to Shuwaikh, can we run in close to the anchored tankers, the ones waiting to load? I'd like to have a good look at them."

"Yes, no problem."

"Will it be daylight?"

"Daylight. It should be between three and four o'clock tomorrow afternoon."

"Perfect."

The captain was perplexed. "Well, what about your plan? What do you want to do?"

Said shrugged, saying, "I can fit into your plan of action without any changes at all. If we're anchored five miles off the north pier by ten or eleven o'clock as you said . . . What time do you want to up anchor and leave?"

Rashid was emphatic. "Midnight. As soon as I get rid of the stuff."

"And get your money."

"Exactly!"

Said thought for a moment and asked, "I might need an hour or two beyond that. If we could anchor at ten, I'd like to have four hours, say until two o'clock. It's important to have that much time. I don't want to be rushed. My men and I will have to work in the dark. It'll be difficult enough as it is."

The captain was reluctant, but he understood the young man's concern. Furthermore, he had become quite fond of Said in the past three weeks, developed a kind of fatherly affection for him. He could bend a little bit. "All right, two o'clock it is. But no later, mind you. If the people who take the stuff off get caught and we're still sitting there . . ." He shook his head.

"I understand," Said acknowledged. "We're both taking risks, big ones. Those extra two hours could make the difference between success and failure."

The frustrated Rashid, still not knowing what Said and his team were going to do, broke in, "Whatever that is you're doing. You still haven't told me."

"That's right. I haven't."

14

30 March   5:04 P.M.
Mina-al-Ahmadi,
Kuwait

A few minutes after five on the afternoon of March 30, the *Mecca* was abeam the south pier of Mina-al-Ahmadi. She was running at half speed at the request of Said. The old freighter made its way slowly past the gargantuan tankers sitting at their maximum height out of the water, ballast tanks emptied, each patiently waiting its call to proceed into its assigned berth for loading. The wait might be a few hours, at most not more than two or three days. The PLO team, armed with binoculars, plotted the location of each vessel on charts Captain Rashid had provided. To Said it was of greatest importance to record the name of each ship, for he was under the strictest instructions to avoid dealing with any tanker carrying the flag of a NATO country or France. To the captain's amazement, Hassan produced a Polaroid camera and took a picture of each vessel they passed. As they left the flock of giant craft, all at anchor with their noses pointed into the stiff wind from the east like a herd of cattle, Said mounted the steps to the bridge.

"Can you show me where will you be anchoring when we come back tomorrow night?" he asked the captain.

The old man's eyes squinted as he looked westerly toward the long piers filled with loading ships and beyond them the towers and tanks of the enormous refinery. He had his bearings. He was just to the north of the north pier, about four miles out.

He turned to face north toward the bow. "Dead ahead about a mile. We'll be about two miles north of the last tanker we passed."

"The *Esso Madrid*." Said was pleased. "Excellent." He opened the book he was carrying, saying facetiously, "You will be pleased to know, captain, that according to this publication of the U.S. Department of Commerce—*Foreign Flag Merchant Ships Owned by U.S. Parent Companies*—the *Esso Madrid* is owned by Esso Tankers Inc. It was built in Japan in 1976. It is 380,000 deadweight tons, has a speed of sixteen knots, and its country of registry is Liberia."

Rashid was amazed. "Where did you get that?" he demanded, pointing to the book.

"Oh, I just happened to find it in my kit when I left Beirut. I also have a copy of the Lloyd's of London Shipping Register which told me that all those ships would be here. It also tells me where they're going next."

Perhaps now Said would let Rashid in on his plan. But there was no need to ask. Not really, because the scheme of the PLO operation had become perfectly clear to the shrewd old sailor, although he guessed there would still be a few surprises in store for him before he saw the last of Said and his people.

He was right.

15

31 March   12:35 A.M.

Indian Ocean

On March 31, just before 10:35 P.M. Zulu, 12:35 A.M. local, the captain of *Splendid* called his communication center from the control room.

"Pots, this is the captain."

"Pots here. Go ahead, sir."

"We're approaching the flotilla. At least we're in VHF range. I'll be bringing her up to periscope depth so we can take a look around and also transmit. Stand by to take a message to the flag officer, Second Flotilla. He's aboard the *Tiger*."

The *Tiger* was the Royal Navy's famous helicopter cruiser. Rear-Admiral Rex Ward, the flotilla commander, had gone aboard her a week earlier to assume effective control of the British navy's show of force to the Soviets. With his flagship were his third and eighth squadrons of the Second Flotilla. The third was led by the frigate *Arethusa*, who had with her one destroyer and five other frigates. The other squadron, the eighth, was led by the frigate *Ajax* and with her were one destroyer and three frigates. To cap off this strongest show of naval force the British had put into the Indian Ocean in decades, the flotilla had, as its center-piece, the Royal Navy's most recently commissioned ship, the light aircraft carrier *Illustrious*, with its squadron of VTOL (Vertical Take-Off and Landing) Sea Harriers and ten Sea King helicopters, the workhorses of the British Fleet Air Arm.

The British flotilla joined the American Fifth Fleet, which had been formed and committed to permanent station in the Indian Ocean in response to the Soviet initiatives in the Middle East. Central to that fleet was the aircraft carrier *Coral Sea*, the only flat top the U.S. Navy could spare out of its total of seventeen aircraft carriers, twelve of which were assigned to the Atlantic and Mediterranean and five to the Pacific. For some years the *Coral Sea* had carried no air wing, but in the crisis of 1980 she had taken one on, assembled from squadrons assigned to carriers in overhaul and other sources. The Fifth Fleet, complete with two cruisers, five destroyers, and six frigates taken from both the Atlantic and Pacific fleets, had steamed into the Indian Ocean in late February. Coincidentally it became the visible enhancement of the president's bargaining power in dealing with Pakistan. Like the British flotilla, which had joined the American force in entering the Arabian Sea in mid-March, the Fifth Fleet was supported by several unseen attack submarines. They were there for the purpose of fending off any enemy surface or subsurface naval forces that might approach.

It had earlier been intended that the American and British naval forces would undertake joint exercises in the Indian Ocean and the Arabian Sea in advance of the Soviet's operation, OKEAN, which was believed to be scheduled to commence in the Atlantic, Pacific, and Indian Oceans sometime between April 1 and April 15. Elements of the American and British forces were assigned to monitor and watch the Soviet naval and air forces during the exercise. Their task was to observe the Russian maneuvering and tactical methods and, at the same time, make them as uncomfortable as possible. Shadowing was harassing activity at which the Russians themselves had become experts.

For years their naval and merchant-marine craft had shadowed and spied on virtually every Allied naval operation, exercise, or experiment such as the launching of submarine-carried ballistic missiles. The Soviets had even gone so far as to play chicken with American destroyers and frigates in international waters. It was time to give the Soviets some of their own medicine.

As it happened, the timing of the planned U.S./U.K. Indian Ocean exercise could not have better suited the Pakistan objectives of President Hansen. Furthermore, as the Soviet reaction to his successful negotiations with Pakistan grew more violent, the presence of the powerful combined naval forces in that flashpoint sector of the world had a salutary effect on the shrill Soviet propaganda machine as it lashed out against the imperialistic intentions of the "warmongering" U.S. president, as the Russians were labeling him. On the other hand, it had a sobering effect on the Soviet military strategists and planners plotting their short- and long-term moves in Moscow. For them and their political masters, the unswerving Marxist-Leninist goal was world domination. They were at undeclared ideological and physical war with the West. The rhetoric was left to the Politburo and the propagandists. The use of force and the Soviet's military, naval, and air power belonged to the admirals and generals. All of them understood and had the greatest respect for the single tool of their own profession—physical force. They were experts in the use or threatened use of powerful sea, land, and air forces anywhere at any time. Behind their planning was the recognized ability of the Soviet Union to deliver intercontinental or tactical nuclear weapons. Therefore, the presence of American and British armadas in the Arabian Sea simultaneously with the preparations for the movement of large-scale American military forces to Pakistan had caused the Kremlin's military brains to pause.

From his control room in the *Splendid*, its captain spoke slowly into the telephone, choosing his words carefully. At the other end, in his communications center domain, Pots scribbled furiously. "Make a signal to flag officer, Second Flotilla, aboard the *Arethusa* . . ." Years ago, as a young lieutenant-commander, Leach had worked for then Captain, now Rear-Admiral Ward when he was Captain, Sea Training at Faslane. Leach was in that part of Ward's shop responsible for working up new submarines and new crews. He could remember the face of the banty admiral, a gray-haired, balding, little man, his gimlet eyes dancing with nervous energy. Ward was a man well able to carry his high rank and responsibility. Too bad he wouldn't be able to visit the old boy on board the *Arethusa*. If he even had a chance to see the British flotilla he would be lucky. The admiral would probably station *Splendid* on patrol, perhaps fifty or hundred miles away from his group of ships. Apparently, the Russians were beginning to rendezvous at the western end of the Gulf of Aden, in and around the port of Aden where they had access to bunkering and provisioning facilities.

In addition to the gathering fleet, satellite photographs had shown the presence of several fuel-carrying tenders for Soviet diesel submarines. Tenders were also found operating out of the ports of Soviet client states on both the east and west coasts of Africa. Almost half of its submarine fleet, some 160 boats, were diesel powered rather than nuclear. It was essential, therefore, for the Soviets to have anchoring, provisioning, and docking facilities in as many foreign ports, in strategically important areas, as could be arranged. Throughout Africa, in the shifting sands of ruthless politics, many nations had forced the Soviets to keep negotiating for access to new ports. Several times, in recent years, facilities they had built or had been using for long periods were denied to them by new, unsympathetic governments. Their successful drive for an increased number of ports of access on both the Atlantic and Indian Ocean coasts of the continent was motivated by the continuing thrust, begun in 1962, to become the world's dominant naval power, an objective completely consonant with the USSR's overall goal of world domination.

Leach had paused as some of those factors ran through

his mind. He began again, "*Splendid* is presently at 60° 5' 12" east, 13° 8' 3" north and reporting for tasking. Happy to be working for you again. It's a long way from Faslane."

Once more the captain paused. He was satisfied. "That's it. Make the signal as soon as we're at periscope depth. Should be about five minutes."

"Aye, aye, sir."

Within Leach's estimated time his search periscope was up, the radar mast and its radio antenna with it. Just as he clamped his face to the periscope, the captain checked his watch: 10:42 P.M. Zulu. Old Ward would soon be reading his signal. Admiral Ward was not old in the conventional sense, only forty-nine as against Leach's thirty-four years. But it seemed that all admirals were referred to as "old men" regardless of their ages.

Scanning the horizon, he called out to the radar watchkeeper, "Anything, radar?"

"Yes, sir. Contact. Surface vessel. Bearing 030, range thirty-two miles."

Leach swung the periscope to that heading. Yes, there she was. It looked like a freighter, its bridge amidships, crane masts reaching skyward like fingers. "Have you got him, sonar?"

Petty Officer Pratt's voice was loud and clear. "Aye, sir, and I just got something else. Contact. Bearing 185, classified submarine, range 1,500 yards . . ."

The reaction of the captain was instantaneous. "Two thousand yards!" he exclaimed, pulling his eyes away from the periscope and turning to shout in the direction of the sonar compartment. "Jesus Christ, Pratt! Have you been asleep! Is that your first contact?" Pratt should have picked up the bogey miles out . . . Unless. The captain realized that he had been feeling a little edgy that morning. Perhaps he had reacted too quickly. He left the periscope to go to the sonar room. He stood at the door looking in at the screen. There was the submarine, its blip shining white just where Pratt said it was, sitting there in a constant, unmoving position. No doubt about it. They had picked up a shadow.

Out of the corner of his eye, Petty Officer Pratt caught

the figure of the captain standing in the doorway looking at the screen. His own face turned again toward the bright sonar images. In a voice which showed his unhappiness at being shouted at when he was not at fault, he said, "I think we've passed over her, sir. She was probably sitting silent waiting for us and started up when we were about fifteen hundred yards past her. That's when I first got her. Now she's sitting where you see her, about two thousand back." The young petty officer was one of the best sonar men in the fleet. And he was right. Leach was wrong to have shouted at him.

"You're absolutely right, Pratt. Sorry. I shouldn't have raised my voice."

Pratt still hadn't turned to look at him, but his right hand lifted and partly turned as he said, "Not a problem, sir." Turning toward his console of electronic gear he added, "The signature's coming up now, sir. It's a Victor II."

Bloody Russian bastard, was Leach's first thought. If he missed his guess, that goddamn submarine would be glued to his tail so long as *Splendid* was in the Indian Ocean. He knew the Victor II class. They were a match any day for the Swiftsure class of British attack submarine to which *Splendid* belonged. The Victor II had an advertised speed of thirty-one knots dived, but he thought it would be far greater. She was bigger than *Splendid*, at 323 feet in length with a displacement of 5,700 deadweight tons as against his boat's length of 272 feet and 4,500 tons. But the Soviet craft's nuclear power plant delivered twice the power of *Splendid*, 30,000 shaft horsepower against his ship's 15,000.

The Victor II was a long way from home. Most of them were based with the Soviet northern fleet operating out of the Kola Peninsula, although some were positioned in the Pacific. Built at the admiralty yard in Leningrad, the big, fast antisubmarine and antiship vessel had eight torpedo tubes in its bow and carried twenty-one of those ship-destroying devices. In addition, it carried a SUBROC type of weapon, probably ten of them, an underwater-launched missile carrying a depth charge which could be nuclear. Like *Splendid*, the trailing Victor could stay submerged for weeks on end, putting as much as 40,000 nautical miles past her keel in a single voyage.

"What's her depth?"

"Looks like 300 feet, sir."

There was nothing the captain could do about it. The Russki would sit there, watching his every move. Even so, it would be no more than a bothersome worry. Not a real threat unless some idiot started a war while they were playing tag in the Indian Ocean. If the captain of the Victor heard about it before he did, *Splendid* would be the first submarine sunk in World War III. But surely no one in his right mind on either side would start a war, Leach reassured himself, as he often had in the past when the possibility of war came into his mind. But in his heart Leach knew he did not believe that no one would start a war. If he had believed it, he would not have been in *Splendid* as its captain on that morning of March 31.

He could sense someone behind him in the passageway. He turned. It was Pots with a message.

"From the admiral, sir."

Back beside the periscope, Leach read, "To the man who sticks to everything, welcome." That was how the admiral used to refer to him in the old days. A play on Leach's name, it used to amuse the old man. Obviously it still did.

"*Splendid* will proceed to take up patrol station across eastern Gulf of Aden, generally in a line running north from Cape Guardafui. Soviet fleet is assembling to the west in area of Aden preparatory to OKEAN. Report when on station, then every six hours from the exact minute of your first on-station transmission. Emergency watch will be kept on assigned frequencies. Use caution. Russian bear is baring teeth at Yanks over Pakistan. Give a wag of *Splendid*'s tail to your dog Victor. We have a whole pack with us."

Leach laughed out loud. Leave it to the old man. He thought, I'll bet the Sea Kings off the *Tiger* are working their butts off, plopping their sonars into the drink for miles around the flotilla. Between him and the Americans, they'll know by this time exactly what the Russkis have under the water up there.

He walked over to the chart table. Putting both hands

on it, he leaned across to look at his navigating officer who was busily tracking the course of *Splendid* and its position. Pilot looked up. "Sir?"

"Fish out your charts for the Gulf of Aden."

Pilot's hands reached out to the bottom of his stack of long drawers. In an instant the marine chart covering the entire gulf was spread smoothly on the table.

Leach looked southward on the map's face. His right index finger traced a line from Cape Guardafui north across the mouth of the Gulf to the shore of South Yemen, another client state of the Russians.

"We're going to take up station there, roughly on that line," he said. "Calculate the course to get there and, when you have a chance, set up a good line for station holding. You know, find some high landmarks on both shores so I can pick them up easily on the periscope."

"I can give you a preliminary course to the Gulf right now, sir," Pilot advised, rolling out his parallel ruler from the side of the chart table. "Try 278 degrees, that will put us into the slot just north of Socotra, the Island of Socotra, here." He pointed to a large island about one hundred miles to the east of Cape Guardafui.

"Good."

Straightening up, Leach returned to the search periscope and had a look around the horizon. The only thing to be seen was the freighter, now slightly closer. Satisfied, he brought the periscope down and gave the order to dive to 500 feet. Once the diving procedures were finished and the ship was on its way down to its ordered level, he gave the change of course that would take them from their northbound track almost due west into the Gulf of Aden.

When *Splendid* was well into her long, banking left turn for her new course, Leach called to the sonar room, "What's our Russian doing?"

Pratt had been expecting the question. "She's turning right with us, sir."

Moments after, when *Splendid* had come straight and level on her course for Aden, the voice of the sonar watchkeeper came again. "Contact. Bearing red 030, classified submarine, range thirty-five miles, speed estimated thirty-five knots, estimated course 355."

Whoever she was, she was not headed for the same place as *Splendid*: the Gulf of Aden. Pratt's reply to the captain's question about her signature was totally anticipated. "She's Russian, sir. Another Victor II." That explained her high speed.

Lowering himself into his chair, he muttered out loud to himself, "Christ, the whole bloody world is filled with Russian submarines!"

16

31 March

Kuwait

As you approach the city of Kuwait from the sea, there is an impression of total flatness. The usually calm waters of the Arabian Gulf blend toward the endless desert sand that holds the streets, buildings, and people within the ancient city. In recent times, tall, sparkling office buildings and hotels have sprung up, crude-oil nurtured, from the sand, in Kuwait's rush to modernity and prosperity. Moving northwest along the channel into Shuwaikh port, an in-bound ship passes Ras Jouza Point on the left, the Kuwait Towers on its shores, by the Dasman and Sief palaces, and the Sheraton Hotel. At the entrance to the port area sit the embassies of East Germany, Somalia, and Morocco. In the southern section of the city, near the tall Hilton Hotel, stands the American Embassy, just off First Ring Road. At the Ras Jouza Point, a stone's throw north of the Kuwait Towers, the embassies of the Soviet Union and the United Kingdom stand almost cheek by jowl, just a few yards from the Afghanistan embassy and its easterly neighbor, the People's Republic of China.

The skyline is broken not only by the new buildings,

but by the traditional minarets whose shape has been copied by the designers of two tall water towers, their concrete forms thrusting up hundreds of feet into the air, each with enormous tanks like balls bulging out at midpoint to hold hundreds of thousands of gallons of desalinated drinking water from the plant at their feet, a short distance from the port entrance.

The early morning sun rose out of the waters of the gulf behind them as the *Mecca* made its way up the channel. By eight o'clock the *Mecca* was berthed, customs clearances had been completed and registration procedures had been cleared up by Rashid with the port authority. Trucks and men of the Kuwait Stevedoring Company had appeared at dockside to assist the crew of the *Mecca* in unloading her mixed cargo.

Shortly after, the PLO team walked down the gangplank to the pier. Once again, their long black *abas* covered their uniforms. Clean *khafias* were on their heads, their plain black *guptas* (headbands) squarely in place. They headed for the Sheraton Hotel. As they were coming into port, Said had spotted the attractive, tall building, its sign prominently displayed at roof level. He had to do some telephoning. The Sheraton, catering as it did to Americans and the flood of Europeans doing business in Kuwait, would be able to cope with his overseas telephone calls without any difficulty. In preparation for this eventuality, he had obtained in Beirut a supply of Kuwait dinars; enough, he estimated, for a good meal and one long distance call to Beirut.

Inside the air-conditioned, marble-floored foyer, Said bought two street maps of the city at the news kiosk. One he handed to Ahmed with a wad of money, telling the three of them to make a tour of the city and meet him back at the hotel at twelve noon for lunch. The second map he would keep for himself. When his telephone calls were finished, he would take a walk around the city.

When they had departed, he talked with the concierge, gave him a Beirut telephone number and a hastening tip of dinars. The concierge said he would let him know when the call was ready. In the meantime if he would take a seat in the lobby, a man would be by with coffee shortly, as was the practice.

It was almost an hour later, shortly after ten, that he was summoned to the telephone. His leader, Arafat, was at his headquarters. He was expecting Said's call, anxious to know about the Haifa affair and the prospects for the success of the Kuwait operation. Said hurried to the booth and gave his mentor a complete report, promising that the first phase would be completed that night. If something went wrong, he would report by a cable he would send when the *Mecca* stopped at Bahrain.

Arafat listened without interrupting. The line was good. No need to shout. When his lieutenant was finished, Arafat complimented him. "You have done well, Said, very well indeed. The Haifa operation was superb, absolutely superb. I'm confident you're going to have great success tonight. May Allah be with you. But let me go back to Haifa. The Israelis are furious. They've attacked our refugee camps by air in retaliation, as you might have expected."

In his telephone booth far away from Beirut, Said nodded silently. He had heard the news reports on the radio. Revenge, and who could blame them. That was the normal pattern between blood enemies. But it was what his chief said next that filled the young man's soul with apprehension.

"However, there is one thing I must warn you about. Our intelligence people tell me that the Israelis know that you and your team were on the *Mecca*. They're convinced that you did the job. They're sending out their best hit team to find you. As far as I know, they don't know where the *Mecca* is yet and right now even if they did, it wouldn't do them any good because they wouldn't be able to get into Kuwait . . . Said, are you still there?"

There was a pause. "Yes, sir, I'm still here. What you are telling me is no surprise."

"All I am saying is be careful!"

"Don't worry. My team is as good as any they have."

"You have to be better, my son."

When their conversation was finished, the line went dead. Said hung up with a vacant stare on his face, turning over in his mind Arafat's words of warning. He would cross that bridge when he came to it. There were many other things to do first. The first phase had to be finished. There would be another long voyage, one that Captain Rashid did not know about yet. And then the final phase at that far distant port.

He straightened up. His team could handle any Israeli hit squad, out-think them, out-fight them, out-kill them.

There was one more telephone call to be made. It was a local call to a number in the city of Kuwait. Once again he went to the concierge, who gave him his bill for the Beirut call. That was paid. There would be no charge for the local call. He could put it through directly. When the connection was made, he asked the embassy receptionist for the military attaché. Said identified himself to that officer's secretary, using the Arabic language. The military attaché, ostensibly a lieutenant-colonel in the army, in reality was a high-ranking officer of the infamous KGB. When he came on the line, Said spoke with him eloquently, fluently, and without accent in the language of his Russian father, a sea captain of the northern city of Murmansk, nestled in a deep and narrow fjord of the frigid Barents Sea in the Arctic Ocean. When Said spoke to the colonel it was as an equal. For not only was Said a lieutenant-colonel in the Palestinian Liberation Army, as Captain Rashid knew him to be, he was also a member of the KGB, the world-grasping octopus of intrigue, intelligence, counterintelligence, and espionage. Said worked to further the world domination objectives of the Supreme Soviet, goals that were consistent with those of the Palestinian Liberation movement.

Lieutenant-Colonel Said of the KGB provided essentially the same report he had given to Yassir Arafat, including the date and time of the execution of the Phase II, 1300 hours Greenwich Mean Time (GMT) on April 26.

The *Mecca*'s crew cast off her lines from the Shuwaikh docks shortly after five that afternoon. Without a cargo, the old boat rode high out of the water. But she would be without freight only until she reached Bahrain, the highly industrialized Arab island nation a day's sail away on the *Mecca*'s route back to the Mediterranean. Her owner's Bahrain agents had contracted for the carriage of two thousand tons of aluminum ingots from Bahrain to Aden.

Rashid had informed Said of the Bahrain stop when he and his team returned to the freighter.

"How long will we be at Bahrain?" Said asked.

"The stuff's sitting on the dock. It shouldn't take us any more than three or four hours to get it on board." The captain thought it was time to raise the question. "Bahrain might be a good place for you people to leave the *Mecca*. It has one of the best-served airports in the Middle East. You can fly direct to Beirut from there. I can bring home any gear you don't want to carry on the aircraft."

"In your special compartment?"

Rashid smiled. "If need be."

"I'll think about it," was Said's evasive response.

He would not think about it at all. He would wait until the *Mecca* was two days out of Aden before he told Captain Rashid that instead of heading back up the Red Sea to the Suez and the Mediterranean, the *Mecca* would be sailing south down the coast of Africa. The two days' warning would give Rashid time to get on the radio and attempt to arrange a southbound cargo out of Aden. If he couldn't, the *Mecca* would have to sail south in ballast. The captain and owners would be fully compensated. That would be made perfectly clear.

Said returned to the bridge as Captain Rashid was getting the *Mecca* under way. They left Shuwaikh harbor, running out the channel past the water towers and the Sheraton Hotel bathed in the golden glow of the setting sun.

The captain had confirmed that the *Mecca* would be dropping anchor off Mina-al-Ahmadi around ten o'clock, as originally planned. From the time the *Mecca* left the Shuwaikh harbor astern, there was little more than four hours for the PLO team to get ready. The cook served them supper at 6:30. By the time that meal was finished, the *Mecca* was steaming slowly southward in total darkness except for her running lights and the faint glow of the flaring natural gas from the Kuwait oil fields far to the west. The four Arabs had to get their gear and weapons out of the captain's secret compartment without disclosing to the crew where they had hidden the material during the long voyage. The captain's men had been surprised enough when they found the PLO four back on board after the *Mecca* had left Port Said.

This time the scenario was different. The move had to be done under cover of darkness. Other than Nabil and the wheelsman engaged on the bridge, the crew would have to be occupied on some part of the ship that would keep them away from the deck. The solution was simple. While the cook had served the PLO group their supper at 6:30, Rashid ordered that the crew would be fed at seven. Furthermore, they would have the best food in the cook's larder and once again some wine, but this time only a liter per man.

With Maan standing guard at the head of the steps on the port side of the cabin deck, the lift-out operation began as soon as he was satisfied that all the crew were seated in the galley and digging into their special dinner. Working furiously, Said, Hassan, and Ahmed had their cache of equipment and Rashid's unmarked sacks of opium up and out of the secret compartment and on the deck immediately aft of the master's quarters. On the bridge above, Captain Rashid kept Nabil occupied during the critical period, going over charts of the approaches to Mina-al-Ahmadi.

Once their equipment was on deck, the need for cover and secrecy no longer existed. They would complete their preparations in the open with the curious crew as spectators. Curious they were. When they began straggling out of the galley, smoking and talking in the darkness, one of the deck hands sauntered up to the forward railing of the cabin deck to look into the black night to see what was ahead of the *Mecca*. As his eyes adjusted to the darkness, they opened wide with astonishment when he saw dark figures moving on the deck below, vague silhouettes against the dim grayness of the wall of the master's cabin. It was those damn PLO people. What were they doing? Calling to his companions to join him, the deck hand and the rest of the crew, including the cook, surrounded the Palestinians. They were amazed at what they saw.

On the starboard side of the deck, Said and Hassan were gently lifting from their styrofoam packages, gray, metallic objects about as big around as a large dinner plate. Their bottoms were flat but the tops domelike. In the center was a dial. To the right of the dial was a thick metal tube some six inches long attached to the surface by a universal swivel. To the left of the dial was a hinged ring just big enough for a large index finger.

The ring was attached to an arming pin which, when pulled out, permitted two internal spring-loaded wires to make contact, thereby activating a high-powered, electric-battery-generated charge which did two things. First, it set up a strong magnetic field in the base of the device, a field that would last indefinitely after the electrical power source terminated. Second, it completed the circuit that activated a tiny radio receiver preset to the frequency selected on the dial face. When the radio received the master signal on the selected frequency, it would trip the detonating circuit. At that instant the device, packed with immensely powerful material, would explode. The thick tube was a telescopic aerial that would extend to a distance of twenty feet.

The metal objects were deadly limpet mines, one of which could shatter the whole of a ship like the *Mecca* and send her to the bottom in seconds. Or it could destroy six Israeli gunboats. Ten of them strategically planted along the hull of a VLCC or ULCC supertanker could turn it into a blazing mass of wreckage in a split second, to sink in a matter of minutes if the ship was loaded and in a matter of seconds if it was in ballast.

On the port side of the deck, Ahmed and Maan took the two inflatable speedboats out of their container bags, unrolled them and inflated them using CO_2 bottles to bring them up to maximum and rigidity pressure. The gasoline-driven outboard motors had to be test run. They were clamped to the wooden shaft of the old ship's railing. The tubes from the red gasoline tanks were inserted into the front of each motor and the gasoline lines energized. With a strong pull on the starter rope by Ahmed, the motors roared into life, billowing huge clouds of blue smoke which disappeared as soon as the engines settled into a steady run.

Satisfied with the performance of the motors, Ahmed shut them off, lifted them off the railing and secured one on the back of each of the speedboats. He set the gas tanks on the floor amidships for balance.

The next test was of the quiet electric motors, the ones they would use throughout the entire operation. The gasoline engines were for emergency getaway purposes only, or if the batteries lost power. The railing was used again as a base on which to clamp the electric motors for testing. Their power lines ran to two wet batteries sitting on the deck in separate metal cases with a leather handle strap for easy carrying. Both electric motors worked perfectly, emitting almost no noise as their propellers spun freely in the night air. But it was apparent that the batteries needed a fast charge in order to bring them up to full power.

After transferring the electric motors to the back of the boats to sit next to their gasoline-driven counterparts, Ahmed and Maan took the batteries and their electrical charge machine down to the chief engineer's workshop. They hooked the charger into the ship's electrical supply, then clamped the positive and negative claws of the charger's wires onto the poles of the first set of batteries. By the time they were ready to launch the operation at ten that night, all four batteries would be up to their full power.

The two of them returned to their speedboats to begin assembling the oars and installing the ropes by which the boats would be lifted by the ship's crane over the side and gently lowered to the water. Up to that point, the crew members had simply stood and gawked at what was going on. Now they started to ask some questions. Said freely answered almost all. There was no need for them not to know. In any event, he would make sure they could not use the information until both phases of the operation had been completed. After that it wouldn't matter. He explained to them how the mines worked; how they clung to the metal surface of the hull of a ship with such a force that it was almost impossible to pry them off; how they were armed and the method of detonation by radio over long distances.

When asked, however, why they were going to mine the tankers, all he would say was, "In the cause of the liberation of the Palestinian people." And to the question of which ships he was going to mine, he would only say, "Those carrying the right flag."

Kneeling on the deck working on the last of the one hundred mines, Said had not noticed that the captain had joined the little group in the darkness as he gave those answers. Rashid was appalled by the lethal power that lay glinting on the deck, with flashes of the red, green, and white running lights reflecting off their shiny surfaces.

"Said, you could blow up the whole world with these!"

"That's exactly what I intend to do, captain, at least come as close to it as I possibly can."

Rashid shook his head. "All in the name of the liberation of the Palestinian people. There must be an easier way."

Said's voice, calm and soft in the balmy night air, was barely audible over the roar of the old *Mecca*'s engines and the thumping of her screw.

The far twinkling lights of the huge refinery at Mina-al-Ahmadi, and the flickering flames of gas from the multitude of its chimneys, appeared on the horizon ahead of the *Mecca* shortly after nine. Then came the first signs of the running lights of the empty supertankers clustered seaward, waiting at anchor. Against the web of loading piers, a multitude of tiny, red, green, and white beams showed the presence of about twenty vessels taking on their loads of heavy black crude or processed liquid petroleum from the pipes of the refinery.

A few minutes before ten, the *Mecca* was coming up to her agreed anchorage station, five miles northeast of the northern pier, about two miles from the northernmost waiting tanker. Captain Rashid had returned to his bridge after taking a look at the mines and the fully rigged speedboats. Nabil was already on the bridge, pacing back and forth behind the helmsman, fearful for his own safety after seeing those dreadful mines for the first time. He was conjuring up in his mind all manner of scenarios for the ships that would have them clamped to their bottoms. Were those wild men actually going to put those mines on those tankers out there? He couldn't believe it. Why? Were they going to blow them up right then and there? If they did, the whole place would blow up: the refinery, the piers, the storage tanks. He could see the entire area going up like an atomic bomb.

As soon as the captain came back on the bridge, Nabil began pleading with him to get the *Mecca* going as soon as the special cargo sacks had been picked up. Leave the Palestinians behind if they weren't back by then, he urged. Nabil was close to panic as he saw Said in a black wetsuit coming up the steps from the port wing of the bridge, an apparition that served to escalate the fear in Nabil's gut. The Egyptian withdrew to the far end of the bridge's starboard wing to get as far away from the PLO leader as he could.

The captain asked for "slow ahead." In the blackness he could barely see the deck hands in the fo'c'sle, ready at their anchor positions. He estimated another three or four minutes before he ordered the engines stopped.

He turned to face Said as he padded toward him. "Are you ready to go?"

Said nodded. "Everything's set, just waiting for the last battery. It should be up any minute."

Suddenly Rashid noticed in the dim light from the engine instruments that Said did not have on his perpetual sunglasses. It was one of those rare moments when he could see, but only barely, into the young man's eyes. He thought he saw a glimmer of affection.

"Rashid," Said said, "this is going to be a dangerous operation. Something might go wrong. I am sure it won't. But I want you to know how much . . . how grateful I am to you. Do you understand?"

The captain's creased face broke into a smile as he laid a hand on Said's black shoulder. "Of course I do. Of course, and may Allah be with you, Said."

Said's eyes dropped away from the old man's for a moment just as Rashid removed his hand. Then those incongruous blue eyes were fixed again on Rashid's. "There is something you must know. I have had to take a precaution. I thought about doing it at Port Said, but it wasn't necessary as you had the opium on board, but now I have to do it. I have to be absolutely sure that the *Mecca* will still be here when we're finished. Once you get rid of your special cargo there will be nothing to keep you here, nothing to make you wait for us."

"But you have my word!" Rashid protested.

"And I accept it." He looked in the distance toward Nabil and judged that he could hear none of the conversation. He lifted his voice so the first officer could get every word. "But there may be others on this ship who will think differently. You're only one man against nine, captain. So to make sure the *Mecca* is still here when I get back, I have planted one of the mines. It's activated. There's the safety pin." He held up the right hand and opened it palm down. Around his index finger was a steel ring. Attached to it and hanging down was the safety pin of the hidden mine. The captain looked at it without emotion, but Nabil, his bulging eyes wide with fear, gasped, "You're mad! You'll kill us all!"

"If the *Mecca* stays here, you have nothing to worry about. If you leave, you're dead. Our transmitter is in my boat. It doesn't matter where you are. All we have to do is push a button." Those words were directed to the trembling Nabil. Said had taken one further precaution. "And we've put your radio transmitter out of commission."

Said turned to Captain Rashid. "I'm sorry," he said.

The black figure disappeared down the steps. Rashid sized up his position and ordered, "Stop engines."

In a state of near mental collapse, the petrified Nabil did not respond. Pushing him aside, the captain pulled back on the telegraph levers to the "stop" position. Immediately he could hear the roar of the engines die as the chief engineer, in his private hell of an engine room below, moved the throttles to idle.

On the cargo deck aft, Ahmed started up the crane motor. When it had settled down, he skilfully moved the levers, swinging its cable and hook over the waiting speedboats. Ahmed stopped it about five feet above the first craft to be lifted. Immediately, three black-suited figures slipped the loops of the boat's lifting ropes—one at the bow, two from each corner of the stern, two from each gunwale, just forward of the middle of the boat—over the sharp tip of the waiting hook. Said raised his right hand palm up, the signal to Ahmed. With the surging sound of the crane motor, the cable began to lift, pulling the ropes taut. Slowly the speedboat with its two motors moved up and away from the deck. At head height, Ahmed stopped the lift without any instructions from Said and pulled the right directional lever on the crane. He swung the boat slowly over the starboard railing to a point about ten feet beyond. Gingerly, he pushed on the lowering lever, watching the speedboat disappear below the deck level and out of sight.

Ahmed's eyes were on Said's hands. The PLO leader leaned over the railing, his black form barely visible to Ahmed in the darkness, but he could pick up the white-brown hands, both of which Said had moved over to his right side, holding them vertically apart and as wide as he could. Below him was Maan standing on the lowered gangway platform, his hands similarly extended. When Maan calculated that the bottom of the inflated craft was about three feet from the surface of the calm, millpond-like black water—it was hard to judge the height in the blackness of the night—he began to move his hands slowly together to indicate the diminishing height of the speedboat. His gesture was copied by Said and seen by Ahmed. Finally the palms of the two outstretched pairs of hands were only a foot apart, then they were together as the bottom of the boat touched the water.

On the gangway platform, Maan was ready. Immediately the boat was in the water, no more than two feet beyond the platform, he leaped into it to take the boat ropes off the cable's lift hook. Those ropes would be left in place but coiled on the floor of the boat for the haul back onto the *Mecca*'s deck when they returned. Maan signaled to Said above him that the hook was clear, sat on the middle seat between the oarlocks, seized the handles of the oars and rowed toward the stern of the freighter to clear the touchdown area for the second boat. It appeared a few moments later, riding over the rail to meet the water gently. Hassan guided it down as Maan had done.

Within ten minutes, both boats were successfully launched. Hassan jumped into the boat from the gangway platform to unhitch it and bring it alongside. This would be his and Ahmed's craft. The next step was to load it with its fifty mines. In three-man chain fashion, Ahmed lifted each one off the deck and handed it to Said halfway down the steps, who carried it the rest of the way to the platform and then to Hassan. Then followed the radio transmitter, their oxygen bottles, masks, flippers, and black gloves. Boat number one was ready.

Hassan rowed it a few strokes away from the *Mecca* to allow Maan to come in with boat number two. In short order it received the remaining forty-nine limpet mines, Said and Maan's diving gear, then Said himself. Maan moved to the bow of the craft, while Said sat in the rear seat to operate the motor and steer. There was no need for them to wait for the other boat. They knew exactly where they had to go, what they had to do. Said moved the throttle on the electric motor to full speed. He looked up toward the *Mecca*'s railing where the entire ship's crew stood watching them, their figures barely visible in the murk. He could distinguish Rashid's broad figure, standing apart from the rest at the head of the gangway. He waved to the old captain, but in the darkness the gesture was not returned.

Silently the black, heavy-laden boat blended into the enveloping night, leaving only a pencil-like trace of white glowing water in its wake which pointed to the lights of the anchored leviathans to the south.

Hassan moved his craft back to the gangway platform where Ahmed stood waiting. When his huge bulk was on board, settled in the stern position, the second boat moved soundlessly into the darkness.

Said had briefed his team thoroughly when they returned to the *Mecca* that afternoon. On the back of one of his maps he had carefully plotted the location of the super-tankers as they had been anchored the day before. Of the twenty anchored ships, he estimated between eight and ten would have moved into the piers of Mina-al-Ahmadi to take on their loads. The remainder would still be at anchor and in exactly the same locations. Every one of the ships was registered in Liberia or Panama and therefore qualified as an acceptable target in that neither of those countries was a member of NATO. In fact, few of the more than 700 super-tankers that roamed the seas of the world carried the flags of the countries of their owners. Instead they flew a flag of convenience, that of Liberia or Panama.

In his briefing, Said attempted to keep the plan of attack as simple as possible. He drew an erratic north-south line on his map, marking on it the location of each of the ten target ships. He and Maan would take the even-numbered ships in the line. Ahmed and Hassan would take the first one and after that the odd ones in the sequence. To avoid being seen, each tanker would be approached from directly on its bow. The likelihood of being spotted by a crew member was remote, in that the accommodation for the thirty or forty crew members was always at the stern of the ship, a thousand feet or more away from the bow. Furthermore, once their boats were running alongside a target ship, they would, in fact, be under the vessel. By this time, each of the tankers had pumped out its ballast and was riding high in the water. A major part of its vast body was exposed, its hull curving sharply at the water line to produce an overhang under which the two small boats would operate unseen from the deck above.

In the calm, windless night, Said could see from the jumble of running lights ahead that the tankers did not all point in the same direction as they rode at anchor. He steered the boat well to the east of the first ship. It was Hassan and Ahmed's initial target. Though Said and Maan were half a mile from it, the massive ship appeared to loom above them. The funnel at its towering stern was floodlit to display its owner's proud symbol: ESSO. They passed behind the supertanker, knowing that at that moment Ahmed and Maan would be at its nose ready to begin their task.

Beyond the Esso tanker, they turned slightly toward shore to their first target some 300 yards south of it, its bow conveniently pointing directly toward them. In the moonless night, the cloaking darkness was softened only slightly by the yellowish glow of the distant flaring at the refinery ashore. So dark was it that a pair of naked eyes on the deck of the fo'c'sle of one of the anchored supertankers high above the water would not have been able to find the black rubber boat, its passengers, or its lethal cargo. The slim line of phosphorus wake might have been visible, but nothing else.

The Esso insignia blazing proudly in the night on the first ship, combined with its peculiar superstructure, had enabled Said to identify her. From his memory of the photographs they had taken yesterday and the ship's position chart he had drawn, he knew she was the *Esso Italia*. She was in the size range of 250,000 deadweight tons and registered in Liberia. That key identification made, his memory of the chart gave him the names and details of the next nine ships in the waiting line. Any other ships would be new arrivals since the day before.

His mind quickly reviewed the ships they would visit that night. Their first target, the second ship in the line, was the *Afran Zodiac*, owned by Gulf Oil, about 227,000 tons, flag Liberia. The third was the *Fairfield Jason*, owned by Fairway Tankers, about 270,000 tons, flag Liberia. The fourth, *Conoco Europe*, about the same size as the *Fairfield Jason*, flag Liberia. He could not remember the name of the owner. The fifth, *Chevron Edinburgh*, owned by Chevron Transport, same size, flag Liberia. The sixth, *Esso Malaysia*, about 200,000 tons, owned by Esso Tankers Inc., flag Panama. The seventh, *Saint Marcet*, owner he had forgotten, about 280,000 tons, flag Liberia. Eighth, the *Mobil Magnolia*, again about 280,000 tons, the owner Mobil Oil, flag Liberia. The ninth, *Charles Pigott*, owner Bank of California National Association, about 270,000 tons, flag Liberia. And the last, the *Amoco Singapore*, owner Amoco Transport Company, about 230,000 tons, flag Liberia. Not a NATO flag in the lot.

The *Afran Zodiac*'s massive anchor chain slipped by so closely that they could have touched it. In a few seconds they bumped against the enormous hydrodynamic bulb that sat under the bow of the ship, its orange paint making it dully visible only when they were making contact. Maan cut the power immediately. The yielding surface of the rubber boat bounced gently off the ship's hull. They were ready to begin. Not a word would be spoken.

Said put on his flippers, gloves, face mask, and, with Maan's help, strapped on his black-painted oxygen bottle. He eased himself over the gunwale of the boat into the water between it and the towering bow of the *Afran Zodiac*. Oxygen tube firmly clamped in his mouth, he reached up and took from Hassan's hands the first limpet mine. He clutched it to his chest with both arms, the flat surface to be magnetized facing away from his body. Turning toward the hull he submerged to a point where he calculated he was about three feet below the water line. With both hands he shoved the mine against the hard metal of the hull. Holding it there with his left hand, he explored with his right the rounded surface of the device, found the ring of the arming pin, inserted his index finger in it and pulled. Instantaneously the mine was both magnetized and armed, clamped firmly to the underbelly of the monster ship.

Only one thing remained to be done. Deftly his hands found the telescopic aerial and pulled it out to its full length, leaving it flush against the hull pointing aft toward the stern. The "wings" at the aerial's tip would lift it to the surface once the ship was under way. Back Said went to the surface, where he hung on to the gunwale rope as the electric motor drove the boat about a hundred feet along under the curved hull toward the stern. There the mining procedure was repeated as it was at similar intervals along the water line, with the last one, the tenth, placed close to the stern under the engine room. They were finished. With Maan's help, Said climbed back into the boat. As silently as they had arrived, the small craft, its electric motor whirring noiselessly, crept back to the bow under the protective overhang of the hull, past the anchor chain and on in the darkness to the *Conoco Europe*.

Said checked his watch. It had taken him twenty-two minutes to mine the *Afran Zodiac*. The time was seven minutes to eleven. Four more ships to do, with a transit time of say ten minutes between each of them and forty minutes to get back to the *Mecca*, that would get them back to her by 01:40, long before Rashid's deadline of 02:00—if nothing went wrong. So far so good.

Guided by the running lights of the anchored ships, they moved past the third ship, the *Fairfield Jason*, both men wondering how Ahmed and Hassan were doing. They should have started on her by that time.

The approach of Said and Maan to the *Conoco Europe* was similar to their handling of the *Afran Zodiac*. The mine planting went as planned without incident, but this time it was Maan who was in the water. Then on to the *Esso Malaysia*, the *Mobil Magnolia* and finally the *Amoco Singapore*.

Said had mined both the Mobil and Esso ships, so it was Maan who was in the water to finish the operation. The eighth limpet mine had been clamped to the hull of the *Amoco Singapore*. The next one would be the last of the forty-nine mines they had brought from the *Mecca*. Said took the boat to the stern under the engine room. That position was also just ahead of the massive six blades of the ship's mighty propeller.

Just as Maan submerged with the final mine clutched to his chest, Said's ears caught the tinkle of the ship's engine telegraph bells. Immediately there was a heavy rumbling from inside the vessel as its powerful diesels accelerated, turning the propeller shaft with rapidly increasing speed. It seemed to Said no more than an instant before the water around him had turned into a churning maelstrom. The vicious blades of the mammoth screw were just below the surface twenty feet away, turning faster and faster, sucking the water ahead of the propeller into its maw with ever increasing force. Said could feel his boat being pulled toward the propeller. Reacting instantly and instinctively he rammed the throttle of his electric motor fully open, pushing its steering arm hard over to port to swing the nose of his craft to the right, away from the spreading whirlpool. But it was too late. The suction overpowered the weak motor of the light craft, even though it had managed to move out away from the ship by a yard before it was overcome by the tremendous power of the water being drawn into the thrashing blades, turning inside their protective circular shield.

The small craft was out of control. Said knew that he was being drawn inexorably into the white, foaming vortex. In one motion he was on his feet and diving out away from the tanker. But as soon as he hit the water he knew he had not escaped. He was being hauled down, tumbling. The oxygen bottle on his back was pulled violently. His arms and legs twisted as he was propelled downward and back in the churning black and white void of foaming water. The noise of the pounding screw filled his eardrums. A sharp pain shot through his left arm and shoulder as he was thrown hard against the side of the ship. Then, as quickly as he had been sucked under, he was thrown to the surface gasping for air in the churning water. He was about thirty yards behind the huge tanker, its vast bulk now beginning to move slowly forward to pick up its anchor and proceed into its assigned loading berth.

Frantically Said searched the surface for Maan. He was nowhere to be seen. But the boat was just a few feet away from him still miraculously intact except for a slash through the fabric of the starboard gunwale. The slash, however, was in only one of the many compartments of the inflated speedboat. The craft was still serviceable. He hauled himself back into it.

Where was Maan? Said did not call out. He could only look and hope. There, just to the left. There was something floating in the water about thirty feet away. Said eased on the electric power, edging the boat up to the shiny black object. As he leaned over the side to pick it up, he recoiled. It was an arm encased in the sleeve of a black wetsuit. Blood was still flowing from the stump, staining the white water. On the index finger was a black steel pull ring.

17

7 April   10:00 P.M.

Murmansk

Fleet Admiral Smirnov had been given explicit instructions by Chairman Romanov to prepare to get his entire submarine fleet to sea. The movement of the boats from their harbors should be carried out in absolute secrecy. It was imperative that no clue be found by NATO intelligence through the use of their satellites—or in any other way—that the undersea craft had left their bases. Romanov had been concerned that, either by the use of radar or infrared photography, the satellites would be able to track the submarines as they moved out. But the admiral had assured him that he could carry it off without detection. He had a special departure plan designed to fool the eyes of the enemy space vehicles.

As to the passage of the Kola Peninsula submarine fleet through the Denmark Strait between Iceland and Greenland and the gap between Iceland and Norway, Smirnov assured the chairman that the test of the sonar interference system, SONINT, from March 11 through March 22 had worked perfectly. He would use it to mask the exit of both the northern and the Baltic submarine fleets commencing April 3. Once he started the SONINT system by satellite signal, it would operate automatically for eleven days and could not be turned off. But the planned period would be more than enough to enable him to get his entire submarine fleet out to sea and for most of it to move south of the Tropic of Cancer and, therefore, out of the area covered by NATO naval forces. Furthermore, by mid-April many of the submarines, particularly the faster nuclear-powered ones, would already be at their stations, either with the Atlantic fleet for OKEAN, or at stations along the Cape tanker route in the South Atlantic and the Indian Ocean. That was as Romanov had instructed.

It was on March 17 that Smirnov had been summoned to Romanov's Kremlin office. There, in the presence of Ustinov and three other voting members of the Politburo, Kirilenko, Gromyko, and army General Yu Andropov, Romanov gave him a briefing and a set of instructions that both appalled and electrified him. The presence of the other members of the Politburo certified that Romanov's orders to him had been approved by the Politburo itself. Smirnov was to have his submarines deployed and in their required positions in the Atlantic and the Indian Ocean no later than April 20. The date of execution of the first stage of the plan, which Romanov had called the Andropov Plan, would be between April 20 and April 26. Smirnov would be informed of the precise date later on. The second and final stage was to be executed on May Day, that most significant of all days in the calendar of communist Russia.

Romanov made sure his fleet admiral understood the background and objectives the Politburo wished to achieve. There was no doubt their action would take them to the brink of a war with the Americans and their NATO allies. As the Politburo and Romanov saw it, however, the Soviet Union had no choice. The new American president and the president of Pakistan had just announced their agreement under which American troops and equipment would be moving into Pakistan beginning May 7. The presence of American imperialist forces there constituted a threat to the Soviet Union which could not be tolerated.

Romanov's first objective was to stop the Americans. If he could not do it through the United Nations or through diplomatic bargaining or by threats he would have to use force and was prepared to do so. That he made perfectly clear to Smirnov.

The second objective was to secure and control a new source of crude oil for the Soviet Union and its energy-starved Eastern Bloc countries. The Andropov Plan was bold, decisive and dramatic. There was no room for error or failure. The stakes were far too high for that. The man with full responsibility for its execution was Fleet Admiral Nikolai Ivanovich Smirnov. Smirnov would sit in his offices in Moscow, from which place he would directly control not only the OKEAN exercise but also the Andropov operation. The key people were his submarine captains. On their shoulders would fall the ultimate responsibility.

The Arctic sun had set at 9:36 on the evening of April 7. With its disappearance, the pace of activity at the Soviet Navy's submarine base in the ice-free port of Murmansk reached fever pitch as the crews of the remaining serviceable submarines prepared to take their ships to sea.

The captain of Victor II submarine 501 pulled the collar of his heavy jacket up to protect his ears from the piercing cold Murmansk night wind. Captain Second Rank Boris Chernavin barked out orders from the tiny bridge at the front of the 501's long hump of a tower, which sat slightly forward of amidships of the powerful nuclear craft. The fore and aft lines were cast off. Silently, gently, the 323-foot submarine, a black, cigar-shaped form, moved ahead and out into the darkness toward the main channel of the Kola Fjord, turning slowly starboard.

When he heard three heavy splashes in the water at the dock the 501 had just left, the captain turned to look back. In the floodlit water by the quay, three huge bundles were bobbing, each with long hoses running from them up to the dock level, where a gang of sailors was busy starting the motor of a large portable air compressor. When that machine was running satisfactorily the hose from the first bundle in the water was connected to it. In short order the bundle began to uncurl under the pressure of the compressed air being forced inside it. Quickly it snapped out to its full length, its bottom flopping with another splash as that section of 501's plastic counterpart opened fully. It was the stern section of the replica. It would take only half an hour to inflate all three sections and join them together.

This deception had been planned by Smirnov personally. During the previous year he had had inflatable plastic replicas made of all his submarines. When blown up, his flat-bottomed, round-bodied decoys presented an image to the eye of the satellite that was exactly the same as that made by the real submarine. Smirnov's departing Murmansk submarine fleet, the remaining 110 diesel and nuclear-powered vessels of the 162 based there, would be replaced immediately by their doubles. Smirnov was convinced that that action, combined with a quick dive of all boats within minutes of leaving their jetties, would fool the satellite cameras.

Chernavin was disappointed. He would have liked to have stayed to see the copy of his ship fully assembled, but in half an hour he and his submarine would be long gone. He would be five miles north up the channel with Zelenii-Mys to starboard, and preparing to follow the lights of the channel marker buoys when the 501 swung eastward toward Waenga.

Boris Chernavin anticipated that, when the OKEAN exercise was finished and the 501 was back in Murmansk, a signal would be waiting for him confirming his posting to the Marshal Grechko Naval Academy in Leningrad. If he received that posting, it meant that he was in line to move toward the top positions in the Soviet navy. His father, a retired rear-admiral, would be pleased and proud if Boris were given the honor of attending the naval academy. Undoubtedly he had been using his not inconsiderable influence among his former naval colleagues to make sure that his son was selected. A captain second rank—equivalent to an American or British naval commander—at the age of twenty-eight when he became 501's captain, Chernavin had advanced rapidly in rank. This, too, was not unusual in the elite submarine service of the 450,000-man Red Navy that he, Boris Chernavin, knew and believed was the largest, best, and most powerful navy in the world.

As the 501 approached the 150-foot deep channel, Chernavin gave the order to dive. Within eight minutes of casting off her lines, the submarine was submerged, invisible, shielded from the probing eye of any satellite by the black surface of the Kola Fjord's inpenetrable water.

Using his active sonar, attack periscope, and radar to navigate, Chernavin moved his ship into station half a mile behind 476, the Echo class submarine that had been berthed just astern of his 501. Ahead of 476 and as far as his sonar screen eyes could see were the electronic white blips of a single file line of twenty-eight submerged nuclear submarines. The unseen column moved noiselessly through the ebony water past the twinkling lights of the multitude of freighters, tankers, and bulk carriers big and small that were at Murmansk to take or deliver cargoes; past the factory ships and trawlers of the fishing fleet in port to discharge its frozen cargo; past busy shipyards. The run north from Murmansk down the Kola Fjord to the Barents Sea was forty miles, with a transit time of about five hours.

By 2 A.M. on the morning of April 8, with Victor 501 bringing up the rear, the silent line of submarines had left the port of Poliarnyi astern. An hour later, well out to sea beyond the entrance to the fjord, Chernavin took his ship down from periscope level to a running depth of 300 feet. The anticipated covering interference had hit his sonar moments after the 501 cleared the fjord. Like all his fellow submarine captains, Chernavin would have to navigate without being able to "see" until the sonar interference stopped. Furthermore, he expected he would not surface for several weeks. In fact, the 501 would never surface again.

18

8 April   6:07 P.M.
Moscow

General Andropov read the lengthy signal from his senior KGB man in Washington. There was no doubt about it. Chairman Romanov must see it immediately, first because of the urgency and importance of the contents and second, because it had demonstrated clearly the high caliber of the intelligence system that the KGB had developed in the United States. That hundreds of thousands of people in the United States at that moment were reading essentially the same information in the *New York Times* in no measure took away from Andropov's pride in the superior capability of his own agency.

The time was shortly after six in the evening in Moscow. When his aide tracked down the chairman's whereabouts, Andropov himself rang Romanov at his sumptuous riverside dacha in that special wooded area on the outskirts of Moscow reserved for high party officials. Indeed, Andropov's own dacha was in the same area. Perhaps he might stop by with the signal on his way home.

A servant answered, saying that the chairman was at dinner, but Romanov had heard the call and came on the line himself when advised that it was Andropov calling. He and Tania were just finishing dinner. Tania's name raised in Andropov's mind the image of a most beautiful woman. Some ten years younger than her husband, she bore a startling resemblance to a movie star of Andropov's youth, the exquisite Swedish beauty, Greta Garbo. Even at his advanced age, the head of the KGB had in no way lost his appraising eye for a fine-looking woman. Yes, a visit to the Romanov dacha, brief though it would be, would be well worthwhile, simply for the opportunity to be with the charming Tania before he went home to his own dumpy wife.

Twenty minutes later, he was at the white-linen-covered table of the family dining room of the Romanov dacha. It was in that richly paneled, intimate room that the Romanovs took supper together when they were not entertaining. That evening its intimacy was enhanced by glowing candles glittering off sparkling silverware, gold-encrusted plates and crystal wine goblets. The glasses were filled with Romanov's special sparkling rosé, an after-dinner delicacy that he sometimes preferred to the biting, smooth Courvoisier cognac with which he usually took his single Havana cigar of the day. Seated between the couple, twirling his goblet of wine, Andropov talked with the lovely Tania. They discussed the escalating crisis with the Americans, about which she proved fully knowledgeable, while Romanov, puffing occasionally on his cigar and taking a sip of wine, concentrated totally on the message which he read in the flickering light of the flames from the three-pointed candelabra. Perching his gold-rimmed half glasses on the bridge of his nose, his mind soaked up the KGB signal from Washington. It was dated that day, April 8:

KGB operatives report the departure of U.S.-Pakistan Task Force (PTF) sea lift. Elements comprise commandeered passenger ships carrying troops; amphibious cargo, transport dock landing, and tank landing ships; also supporting ammunition, combat stores, hospital, replenishment, and repair ships; plus recently acquired container ships. All PTF vessels left port between 0600 and 1100 hours local time departing from Mayport, Florida; Charleston, South Carolina; Norfolk, Virginia; Little Creek, Virginia; Brooklyn, New York; Newport, Rhode Island; and Boston, Massachusetts.

All elements PTF expected to rendezvous off Bermuda to proceed in convoy to Karachi, escorted by two multi-purpose and two ASW [antisubmarine warfare] aircraft carriers, ten destroyers, and ten frigates.

PTF carrying three infantry, and one armored division plus the 25th Infantry Division from Pacific Command's reserve in Hawaii, plus all tanks, vehicles, supporting equipment, and supplies. Estimate 100,000 troops in PTF sea lift. Estimated arrival time off Pakistan: May 6.

Commencing May 7 concurrent with first landings in Karachi, U.S. will also commence airlift of 82nd Airborne Division, plus two 1,800-man Marine battalions to strategic inland points along Pakistan borders with Afghanistan and Iran. 82nd Airborne has 16,000 men, 50 light reconnaissance tanks and approximately 100 helicopters, 33 of them mounting anti-tank missiles.

Twenty-six fighter/attack squadrons of Tactical Air Command (TAC) earmarked for PTF to deploy as soon as support facilities available after initial landings. Until arrival TAC squadrons aircraft from Indian Ocean Fifth Fleet augmented by convoy escort carriers will provide air support.

Detailed information on identity all units in PTF will follow.

Chairman Romanov handed the message to Andropov saying, "Let Tania take a look at that."

As the KGB chief gave the document to her, Romanov slipped off his glasses, contemplated his half-smoked cigar, and topped off the goblet of wine. "You have to hand it to the Americans, Yu. They've pulled their task force together and put it to sea in three weeks. That's not bad for an ad hoc operation."

Andropov grunted. "Ad hoc is right. The Americans never cease to amaze me with their inability to plan ahead for this sort of crisis. They seem to be completely incapable of doing any strategic long-term planning."

"Perhaps," Romanov suggested, "that is because they change their leadership every four years—or eight—and the president and his administration are always worried about the next election. Whereas our system is built for stability. The same people stay in the Politburo, some of them, such as Brezhnev and Suslov and, of course, Gromyko, for over two decades."

"Indeed that may be one of the reasons," Andropov agreed, lifting his glass to look at the perfection of the ruby colored wine against the flame of the nearest candle. "But what I'm talking about, Grigori, is that in place of intelli-gent long-range strategic planning they place reaction. That's the nature of the American people.It's the nature of their government, and, therefore, it's the nature of their military. In the last two and a half decades, while we were building our navy—Gorshkov was doing it—into the largest and most powerful in the world, the American navy has declined from some 900 ships to fewer than 500. Its reserve fleet is down from over two thousand ships to about 300, many of them ready for the scrapyard. If that wasn't enough, their bases around the world have gone from a hundred down to fewer than thirty."

"To our advantage," Tania commented. She had finished reading the message.

"To our advantage, indeed. And we will press that ad-vantage at every turn. Let me give you another example. When Carter threatened to use military force to keep us out of the Persian Gulf, the American Joint Chiefs of Staff and the defence secretary told him that about the only force they could deploy quickly into the Persian Gulf was their Airborne Division, the 82nd. It's mentioned in the signal." He pointed toward the document on the table in front of

Tania. "On the recommendations of the Joint Chiefs of Staff, the secretary proposed putting together a seven-ship force loaded with combat equipment, mothballed but ready to go on short notice—tanks, trucks, guns, that sort of thing. That logistics force was to be positioned at Diego Garcia from which it could sail . . ."

"Where is Diego Garcia?" Tania asked.

"It's an American base on a British island about a thousand miles south of India. It would be about a five-day sail from there to the Persian Gulf to rendezvous with combat troops airlifted in, their so-called Rapid Deployment Force. Their target was to be able to get 13,000 men and 300 tanks into the Persian Gulf on a week's notice. What happened? They put three ships at Diego Garcia. They're still there, totally vulnerable to our submarines. And the rapid deployment force was a dream, just a dream. So, today, again to our great advantage," he acknowledged, "the Americans have had to throw together an ad hoc task force, get it to sea and spend twenty-eight days getting it to Pakistan, let alone ashore."

Romanov asked his wife, "Could I see the message again, please?"

When he had it in front of him, he checked one point on the first page and then asked Andropov, "When will our submarines start tracking them?"

"Smirnov tells me that the first contact will be made at their rendezvous point near Bermuda. The tracking process, both by submarine and satellite, will begin at that location. By the time the Americans round the Cape of Good Hope—they will stay well south of it to keep out of the tanker lanes, and going north in the Indian Ocean they will stay well to the east—by that time we should have twenty-five to thirty submarines tracking them."

The chairman nodded silent approval.

He asked, "What about the OKEAN exercise? Will Smirnov move his Atlantic fleet down to intercept?"

"No. OKEAN begins on the fifteenth of April, as you know. According to my plan," he paused to emphasize the word *my*, "all of our serviceable submarines have moved out of the Kola Peninsula between the third and the seventh under the SONINT interference cover. The last left yesterday. They should be south of the NATO coverage area, the Tropic of Cancer, by the fourteenth or fifteenth. The Atlantic OKEAN fleet will carry out its exercises in that area for the following two weeks. Smirnov wants to keep them there as a decoy to the satellites or any snooping American or British surveillance ships that cross the Tropic of Cancer on their own. In the meantime, the major part of our submarine force will deploy to their stations in the South Atlantic and the Indian Ocean. On the other hand, our Indian Ocean OKEAN attacking and defending fleets are scheduled to leave the Gulf of Aden a week from now. They will conduct coordinated naval and air exercises within seeing range of the American Fifth Fleet and the British flotilla to show them that we have powerful muscle. Then they will turn south to intercept the American task force, to give it some expert harassment during the last four or five days of its approach to Pakistan."

Romanov was pleased. He rammed his cigar butt into a silver ashtray, exclaiming, "Excellent! But if the Andropov Plan works . . ."

The KGB head preened slightly at the mention of his scheme.

"If it works, on May Day there won't be any American task force approaching Pakistan to harass, will there, Yu?"

With a smug smile General Andropov could not but agree. "No, sir, there will not!"

Her glass raised on high, Tania made a simple toast. "Let's drink to that."

Her husband, one of the two most powerful men in the world, and his proud minister enthusiastically stood, touched their glasses to each other's and hers as Grigori Romanov toasted, "To the Andropov Plan. To its glorious success!"

19

1-10 April

Port of Manama, Bahrain

and Gulf of Aden

The lethal mines of Lieutenant-Colonel Said Kassem and his PLO team had been planted on the ten hulls of the chosen supertankers of Mina-al-Ahmadi on the night of March 31. By the evening of the next day, the *Mecca* was docked in the Port of Manama, the bustling capital of the island nation of Bahrain, taking on a cargo of aluminum ingots consigned to Aden for transshipment. The Palestinians, grieving for their lost comrade and concerned that the *Mecca*'s untrustworthy crew members should not be given a chance to slip ashore to pass information about the mining to the authorities, had forbidden any of the crew to leave the ship or talk to the local stevedores loading the old freighter.

The loading had gone rapidly and the *Mecca* left Bahrain immediately after the cargo was on board, making her way out of port eastward beyond Muharraq Island and past the enormous Arab shipbuilding and repair yard with its massive dry docks, big enough to hold and repair the largest supertankers afloat.

On April 8, when the *Mecca* was three days sail away

from Aden, Said informed Captain Rashid that after she discharged her cargo at Aden, she would then have to sail back around the Horn of Africa and south down the Indian Ocean to Durban. He hastened to add that these arrangements had been made by Arafat with the ship's owners in Beirut.

Furthermore, the captain as well as the crew would be paid a substantial bonus for making the long voyage to South Africa. Captain Rashid was not disturbed by the change of plans. After all, he was in the freighter business for the purpose of making money. So long as he and his owners and crew were being paid, he would take the *Mecca* anywhere. Said had informed him of the change of plans before they arrived at Aden, so Rashid could communicate with the ship's agents at that port in order to arrange a cargo for the run down the African coast. Hassan had made the VHF radio transmitter temporarily serviceable. The message was passed to Aden through the harbormaster at Merbat on the south coast of Oman, as the *Mecca* passed abeam of that port some ten miles off shore.

Splendid had been patrolling the Gulf of Aden for nine days. When she had arrived at her station in the fifty-mile-wide stretch of the gulf between the northeast tip of Somalia and the shores of South Yemen, Commander Leach had elected to use a racetrack pattern for his patrol. The pattern changed from a port racetrack to a starboard one at the beginning of each watch.

When setting up his patrol pattern, Leach had been concerned by the fact that, while the gulf was about fifty miles wide, only twenty-six miles of it were in international waters. If he went closer than twelve miles from shore to the north or south he would be in the territorial waters of South Yemen or Somalia and would be subject to arrest or to being driven off with whatever force was available to the offended nation.

The navigating officer had also pointed out to him that the water was extremely shallow at the northern end of the proposed racetrack pattern. The depth was no more than a hundred feet. There would be little maneuvering room for a vessel as large as *Splendid*. She was some fifty-five feet high from her rounded bottom to the top of her tower. When her periscope was up, another twenty-five feet were added. In such shallow waters the submarine would be highly vulnerable.

Within twenty-four hours of taking up her slow-moving station at the mouth of the gulf, *Splendid* and her crew had settled down to a routine that was to last for days. During her ponderous moves back and forth across the gulf, Leach kept his boat at periscope level, popping his glass eye up over the surface for a good look at whatever was going by, whenever the sonar or radar watchkeepers indicated that a passing vessel was at its closest range. Occasionally, in order to take a photograph of an inbound Red Navy ship at close range, he would accelerate *Splendid* temporarily to get as close as possible to the vessel. At the right moment up would go the search periscope and the photographs would be taken quickly. Immediately the periscope would disappear below the surface, having been duly noted by the radar operators on the photographed vessel. The sonar operators of the photographed ship, their equipment having failed to pick up the *Splendid* at her slow rate of three knots, would, at the time of her acceleration, have been startled to find a target bearing down on them from nowhere, which then disappeared from their screens as quickly as it had appeared.

Thirty seconds before the exact minute assigned for *Splendid*'s reports to the admiral's flagship, her radar mast with its radio antenna would appear above the surface for the transmission to be made. At such close range to the flotilla and being under direct operational control of its flag officer, it was necessary for Pots and his team to maintain round the clock, ears-on, alert monitoring of the flotilla's operating radio frequencies. All signals made for the *Splendid* during her period on the station had to be picked up. There could be no lapses. There were only a few messages.

There were no lapses.

Pots' team of watchkeepers were able to monitor all

the messages passing around the Royal Navy flotilla and its exchanges with the U.S. fleet. Leach was therefore able to keep abreast of what was going on. Every morning the captain had the communications officer brief him and the first lieutenant, and as many off-watch officers as wished to sit in, on the flotilla messages that had been monitored. Not all of them, of course, but those that the communications officer considered to be the most relevant and important.

The Victor II Soviet submarine still maintained her surveillance station on *Splendid* by pinging at her from time to time with active sonar. The Russian boat kept her position just to the west of the British ship's racetrack course. The Victor, operating at three knots, the same speed as *Splendid*, was also noiseless. The British ship reciprocated by occasionally driving her pinging active sonar waves out to bounce off the Red sub and return. It was done to confirm that the other was still there and pinpoint where she was.

Midmorning on April 9, as *Splendid* was reaching the northern turning point of one of her countless patrol runs across the Gulf of Aden, sonar reported, "Contact. 075, 11,000 yards and closing. Course 265. Making about ten knots. Sounds like some kind of a freighter." Then he added, "In forty-five minutes we should both be at the same place."

In his bunk, reading a sex-filled mystery paperback, Marcus Leach listened to the report. He decided that for amusement he would take a look at the freighter as she passed by. It would be worth a laugh to scare the hell out of her crew by sticking the periscope up right under their noses. He set the alarm on his wrist watch for forty minutes ahead and went back to his stimulating reading.

Thus at 0936 hours GMT in the sunny morning of the ninth of April, a periscope suddenly appeared about thirty degrees off the port bow and a hundred yards south of the *Mecca*.

The captain of the submarine would have been disappointed if he had realized that he had not startled the captain of the ancient freighter. The powerful magnifying lenses of the attack periscope clearly picked up the image of the weatherbeaten old captain as he stood on the port wing of his bridge, eyes focused nonchalantly on the shiny submarine eye watching him. No, he wasn't startled. A sailor who has spent a lifetime on the Mediterranean has also had a lifetime of perceiving periscopes and, in so doing, making rude gestures at them. Which is what Captain Rashid did, his hand clenched, knuckles away from his face and two fingers making a V sign as he lifted his fist upward several times, making one of the world's most universally recognized obscene gestures.

At the operating end of the periscope, Marcus Leach laughed. "Up yours too, captain!"

Watching the stern of the battered ship move westward, Leach finally caught the word painted on her fantail. So it was that the name *Mecca* was recorded in the log of the *Splendid* for the first time. She would again be recorded on the eleventh of April as she steamed out of the gulf.

What was not recorded in that log was what was not known: that the fate of the *Splendid* was linked to the nondescript *Mecca* and three of the men aboard her.

The *Mecca* put into Aden on the morning of April 10. The turnaround took a full day. The agent had obtained a cargo of baled cotton. Between the discharging of the ingots, the loading of the cotton, the bunkering to top up fuel tanks, the taking on of water and provisions, the time requirement was such that it was impossible to get under way until the morning of April 11. The departure was further delayed because Said refused to let the captain take the ship into dock. As at Bahrain, Said had to keep the crew on board and away from any opportunity to pass information about the mined tankers. So the *Mecca* was secured in the inner harbor to a buoy and dolphin berth connected to shore by submarine pipeline for bunkering purposes. A procession of vessels—a water barge and several small craft loaded with provisions—made their way to and from the *Mecca* and the shore. Included in the supplies which the captain had requisitioned through the agent was a set of marine charts that would take him south into waters he had never sailed before. They would take him safely down the steaming coast of Africa, parallel to but away from the busy shipping lanes used by the endless procession of crude oil and petroleum supertankers plying between the Arabian Gulf and ports in Western Europe and North America.

For Nabil, the prohibition against going ashore at Aden was enough, to put him over the brink. He had witnessed the launch of the PLO mining operation against the supertankers. As part of *Mecca*'s crew, was he implicated? Nabil had also been shaken by the death of Maan.

The crew had been confined to ship at Bahrain. There had been the jolting, close-in appearance of a threatening periscope. Now there was the Aden situation and on top of that the news that the PLO would force the *Mecca* to sail down to Durban. Nabil was ready to quit. He'd had enough. He told Rashid so.

"I understand, I understand." The captain was sympathetic. "But I can tell you, Nabil, Said won't let you off this ship. He can't afford to. You know too much. I haven't told you this—they're giving us a bonus to do the Durban trip."

Nabil's sullen expression vanished instantly.

"A bonus! How much?"

"How does three months' pay sound?"

A broad, toothy smile lit up the Egyptian's face.

Rashid never ceased to be amazed by what money could do.

20

8:23 GMT 12:23 P.M. Local Time
Gulf of Aden

At 0823 hours GMT on April 15, Captain Leach was in *Splendid*'s wardroom taking early breakfast when the broadcast loudspeaker on the bulkhead behind him made a clicking, scratching noise that alerted him.

"Captain, this is sonar." The excited voice of the usually placid communications officer reported, "Contact due west. I classify what looks like the whole goddamned Russian navy, range forty-five miles, closing. They're steaming eastbound in a column, sir. There are four abreast in the lead."

Leach banged down his knife and fork. In a few strides he was in the sonar room, his mouth agape at the bright white dots entering the dancing sonar screen on its left side, moving steadily in the direction of the white dot at its center—the position of *Splendid* herself as she moved northward in her patrol track.

In the control room he called for Pots on the double. A message was made to the flag officer reporting the situation. "Pilot, when will the vanguard be here, your best ETA?"

The reply was immediate. "Two hours five minutes, sir, give or take five."

"Right." Leach's eyes went up to the clock. "Estimate vanguard our position at 10:30 Zulu," he added to the message.

By 10:00 GMT the approaching Russian fleet was painted on the sonar. Their acoustic signatures had been identified by the computer. But seeing them on the sonar screen was no match for the sight of their majestic advance up the gulf under a clear blue sky across flat, azure waters chopped slightly by a spanking breeze. Leach's search periscope was up, its powerful magnifying lenses drawing the vision of the huge fleet almost on top of him. He could see the nuclear-powered aircraft carriers *Minsk* and *Kharkov*, each with its twelve STOL Forger fighters and a clutch of huge Hormone helicopters on its decks.

On each flank of the front line rode two Kashin class destroyers, the *Skory* on the port and the *Strogy* on the starboard. Out ahead of the line swarmed a dozen Hormone helicopters ranging back and forth at, Leach estimated, about 500 feet. As he watched, two of them made for *Splendid*'s location. They knew where she was. They had picked up her periscope and radar mast on their own radars. Furthermore, their crews would be able to see her black bulk outlined just below the surface of the clear Aden water.

Splendid had just completed her southbound turn at the northern end of her track. Leach had brought his craft to a halt to watch the oncoming procession. She sat in only 150 feet of water, her bottom just 70 feet off the floor of the Gulf of Aden. She had, therefore, no depth maneuvering room. On the other hand, Leach was satisfied she wouldn't need it. They were in international waters, albeit it only a few hundred yards outside Yemen's territorial waters, as Pilot confirmed. A state of hostilities did not exist between the United Kingdom and the Soviet Union. He was standing well north of the track the Soviet fleet was making. For those reasons he believed he had no cause to be concerned about being in such shallow water. On the other hand he remembered the admiral's signal that the Russian bear was showing his teeth.

It was time to let his crew share in the sight. After all they had come a long way and had endured the boring agonies of the Aden patrol.

"Coxswain?"

"Sir." It seemed that the coxswain was at his elbow in a split second.

Leach took his face away from the eye piece. "I want all the ratings to see this."

The coxswain's eyebrows shot up. "All of them, sir?"

"That's right, all eighty-four of them. And if you're quick about it, you too. You've got ten minutes to do it. Just a few seconds for each man. Then I'll run the officers through."

In eleven minutes and fifteen seconds flat every member of the crew of *Splendid* had had a short peek at the magnificent, stately line of the mighty Red Navy fleet steaming down the Gulf of Aden, an eight-mile-long column of ships gleaming gray-white in the morning sun. Behind the first line came the 30,000-ton cruiser, the *Khirov*, the Soviet's first nuclear-powered fighting surface ship. Its new generation surface-to-surface and surface-to-air missiles, its two large guns, its antiaircraft cannon submarine tracking rockets, and torpedos bristled on its decks and superstructure. At the sides of the *Khirov* were a new Kresta III cruiser, the helicopter cruiser *Leningrad*, and one of the first of the Sovietsky Soyuz class of cruiser, just commissioned. Following in the line were destroyers of the Kashin class, Krivak frigates, Tarantul missile corvettes, and several of the smaller Nanuchka missile ships. Bringing up the rear of the seemingly endless column were the replenishment and cargo vessels, among them the tanker *Boris Chilkin*.

After he had had his view through the periscope, the last man to look asked his captain, "Where do you think their attack submarines are?"

"Out in the Arabian Sea or somewhere in the Indian Ocean waiting for them. They wouldn't have come down through the Suez." Leach knew that three-quarters of the advancing Russian armada had made its way from the Soviet's northern bases south through the Atlantic, then east through the Mediterranean and down the Suez Canal. Some elements had come in from the Pacific, it was true, but the bulk had come from the Red Navy's northern and Mediterranean fleets.

Leach estimated that the northernmost of the four ships in the front line would pass about one mile immediately south of *Splendid*. He would use the ship's camera to take as many pictures as he could as the procession marched past. For a moment he toyed with the thought of surfacing but to do so would be to go against the order of the admiral. That one had come in just after they had taken up their station. It was almost as an afterthought on the flag officer's part. Leach's periscope was trained on the first line of ships, now about a mile west of his patrol line steaming at twenty knots.

A shot of adrenalin moved into Leach's system when he heard sonar watchkeeper Pratt's voice say, "Contact. Four small ships have moved out of the column at the far end of it, sir. They're moving in line astern traveling fast closing at thirty knots. They're heading directly for us, range three miles. Bearing 065."

"Have you got them, radar?"

"Aye, sir."

As he was swinging his periscope toward the oncoming craft he barked, "What are they?"

"Code signature is Grisha class."

"Christ!" exclaimed Leach. The Grishas were real trouble. The Russians called them *maly protivolodochny korabl*, meaning small antisubmarine ships. They carried four torpedo tubes with twenty-one torpedoes on board. Even though they were described as small they were, at 236 feet, almost as long as *Splendid* and, like her, fast.

What the hell were they up to? Peering through the periscope he caught the V of white foam from the lead Grisha's sharp, pitched-up bow cutting through the water, and behind it guns, rockets, and the twirling radar on the short tower bridge amidships. Behind her he could see hints of the three more following in line astern.

"Range one mile, sir."

The captain was still puzzled. Again, what were they up to? Were they going to attack with rockets or depth charges or torpedos? If so, *Splendid* was dead. But there was no war on. Killing *Splendid* would start one. They could ram her and then claim she had been in South Yemen territorial waters. But the Grishas were too small, too shallow in draft to ram his ship at periscope depth; and even if they could ram they would destroy themselves.

It had to be a practice run. It was a chance for those lethal antisubmarine craft to exercise their skills. That was it, Leach decided.

"Search periscope down. Up attack periscope and give me only two feet above the tower. Repeat—the tower. Radar mast down." He wanted to watch the Grishas from the underside on their run in. Putting the attack periscope up only two feet would still give them plenty of clearance.

"Search periscope down. Attack periscope two feet above the tower. Radar mast down, sir."

Leach could hear the rumblings of the Grishas' powerful engines growing steadily louder. Suddenly the noise dropped off almost completely. From the sonar room came the report. "They've reduced speed, sir. Five knots. They're still in line astern about a hundred feet apart. They're pinging us . . . they're dropping something off their sterns. Can't tell what it is, sir."

Strange, thought the captain. His eyes were glued to the periscope, its lens looking starboard and back to the northwest. A Soviet ship was coming in on his stern. Yes, there was the belly of the first craft.

"Range fifty yards, sir."

Leach's eyes followed the long, narrow line of the keel of the first approaching Grisha. His periscope was tilted upwards, almost vertical. As the stern and the rudder and turning twin screws passed over, Leach saw something he had never before seen. Just under the surface, the Soviet warship was towing a boom about thirty feet wide. At six-foot intervals along the boom were what looked like heavy steel cables that curved out and down like bows behind the vessel as they were being pulled through the water. Leach moved his periscope from the near-vertical to the horizontal as he tracked the cables down deeper and deeper into the darkening water. The cables were coming closer and closer to his ship. There at even level with the periscope he saw the first sharp-pointed, massive grappling hooks attached to the cables. Quickly he moved the periscope to its maximum downward facing position. Below in the murk he could see huge cement weights, six of them, holding the cables down moving at a level well below the bottom of the submarine. He could scarcely believe his eyes.

"Down periscope and be quick about it!" he shouted. "They're going to grapple us! Telegraph engines full ahead!"

The first singing of the cables against the round smooth hull of the submarine had started just as the periscope hit the bottom of its well and the first surge of *Splendid*'s propeller hummed through the submarine.

The whistling of the cables rubbing against the metal was replaced by the clanging of heavy metal as the first set of grappling hooks made their way up the side of the ship at the stern. Suddenly the noise stopped. At the same instant the control wheel in the planesman's hand moved a full turn to the left and toward his chest. He was powerless to prevent the shifting of the wheel.

"The wheel, sir! The wheel!" From behind him the officer of the watch leaned forward to join him in attempting to straighten up the wheel and shove it forward. It was locked.

Christ, they've got the stern hydroplane and the rudder, Leach thought.

The thrust of the submarine's motor was beginning to move her forward when the sudden, full-power roar of the Grisha's twin engines burst through *Splendid*'s hull. In an instant the drive of the Russian ship, pulling the submarine's stern to port, met the forward thrust of *Splendid* under full power, forcing the two straining vessels into a straight line, the submarine pointing south, the Grisha on the surface pointing north. Her stern was almost under water, pulled down by the weight and thrust of *Splendid* and her own propelling, powerful screws. Something had to give.

On the surface, the other three Grishas, their grappling gear at the ready, stood off to the west a hundred yards away. Their crew members gaped at the scene in front of them as their lead ship struggled to overcome the unseen submarine like a fishing vessel trying to overpower a large whale.

With a ripping, tearing sound and the screech of metal forcibly being parted from other metal, the stern davits of the ship to which the cable boom was attached gave way, taking with them the entire stern plate of the vessel. Like a surfboard flat in the water the stern plate took off in a southward direction. It disappeared under the waves as *Splendid*, loose from the clutches of her would-be captor, accelerated through the shallow water, her propeller unimpeded. She trailed behind her the prickly grappling hooks, cables, boom and the twirling stern plate of the Grisha.

In her wake on the surface, the sixty members of the damaged Grisha's crew were preparing to abandon ship as the sea flooded into her aft section. The stunned captains of the other three antisubmarine craft abandoned the chase in favor of rescuing their comrades from their sinking sister ship.

In *Splendid*, the coxswain himself was behind the control wheel. The captain and the first lieutenant hovered anxiously over him. With the wheel hard over to the left and back, the first move of the freed boat was to port. The coxswain fought to bring the wheel around to the right and forward. The captain, standing to his right, helped turn the wheel while the first lieutenant from the left and behind shoved forward on it. Under the pressure it began to turn slowly. Then in an instant the wheel was turning normally. The rudder was free and so were the hydroplanes. The coxswain shoved the wheel forward just in time to prevent the huge craft from leaping out of the water. Instead, the top of her tower porpoised a hundred yards south of the milling Grishas and disappeared again under the comforting blanket of the deepening gulf toward the last of the ships in the Soviet column. The lead ships of that mighty line steamed unwaveringly toward the entrance to the Arabian Gulf where the American Fifth Fleet and the Second British Flotilla awaited them.

21

15 April   6:45 A.M.

The White House

Washington, D.C.

Soon after he moved into the White House, John Hansen decided that he would use the president's study as his main workroom. He needed a place where he could leave files and documents, publications and books, anything he was using, on top of his desk or on the tables. He would use the Oval Office in the west wing for the never ending official and formal meetings with heads of state, cabinet members, ambassadors, congressional leaders, delegations of plain ordinary folks, and for the signing of legislation. The desk in the Oval Office was always clear, whereas the desk in the study, a similarly oval-shaped room, was always cluttered.

The president's study was conveniently situated in the family quarters of the White House on its second floor. At the southwest corner of the family quarters was the suite of bedrooms. A door led from the main bedroom directly to the east into the study. Because of its accessibility, John and Judith Hansen both used it as part of their living area as well as a work place for John. It was also a room in which he could have informal working meetings with his own staff or to have department heads in for discussions or briefings. Hansen felt more at home there than in any other part of the White House.

On Monday, April 15, when the early golden rays of the morning sun filtered through the tall, arched windows in the curved bay of the study, the president was at his desk still dressed in pajamas, dressing gown and slippers. He was sipping his first cup of decaffeinated coffee while absorbing the front page of the *New York Times*. He always believed there was no better way of staying aware of what was going on in the country than religiously reading the *Times* and the *Washington Post*. The *Post* would be next.

For the week ahead, the working hours of every day were booked. Two meetings were scheduled of the executive committee of the National Security Council, one for Tuesday and another for Friday. It was essential to keep them abreast of the developing confrontation with Romanov. The meetings provided up-to-the-minute briefings on the CIA's information and assessment of the Soviet Union's political and military activity, its Eastern Bloc satellites, the countries of the Persian Gulf and the Middle East, as well as the active hot spots in Africa where the Cubans were still playing their intervention games on behalf of their Soviet masters.

At its meeting the previous Friday, the executive committee had been briefed on several matters. The first was the progress of the huge convoy of American naval and merchant ships, the biggest assembly of American vessels to be put to sea since World War II. The main event during the week of April 8 was the departure of the task force for Pakistan. Bringing the men, equipment, ships, and supplies together over the three-week period from March 15 had been a monumental undertaking on the part of the Pentagon. The military hierarchy coordinated all the supporting government departments and the key American shipping firms that could provide the passenger ships and freighters needed to augment the navy's resources. The Pentagon people had worked day and night. Selected reserve army and air force units across the country were put on active service, some of them to participate in the task force itself and others to take the places of regular units and personnel designated to go to Pakistan. During the organization period, the president had put unrelenting pressure on the Pentagon and the secretaries of the various departments. In addition, he personally leaned on the leaders of the major industries which would provide the supply of food, fuel, ships, equipment, and transportation facilities to carry goods to the task force's embarkation points up and down the east coast.

Hansen's pursuit of support for the task force had been ruthless and relentless. The president had told the Soviets and the world that the American armed forces would be landing in Pakistan on May 7, both by sea and air. It had been decreed as a national goal and objective by the leader of the United States, the most powerful nation on earth, a nation that had rallied behind its leader's statement of a national purpose when John Kennedy said it would put a man on the moon. America would perform. That spirit was made evident, not only in editorials of the nation's media, but by the expeditious ratification by Congress of the Pakistan agreement. On March 25 it received the near unanimous approval of both the Senate and House and with little bickering over the contents of the document. Hansen had received word shortly after meeting with the Soviet ambassador, Kuznetsov, when he handed the ancient Soviet diplomat his reply to Romanov's belligerent note of March 16.

In scenes reminiscent of departures in World Wars I and II, with bands playing, flags flying, and families and friends standing on the docks waving goodbye to soldiers departing on troop ships, the warships, transports, and other vessels of the task force left the harbors along the eastern seaboard amidst the hooting signals of hundreds of craft and the dipping of flags in salute. The force was on its way exactly on schedule. It left behind a nation galvanized for the demanding, costly chore of resupplying and maintaining that force across thousands of miles of ocean infested by Soviet submarines and surface surveillance warships.

The navy could not tell the president where the Soviet submarines were located in the Atlantic because the Russians had reactivated their sonar interference system, SONINT, on April 3. SONINT had stopped operating the day before—April 14. The onshore computers, hooked by cable to the NATO and U.S. sonar nets on the bottom of the North Atlantic, quickly spewed out the location and type of the seventy-eight Russian submarines operating in that ocean. The navy could not account for the other twenty-two that were in the North Atlantic the day SONINT was reactivated. They could have returned to their bases.

"Or they could have moved into the South Atlantic beyond NATO jurisdiction, where we don't have a sonar system," the president had interjected when Defense Secretary Robert Levy called to bring him up-to-date, late in the afternoon of the fourteenth.

Levy agreed. "That's right, we really don't know where the hell they are. My guess is we'll find them shadowing the task force. We should be getting reports from the flagship of the escort anytime now. It looks as though they're set to begin their OKEAN exercise, probably on the fifteenth. As you know, they've been assembling in the South Atlantic off Senegal."

"South of the Tropic of Cancer?"

"That's right, Mr. President. And in the Indian Ocean they're assembling in the Gulf of Aden. The defending fleet there is about 300 miles southwest of Bombay. In the Pacific, their attack fleet is to the east of the Mariana Islands and the defending fleet is about one hundred miles west of Wake Island."

"Where is the defending fleet in the Atlantic?"

"It's steaming southbound off the Canary Islands. When the exercise begins, if past performances are any indication, the attack fleets, with air support from their own carriers plus big long-range antisubmarine aircraft, will launch coordinated, simultaneous attacks against the defending fleets in the Atlantic, Indian Ocean, and the Pacific. The whole thing will be run from Moscow by Admiral Smirnov himself."

"What about their submarines in port? What's the satellite count on those?"

"They tell me the satellite photographs show that everything's normal. The majority, the usual number, are tied up at their bases on the Baltic and the Kola Peninsula. Don't worry, Mr. President, we're keeping an eagle eye on that situation." He added, "But I'd hate to think what 381 of those things could do if they were turned loose."

The president agreed. "It boggles the mind. The fact is they've got them, Robert. They've built them for a reason. Some to lob nuclear ballistic missiles at us from hard-to-find moving platforms. But most of them are for destroying ships—other submarines, surface ships, freighters, anything that moves on the high seas, particularly the ones that worry me most, the tankers that carry the crude oil."

The report he had requested from GAO on the consequences of a crude oil cut-off to North American and Western Europe had been delivered to him just before he left for Camp David en route to Diego Garcia. Even though it was only a preliminary rough cut at the answer, it had shaken him badly when he read it. He was even more shaken when he went through the final in-depth report that arrived on his desk on April 11, the same day the United Nations General Assembly dealt with the Pakistan agreement. The report could not have painted a blacker picture. When he had finished reading it, he could not help but agree with the conclusion: that for Western Europe and the United States a complete cut-off of crude oil for an extended period beyond thirty days would have disastrous consequences for the economy, culture, and civilization of the Western world. It would be a calamity second only to an all-out nuclear attack. The report had only reinforced his determination to go into Pakistan. From that all-important launching area he could defend the oil-producing nations of the Persian Gulf if need be. He had ordered the final GAO crude oil cut-off report to be circulated among the members of the executive committee of the National Security Council. It was essential that every one of them should have a full understanding of what it said about the potential for catastrophe if America were once again to back down from the Soviets who threatened the Persian Gulf.

As the president had expected, the Russians were putting on diplomatic and propaganda pressures, everything in their arsenal, to force Hansen to stay out of Pakistan. On Thursday, April 11, 112 members of the General Assembly of the United Nations had voted in favor of the Soviet-sponsored resolution condemning the U.S.-Pakistan agreement on the grounds that the entry of United States forces into Pakistan would constitute a grave and unacceptable threat to world peace. In addition to the censure, the resolution demanded that the United States recall its task force. President Hansen had expected the Soviets to take their case to the United Nations. Furthermore, he expected the result. In no way did it deflect him from his determined course of action.

The president took a sip of coffee and turned to the second page of the *New York Times*, his eyes quickly running over each of the columns of interest to him. He had developed an excellent speed reading technique years before when the volume of paper he had to cope with reached the saturation point. At the bottom of the page was a small article which he almost missed. The headline was "General Critical of Pakistan Plan." Hansen couldn't believe what he was reading.

General Glen Young, chairman of the Joint Chiefs of Staff, said in a speech last night that there were high risks in sending a military task force to Pakistan. Young said that it would be impossible to support the task force for more than thirty days. The logistical problems of moving material to support a 120,000-man force 13,000 miles away from the United States could be beyond the capacity of the available American merchant fleet. Young had expressed his objections when the president decided to enter into negotiations with Pakistan.

In five minutes the president had the chairman of the Joint Chiefs of Staff on the telephone. He had found him at home.

"General Young, have you seen the *New York Times* this morning?"

"No sir, I haven't," the startled general replied.

"Let me read it to you." When the president had finished, he demanded, "Is that report correct, general?"

"It's fairly accurate, but the quote wasn't from my text, Mr. President. It was in a question-and-answer period. As you know, I put forward those objections right from the very beginning . . ."

"And I overrode them, general! I want you to understand one thing. I am the commander in chief of the armed forces of the United States of America and I'm *your* commander. I heard your opinion and I decided to take a course of action that goes against it. When I give you an order that's the end of the matter. You obey the order!"

At the other end of the line Young's voice was remarkably cool. "I did obey your order, Mr. President, even though I disagreed with it."

Young was right, he had done what he was told.

"What about your colleagues? What do they think?"

"They're with me. But we're professionals, Mr. President. We do as we're told. You also have to keep one other thing in mind. We're Americans. We're just as concerned as you are about freedom and democracy and the security and safety of the American people. Apart from yourself, Mr. President, no other four people in the country have any higher responsibility than we do in that regard."

Hansen had to agree. "I can't quarrel with that. But there's one thing you haven't mentioned, general, perhaps two. One is the matter of loyalty. That's the least I can expect, as the commander in chief, from you and the chiefs of staff, every one of them. The second is that I expect you to keep your mouth shut publicly about my decisions with which you don't agree. You know the rule better than I do, general. The elected politicians run this country, make the decisions. You in the military do what you're told. If you want to criticize me in public, particularly about a matter as important as Pakistan . . . Let me put it another way. I'll be as direct as I can. The next time you go public against me, I will expect your resignation." Hansen's voice was cold with fury.

That fury was increased by the arrogance and the tone of his chairman of the Joint Chiefs of Staff. "Next time it will be there in advance, Mr. President."

22

19 April

Diego Garcia

It had taken *Splendid* four days to reach the island of Diego Garcia after her encounter with the vicious Grisha. She arrived at the largest of the islands in the Chagos Archipelago in the late afternoon of April 18 after a submerged voyage from the Gulf of Aden.

Immediately she was clear of the Grisha, Leach had made for the lee of Socotra, at the southern edge of the approaches to the gulf. The battered submarine, trailing cables, grappling hooks, and the stern plate of the sunken Russian ship, had reached the island within a few hours. There, in calm water, the senior technical officer, the STD, and his engineering artificers had tackled the cables with blowtorches that functioned just as well in the water as out of it. It had taken them less than three hours to cut and hack their way through the tough, entwining steel cables draped over the hydroplanes and across the fin and rudder sectors.

Fortunately for *Splendid* the four hard, brass, sharp-edged blades of her propeller were turning at full revolutions when the cables from behind the Grisha swung from their line on the port side of the submarine to directly astern at the moment when the power of each ship was pitted one against the other. At that instant those blades had sliced cleanly through all of the taut cables with the exception of two that had cut through the forward edge of the ship's fin just below the top of it. Those two had trailed behind, clear of the propeller, dragging with them the boom and the stern plate of the ill-fated Russian antisubmarine craft. The stern plate, an unusual prize of hardware, was hauled aboard *Splendid* to be kept as a souvenir of the boat's first victory. It had to be cut up into sections so it could be brought inside the ship. It mattered not. It would be patched together later to hang in some place of honor back at Faslane.

Leach stood on the deck of his boat to watch the cable clearing operation and also to take a good look at the damage that had been done.

The long diagonal gash through the skin of the forward edge of the fin near its top could be easily patched, as could the cuts in the forward edge of the starboard hydroplane. What really troubled him were the deep gouges in the leading edges of each of the propeller blades. But he knew they were there the instant he felt the blades of his propeller carving through the cables when *Splendid* extricated herself from the clutches of the Russian ship. Coincidental with the cable severance, an unusual growling noise from the stern section reverberated through the boat. Experience told Leach that the cables had damaged the propeller. There would be gouges and nicks which had thrown the propeller off its delicate balance causing a constant vibration in the shaft at high revolutions. The vibration was uncomfortable at thirty knots. In fact, at that speed the captain thought it was dangerous. But at twenty knots it had diminished to the point where it was almost unnoticeable.

When the engineering crew had finished with cable clearing work, Leach signalled his report to the flagship of the second flotilla. In it he expressed his concern about the propeller and the inability of *Splendid* to operate at speeds above twenty knots without causing severe damage to the bearings of her driveshaft and the gear mechanism locking it to the motor.

The response signal from the admiral congratulated him on his success, noting that "your victory over the Grisha and your escape from the clutches of the Russian fleet are in keeping with the worthy fighting traditions of Nelson and the Royal Navy. My congratulations to you and all the crew of *Splendid*. Proceed to Diego Garcia. Replacement propeller will await your arrival. Installation facilities (U.S.) available to complete screw change. Advise when change made. First Sea Lord signals: 'Pray tell *Splendid* crew proud of splendid action.' "

When *Splendid* sailed on the surface slowly southeast through the main pass to the entrance to the Diego Garcia lagoon through the hot steamy rain of the midafternoon of April 19, the American base commander and his men were ready and waiting for her. Their dry dock was flooded, its gates open. As soon as her main ballast and trim tanks were clear of the last trace of water and she was, therefore, some two hundred tons lighter than her normal diving trim, Leach moved her gradually into the dry dock. She was assisted on her tail by the gentle nudging of a small power boat that, with its heavily padded bow, pushed or pulled at the stern of the *Splendid* as she made her way into the vast rectangular box until she lay directly above the huge steel cradle upon which she would sit when the water was pumped out of the dock.

Before the sea water was drained away from the tube-like hull of the *Splendid*, a hose, carrying an inbound water supply to provide the coolant for the nuclear reactor, was put aboard. Its long line snaked out from the top of the dry dock coupled with a return pipe that would be filled with the discharging coolant water, heated as it passed through the nuclear power plant. In addition, a maze of cables, wires, hoses, and pipes were fed into the body of *Splendid*, giving her life-sustaining power like intravenous tubes implanted into the human body to sustain it against the onslaught of a major operation.

Satisfied that the submarine was properly positioned, the dock master closed the gates behind her and began his pumping procedure. By midnight the dry dock was emptied of water. Under the glare of a hundred floodlights, the *Splendid* sat high on the cradle, dry and naked as the day she was launched. Her crew began to climb down the half-dozen ladders the Americans had put in place from the floor of the dry dock as soon as the water level was low enough for them to enter. His crew following behind him, Leach was the first one down, followed by Able Seaman Smith, once again flashlight in hand, and by the rest of the crew. All were anxious to take a look at the damage those bloody Russkis had done to their ship. At the captain's order, the aft ladder was moved from its position near the tower to the stern. Its padded head rested on each side of the point of the conical cap covering the center of the propeller, where it was fitted onto the drive shaft like a spinner at the center of the propeller of an aircraft. Taking the light from the boy seaman, the captain, in his white shorts, an open, white short-sleeved shirt, white rubber-soled shoes, hatless and, like the rest of his crew, soaked to the skin in the constant, warm rain, carefully made his way up the rungs of the ladder. It was steadied at its base by the ever-present coxswain and Smith.

At the top of the ladder Marcus Leach was not prepared for what he saw. Along the sharp leading edges of each of the huge brass blades were four deep gouges at varied intervals. To him a deep gouge was anything over a quarter inch. Those were that depth if not slightly more. That was bad enough. What really gave him a jolt was that on the blade to his right and slightly above him, the four gouge marks were grouped close together, perhaps half an inch apart. From that area about five feet out from the propeller hub, a hairline crack, thin but clearly visible under the beam of his flashlight, ran diagonally upward across the shiny face of the blade toward its center. Leach was not an engineer but he guessed, and was later told he was right, that if the cable impact had been any greater, or if he had attempted to drive his ship toward Diego Garcia using his propeller at high revolutions, the enormous strain on the propeller would have caused the loss of the outer half of that massive brass blade. The result would have been catastrophic. The vibrations caused by the unbalanced propeller spinning at high speed would probably have torn the drive shaft out of its bearings, shattered the electric motors, and opened the stern of the craft to an instant flood of high-pressure ocean water. As it was, *Splendid* had survived, but only by the depth of a crack.

As promised by the admiral, *Splendid*'s new propeller was waiting for her when she arrived at Diego Garcia. The bright, polished metal masterpiece had been flown in by Royal Air Force Hercules transport that morning.

At the bottom of the ladder Leach handed the flashlight to David Scott, his senior technical officer (STO), usually referred to on British submarines as Chief. He was waiting with his clutch of officers and engineering artificers, the men who were responsible for changing the propeller and making *Splendid* seaworthy again.

"It's worse than I thought, Chief. Take a look at the top right-hand blade. It's got a nine-inch crack running back from the leading edge."

Chief was surprised. "I had a good look at the blades when we got the cables off. I didn't see anything then."

"You may have missed it. After all, when you were taking a look you were several feet under water. Or the crack might have developed during the run across. Either way it's there and we're just bloody lucky the whole goddamn thing didn't come apart."

Work began on the propeller change at first light the next morning. While the rest of the crew worked away at maintenance chores in their own shops, a gang was put to work at cleaning off the sea-green growth that had already accumulated on *Splendid*'s hull. That night Leach and his officers threw a barbecue cookout on the beach, complete with a roaring bonfire from pieces of packing crates, the only source of wood on the island. All hands got into the grog the captain supplied, but only three or four had to be assisted up the ladders back to their bunks.

On April 21, *Splendid*'s Chief pronounced her fit and ready to go. All the umbilical cords were removed with the exception of the water pipes for the nuclear reactor. They would come off as soon as she was afloat. The dry dock's seawater valves were opened to begin the flooding that would lift the boat up and out from her cradle as the level of the water in the dock rose to that of the surrounding lagoon. It was an exciting moment for all hands and especially those who were off watch and were permitted to be on deck as she was coming up, rather like the launching of a new ship. Within the hour, appropriate farewells having been said to the dry dock and base crews on that lonely island, *Splendid* was making her way out of the Diego Garcia lagoon.

At Leach's request, Chief stayed in the control room during the initial dive after leaving Diego Garcia. The captain took her down to two hundred feet, having called for revolutions to make fifteen knots. When they were settled at two hundred feet he ordered, "Telegraph full speed ahead."

"Full speed ahead, sir."

He turned to his STO, saying, "Well, Chief, this is the moment of truth."

Slowly the whispering purr of the electric motors and spinning propeller blades increased as the power moved toward full output. Suddenly they could feel it: a high frequency vibration from the stern that mounted in volume as the propeller reached its maximum revolutions per minute.

"Stop engines!" the captain ordered.

Immediately the motor was cut back, the vibrations stopped.

"Well, chief?"

Lieutenant-Commander David Scott shook his head. "It's no go, sir. There must have been some damage to the main bearings. I'm not sure what it is but obviously it's something I can't fix. It looks to me as though you can make about twenty knots but when you get your rpm's beyond that . . ." He shrugged.

"Bloody hell!" the frustrated Leach spat out. "If I can't

have full power my boat isn't operational." He leaned against the periscope drawing his hand across his forehead as he came to the only decision he could make. With a voice of resignation he said, "There's no choice. I'll have to take her home."

Chief ventured, "The admiral won't be very happy, sir."

"Up the admiral!"

23

23 April   9:00 A.M.
South Atlantic Ocean
off Cape Verde

Captain Second Rank Boris Chernavin was in a foul mood. There were three reasons. The first was that his ship and crew had not performed well during the OKEAN exercise. The second was that he was not getting along at all well with his zampolit, the ship's political officer who, unfortunately, was of equal naval rank. And the third was that he and the zampolit had been through a bottle of vodka together which had resulted in a shouting match that had ended at two o'clock in the morning when the zampolit stormed out of the captain's cabin drunk and furious. The captain had a skull-pulsing hangover.

The zampolit was a new man by the name of Vargan. Short, heavyset, about fifteen years older than Chernavin, bald, round-faced, he exuded a perpetual underarm odor which always preceded him. He had joined the 501 just a week before the Murmansk departure. In the ensuing seven days he had succeeded in causing a turmoil among the crew and much frustrating annoyance for its captain.

There was a zampolit on every Soviet warship. He directed the ideological indoctrination and monitored the political reliability of the officers and men. He directed socialist competition. He insured that party decisions were carried out. He enforced discipline—at least he was supposed to. And he acted as both "chaplain" and social worker for the crew to promote morale. The Communist party set up groups within the naval command structure, of which the captain of a ship and his line officers formed one part and the political officer and the party organizations the other. As Chernavin saw it, the system was designed to create havoc. Vargan, a man with limited naval experience, had become critical of the way he, Chernavin, was handling the crew during the OKEAN maneuvers. As a member of the party, the captain was as susceptible to its criticism and discipline as any other member. The opinionated Vargan, totally incapable of taking criticism himself, had become quite liberal with his attacks on Chernavin during their drinking bout. When the captain had protested, saying that Vargan had no naval background against which to make any valid criticisms, the zampolit had pounded the table announcing that he had had ten years at sea; that he shared with the captain the responsibility for the successful operation of the boat and its performance; that how the 501 and its crew performed was all-important to him and his career in the socialist competition by which his future would be judged.

Chernavin knew the little man was right but in his drunken state he had become angry and lost control. Matching Vargan in volume and waving his hands for effect, he told the zampolit in no uncertain terms that he, Chernavin, was the captain of the ship, he was the naval officer and he did not need some know-it-all amateur to tell him how to run his boat. From that springboard the voluble, highly heated, profane argument had proceeded until the drunken little man left the captain's cabin in a fit of fury. Chernavin would have to do something to smooth the waters, but not until he was on the other side of his hangover.

The main rankling factor was that Vargan was right about the ship's performance.

The 501 was designated as part of the attacking force in the Atlantic segment of the OKEAN exercise. Chernavin's orders were that he was to rendezvous with the attacking fleet one hundred miles west of Cape Verde off Senegal. He did not yet know where the defending fleet was. From that time he and his ship would be under the direct command of the flag officer of the attacking fleet, although subject also to direct orders from naval headquarters at Moscow. There would be similar fleets attacking and defending in the Indian and Pacific Oceans.

During the briefing that was given on OKEAN before the departure from Murmansk, he noted that there would be assigned to the exercise over two hundred surface and submarine warships, from aircraft carriers and battle cruisers to ships as small as the Grisha class corvettes, plus provisioning and at-sea maintenance and engineering vessels. Out of the 381 serviceable submarines that would be at sea during the period, only about a hundred would be used in the exercise. Their numbers would probably be known to the Americans and British, who would be shadowing them. But the rest of the submarines at sea would lie hidden, quiet in the exact locations in the Atlantic, South Atlantic, and Indian Oceans to which they had been assigned.

The 501 had been tasked to hold the attacking fleet's antisubmarine defense zone, *zona protivolodochnoy oborony*, in that instance the water expanse around the attacking fleet in which antisubmarine defense forces engage in the search for, and destruction of, enemy submarines and fulfill their mission of protecting the fleet from underwater attack. The 501 had been assigned a distant sector ahead of the attacking fleet as it advanced northward to discover and destroy the defending fleet. Somehow a defending fleet attack submarine slipped undetected through the 501's assigned area and had gone on to launch its practice torpedos against the attacking fleet's flagship. Chernavin had taken to task the sonar michman-warrant or chief petty officer who complained that he had only new, inexperienced watchkeepers on the sonar and that until they had gained more experience it was likely the same thing would happen again. No question they should have seen the incoming submarine but he was off watch when it happened. He would do his utmost to improve the capability of the sonar crew.

It was with difficulty that Chernavin explained to the exercise umpires the reason for the failure of 501. A message had been received from the flag officer himself on the afternoon of April 22 expressing his extreme displeasure at having been "sunk" and warning that he would expect face-to-face explanation from Captain Second Rank Boris Chernavin at the earliest opportunity.

For all these reasons the captain of the 501 was in a foul mood, exacerbated by the faulty focus of his eyes. To make matters worse, his orders were to open his top secret instructions this morning. At the same time, 0900 hours, all other Soviet submarine captains would be doing the same thing. The instructions were from Fleet Admiral Smirnov, the commander in chief.

Chernavin twirled the dial on his cabin safe. Twice he missed the combination setting. Finally he succeeded. His shaking hands opened the large red envelope so supremely official-looking with the commander in chief's red crest embossed on its upper left-hand corner. He extracted a two-page, neatly typed document, the admiral's orders for Operation Sink. He laid the order in front of him, put both elbows on the desk top and leaned his forehead on both hands. He began to read.

As his eyes moved slowly down the first page, he straightened his back, raising his head from his hands. The first three paragraphs were background on the escalating confrontation between the Soviet Union and the Americans, brought to a head by the planned arrival in Pakistan of the first American troops on May 7. The preamble also covered the Soviet Union's urgent need to secure a new supply of crude oil. Domestic production in the Siberian fields was falling off with no new discoveries of magnitude coming on stream, while the demands in both the USSR and her Eastern Bloc satellite countries were escalating.

The signal told Chernavin that his ship, the 501, was part of a comprehensive scheme known as the Andropov Plan through which Chairman Romanov intended to deal with both problems at the same time.

The tasks of 501, including details of how they were to be executed, were set out in precise form—the place, the date, the exact time, the direction of the approach, precautions against being observed, the aiming point for the surface-to-surface rocket and the spacing of the torpedos.

The date specified for the execution of Chernavin's task was still eight days off, on glorious May Day at precisely 1200 hours GMT.

When he had finished reading the complete message his befuddled mind reached the conclusion that Chairman Romanov was either a genius or he was mad. It did not occur to the submarine captain that Comrade Romanov, the general secretary of the Communist party and chairman of the Supreme Soviet Presidium and marshal of the Soviet Union, might be both.

24

26 April   Noon

Durban, South Africa

At noon on April 26, the *Mecca* arrived off Durban, her fuel almost exhausted. The crew had been confined to the dreadful old ship for so long without putting a foot ashore that their tempers were almost at the breaking point, their resentment of the Palestinians at a dangerous peak. Even Captain Rashid, a man of infinite patience, would be delighted when he got rid of Said and his two remaining men. He yearned for the day when the *Mecca* was back in the familiar waters of his beloved Mediterranean. Why the PLO had come this long distance he had no idea. If they had wanted to come from Bahrain to Durban, why hadn't they flown? But he thought he knew why. It was that damned transmitter they had used to blow up the Israeli gunboat in Haifa harbor. You couldn't carry it on a commercial airliner. It would be next to impossible for it to remain undetected. So what better way to get it where you want it when you want it than to take it on the *Mecca*. Was that really why they'd come all the way to Durban? Rashid was only guessing. He had no way of knowing. He would soon find out whether he was right or wrong.

By 2:45 in the afternoon (12:45 GMT), the *Mecca* was five miles to the north-northeast of Durban's harbor, the Bay of Natal, making for the entrance to the port. On the starboard wing of his bridge, the captain could see white sandy beaches, and behind them the office buildings and churches of the city center. Rising beyond were the high hills of Durban, laced with roads and expressways. He caught the glint of houses among the green of the trees. It was a big city, much bigger than he had thought. He would enjoy spending a week ashore here, for that was what he had promised himself. A full week in the best hotel. Clean clothes, good food. With luck, an amiable bedmate. Why just one? Perhaps two or three. That is, if Said would let him ashore. Surely, he would be rid of the PLOs here at Durban.

Aft in the fantail of the stern, Hassan was going through the same testing procedures on his UHF transmitter as he had off Haifa, the night they blew the Israelis to shreds. Even though the old ship was pitching in a quartering sea as she plowed toward Durban, Hassan had elected to set up his transmitter on the same wooden table he had used weeks before in calmer water. Ahmed had once again appropriated it from the galley and with great ease carried it from the port to the starboard side of the cabin deck. Hassan wanted the radio to be out in the open when he pushed the orange detonate button so that his radio transmission would reach its maximum range of a thousand miles, stretching roughly northward into the Mozambique Channel between the island of Madagascar on the east and the African mainland on the west. It would also carry southwest another thousand miles almost to the Cape of Good Hope. In that two thousand-mile expanse of Indian Ocean, scores of supertankers either filled with cargo or in ballast butted through the seas. Among them were ten which, unknown to their masters, had a common cargo other than crude oil or liquid petroleum—Russian-made, armed limpet mines waiting to be detonated by a radio signal. The first of the ten was just passing Cape Town and entering the south Atlantic. It was the *Amoco Singapore* whose propeller had claimed Maan. The last of the ten, the *Esso Malaysia*, was still in the Mozambique Channel. Each of the ships had clear horizons around them. No other tankers were in sight.

Had Captain Rashid, or for that matter, his first officer, Nabil, looked aft between 2:45 and 3 P.M. local time, they would have seen the three PLO soldiers clustered around the black box of the high-powered radio transmitter. At eleven minutes to three (12:49 GMT) Hassan had finished his testing. He was satisfied. Without looking at either Said or Ahmed he said, "We go."

Using Ahmed's accurate LCD watch which had been set against precise hour signals from the Durban radio station, Hassan began a countdown at thirty seconds before 13:00 GMT. At the instant the tiny figures 13:00 came up, Hassan's forefinger depressed the orange button on his black box. For the three PLOs on the *Mecca*, it was an anticlimactic event. If they could have seen an upward rolling ball of flame, as at Haifa, then they would know they had succeeded. But to push a button three miles off Durban with no certain knowledge of what was over the horizon? For the operation that had begun almost two months earlier on March 9—and cost so much—to end simply with the push of a button was strangely disappointing.

Hassan took off his earphones, turned to his left to look at Said, then to his right at Ahmed. He shrugged, turning the palms of his hands upwards. It was done. Was it a success or failure?

Simultaneously with his gesture there came from the southeast a rolling sound like distant thunder. It seemed to go on and on. Almost at the same time and blended with it, came another heavy drum roll sound from due east, followed by even louder rumblings from the northeast.

To those in Durban who heard the far-off noises, they were no more than the peals of remote thunder far out across the endless stretches of the Indian Ocean, not a matter for even the slightest concern.

For the PLO team, however, they were the drum rolls that signalled glorious victory, unparalleled in the history of the Palestinian nation. Among the trio on the fantail of the *Mecca* at that moment, there was elation as they embraced each other. There were tears in their eyes—tears of exaltation and joy and of grief and anguish for Maan, whose life had paid for that supreme moment of satisfying, sweet triumph.

Within the hour, the old *Mecca* was in the calm waters of Natal Bay. The captain skilfully edged her hull up to the Maydon Wharf at the west end of the port, within sight of the Congella Monument and within earshot of the heavy traffic on the southern freeway a hundred yards to the west. A steady, light drizzle had begun as they entered Durban's harbor under a low, overcast, gray sky. Said and his companions stood out of the rain on the passageway under the starboard wing of the bridge. They would be gone as soon as the gangplank was in place, on their way back to Beirut by commercial airliners as quickly as they could make reservations. Said expected they would have little difficulty in getting seats on a Lufthansa or British Airways aircraft to Frankfurt or London, then they would double back to Beirut. He would know soon enough what arrangements he could make.

Captain Rashid would take back to Beirut the team's radio transmitter, its deadly work completed at least for that mission, and the rubber boats, motors, the automatic weapons, and the scuba gear. Each man would keep his pistol in a holster inside his shirt. At the airport, the guns would be put in their dunnage bags to be checked as luggage.

Said remembered Arafat's warning about the Israeli hit squad. He cautioned Ahmed and Hassan to keep their guard up, but he really didn't believe the Israelis would try to get at them in Durban. South Africa would be offended by any attack on their soil. Furthermore, Durban was thousands of miles from Israel. The place where he, Ahmed, and Hassan would be most vulnerable was close to Israel, in Beirut itself.

They had said their farewells to the crew. It had been an especially difficult moment for Said and the old captain.

The two men had become quite close during the month-and-a-half they had been together. Rashid promised he would see Said back in Beirut, probably in a month.

The three Palestinian Arabs stood under the bridge in their freshly laundered khaki shirts and trousers. They did not wear headdresses: it would not be appropriate to wear the *khafia* in Durban. They watched the taxi they had called for on the ship's radio driving along the wharf from the north. Its lights blazed in the rain as it passed between the rows of warehouses and the freight sitting on the dock that was being loaded on or taken off the other ships alongside the Maydon Wharf. The taxi rolled cautiously by crews of stevedores, trucks, and fork lift vehicles and under the swinging cranes of that busy dock. On the wharf, also waiting for the gangplank, stood a South African customs and immigration officer looking miserable in the teeming rain. He wore plastic rain gear over his uniform and cap. The taxi stopped behind him near the open doors of the dark and empty warehouse just a few feet beyond the wharf's edge.

Finally the crew had the fore and aft lines secured to the dock. The captain left the bridge to stand beside the Palestinians as the gangplank went down. He greeted the South African officer as he came on board. Rashid invited him to his cabin to begin the inspection of the ship's papers, but asked if he would mind first clearing three members of his crew who were leaving the ship and going back to Lebanon. The affable South African inspected their passports and innoculation certificates. They were in order. He stamped the passports. They had no goods to declare, but the officer asked Ahmed to open his bag for inspection. Satisfied when that was done, he gave them permission to go ashore.

After a final handshake with Rashid, the trio began to move down the gangplank, their bags swung over their left shoulders, making for the waiting taxi. Its lights were still blazing. Its windshield wipers methodically moved back and forth, sweeping off the gray drizzle.

The gangplank was tilted down at a shallow angle

from the deck to the rain-soaked dock. The eyes of the three
men were on the wet, slippery gangplank as they sought to
keep their footing, steadying themselves with their right
hands on its rope railing. None of them saw the movement
of two shadowy figures in the dark recesses of the
warehouse directly ahead. Nor did they see the glint of
black gun metal.

Rashid had opened the door to his cabin and was stepping aside to allow the customs officer to go in ahead of him
when he heard the first thunk. Instantly, he knew what it
was. The muted sound of a rifle being fired through a
silencer. As he wheeled to look for the source of the sound,
there was a staccato of thunk noises. Flashes from the firing
guns winked brightly against the darkness inside the
warehouse. The first high power bullet smashed through
Said's heart and out into Ahmed's stomach. The second
entered his right eye, cutting a neat hole in the lens of the
mirror sunglasses, tearing out the back of his skull. That
bullet ripped through Ahmed's chest.

Rashid looked on in stunned horror. The aim of the
rapidly fired bullets shifted slightly to Ahmed and, behind
him, Hassan. On impact, the force of the shells propelled
the victims up and backward, their arms and legs flailing in
the throes of death. Ahmed lurched outward over the rope
railing, then fell to the dock on his back.

Hassan was driven straight back up the gangplank, his
body falling heavily against the deck and the wall of the
master's cabin. His blood-stained dunnage bag fell beside
him.

Said's shattered form lay askew on the gangplank,
twitching convulsively. Then it was still. The blood from
his wounds coursed down the gangplank, mixing silently
with the soft rain water.

25

26 April   13:00 GMT
Cape of Good Hope

At 13:00 GMT on April 26, *Splendid*, bound for Faslane and home, was keeping twenty knots and 150 feet. She was 311 miles south of Cape St. Marie at the southerly tip of the island of Madagascar, steering 245 degrees, making for the Cape of Good Hope. Had *Splendid* been on the surface at that moment and her captain on the tower bridge, he might have heard rumbling explosions rolling over the horizon from ahead of his boat and along its starboard side. And moments later at those same points of the horizon he would probably have seen three or four dense black clouds of smoke creeping up into a cloud-pocked sky.

It was not, however, until 17:00 Zulu that evening that Commander Marcus Leach and his crew discovered that they were in the area of what was already being described as the worst marine disaster in history. As was his practice, Leach had the six o'clock (U.K. time) BBC world news piped through the ship's broadcast system so the entire crew could hear it.

In his cabin, working again at his paper war, the captain stopped writing in order to concentrate fully on what he was hearing as soon as the mellifluous British voice of the BBC announcer, scarred by the static of the long distance over which it was carried, began to read the first major news item:

In what is being described as the most vicious, destructive act of terrorism in history, ten of the world's largest supertankers were sunk today off the east coast of Africa, and in the Atlantic another fifteen supertankers have disappeared without trace. In Beirut early this afternoon the Palestinian Liberation Organization announced that it had carried out the sinkings, claiming that it was a blow struck for the liberation of the Palestinian people and for the return to them of their lands.

All of the ships in the Indian Ocean were in the heavily traveled Cape of Good Hope sea lane moving south out of the Persian Gulf, fully loaded with crude oil or petroleum products for destinations in Europe and North America. All were from two to five hundred miles off the African east coast and along a line between the island of Madagascar on the north and the Cape of Good Hope on the south. The explosions that destroyed the vessels caused each of them to burn sending huge pillars of smoke into the air which could be seen for miles. Ships that raced to the locations of the sinkings reported that all of the tankers sank within half an hour after the explosions had ripped through them.

In the South Atlantic, fifteen supertankers have disappeared without trace, apparently also victims of the PLO terrorists. Lloyd's of London has reported that all fifteen tankers had delivered their loads of crude oil or petroleum products to Europe and North America and were sailing back to the Persian Gulf in ballast. All the ships were in the sea lanes from the northernmost off Senegal to the southernmost off Cape Town. Lloyd's has also reported that satellite photographs taken of that part of the South Atlantic this afternoon show no traces of any one of the fifteen supertankers.

Lieutenant-Commander Paul Tait, the first lieutenant, stuck his head in the captain's doorway to make sure Leach was awake and listening to the grim BBC report. Silently Leach motioned to him to sit on the bunk.

Authorities estimate that apart from the hundreds of millions of pounds lost in ships and cargoes—a preliminary estimate puts that loss in the range of one to one-and-a-half billion pounds—there were approximately one thousand men and women on board those ships as crews.

To this moment no survivors have been reported. Lloyd's has said that there are no British crews on any of the ships, all of which carried the flags of Liberia or Panama where they are registered, although all the ships are believed to be owned by United States interests. The prime minister has denounced the action of the PLO . . .

Leach knew what the prime minister would be saying. He turned to Tait as the BBC announcer moved on to other world news.

"Well, Paul, what do you think of that?"

"Incredible. Absolutely incredible. Twenty-five tankers. What in hell is the PLO trying to prove?"

"More to the point, how did they do it? Had to be mines, radio-activated mines. Probably got them from the Russians. The Atlantic ships were in ballast. Put a hole in one of those and she'll go down in less than a minute. The oil in the loaded tankers will usually keep the hull afloat for maybe a half hour or so, depending on the type of explosion."

Tait agreed. "I saw a loaded one go down about a year ago. Some sort of big blast had hit her. Lloyd's thought it was an owner's plot to collect insurance. Anyway, she was down in forty-five minutes. Burned like hell until she went under."

Both officers talked with one ear cocked to the BBC

newscast just in case there was one other item that they might be interested in. There was.

Just as he was summing up the main points of the news, the announcer stopped momentarily and began again:

I have just been handed a bulletin. The PLO leader Yassir Arafat has denied responsibility for the fifteen tankers that have disappeared in the Atlantic, saying the PLO army was responsible for sinking only those that went down today in the Indian Ocean. This is the end of the BBC world news.

"I wonder if anybody will believe him," Leach speculated. "As I said, my guess is the tankers that went down in the Indian Ocean were mined. Limpets. Radio-activated. He could have had one team look after the ships he knew were going to be in the Indian Ocean and another to set up the mining of the tankers they knew were going to be in the South Atlantic on their way back. It takes about eighty days, almost three months, to take one of those big brutes, sail it out of the Persian Gulf, around the Cape up to Europe, unload it and get it back to the Persian Gulf. They're all on tight schedules. All you have to do is have a bright brain in London checking the daily Lloyd's Shipping Register." That unusual publication records the daily position of all ships at sea. "With a ruler, a map of the world, and a sharp pencil, it wouldn't take a genius to figure out what cluster of tankers were going to be in a particular part of the South Atlantic in ballast on a given day headed for the same Arab port in the Persian Gulf. Then you dispatch your team to that country with their mines. As long as there are ships there will be ways of smuggling men, mines, or anything else. They wait for their preselected tankers to arrive and while they're still empty waiting to be loaded, presto, the mines are planted."

The first lieutenant was still not satisfied. "But if he did it that way, why would Arafat deny it? He's accepted the blame for the ten in the Indian Ocean. Why would he say he didn't do the Atlantic job?"

Leach shook his head. "I don't know. First of all, I don't understand the Arab mind. Secondly, the pressure of negative world reaction he's undoubtedly been getting from all quarters might have made him panic. After all, who can find out the true story when the Atlantic tankers have disappeared without trace. When they're in ballast filled with water, a good explosion can send one to the bottom in forty seconds. And it's likely they're all at the bottom of the Atlantic trench where no one can get at them to see what did them in."

"But if there's one on the continental shelf in two or three hundred feet of water . . ."

The captain agreed. "He would have to take his chances on that."

Tait didn't pursue that statement. He had one of his own to make. "My guess is that the Soviets are involved on the Atlantic side."

The captain snorted his derision. "The Soviets! No bloody way. They would be risking World War III doing that." He was emphatic, shaking his head vigorously. "No bloody way. It's those goddamned Arabs, those Palestinians. It has to be!"

26

26 April   7:55 A.M.
The White House
Washington, D.C.

President Hansen had just settled in behind his desk in the study. It was five minutes to eight on the morning of Friday, April 26. Jim Crane would be along at eight with the day's agenda and some of the files for the meetings ahead. Hansen opened his file entitled *Department of Energy Proposals for Revising Gasoline Rationing Plan*. His first formal session in the Oval Office that morning, scheduled for nine o'clock, would be with Energy Secretary George Enos and his senior staff. The president had read their submission, but decided to reread the recommendations contained in the beginning of the document. He had just opened it up to the first page and started to read when Crane, who was never early, burst in waving a piece of paper.

"You should see this, sir!" he exclaimed anxiously.

As Hansen read what was printed on it, he could understand Crane's anxiety. It was a newsroom telex from Reuters reporting the tanker sinkings off Durban.

The president couldn't believe it. "Ten loaded supertankers, all at the same time! What in hell is going on?" His rhetorical question was partly answered when a later wire report announced Arafat's claim for a PLO victory in sinking the supertankers. Within the hour word came of the disappearance of the additional fifteen vessels in the South Atlantic. Close on the heels of that news came Arafat's repudiation of responsibility for the South Atlantic sinkings. That was followed by reports of the names, ownerships, and flags of the twenty-five tankers. Every one of them was American owned. All carried the flag of Liberia with the exception of one which flew the flag of Panama. Those that were sunk in the Indian Ocean were loaded. Those in the South Atlantic were in ballast southbound for the Cape of Good Hope and round it into the Indian Ocean and the Persian Gulf. No communication or signal of any kind had been heard from any one of the twenty-five ships. The fact that all of the tankers appeared to have been hit at the same time, 1300 hours GMT, merely served to confirm Arafat's claim that it was a major PLO victory in its war for recognition, for its own land, and for the freedom of its people.

It was Arafat's denial of the PLO's involvement in the South Atlantic sinkings that sent the alarm bells through President Hansen's mind, the Pentagon, and the CIA headquarters. The "what if?" question immediately surfaced. What if Arafat was telling the truth and the PLO was not involved in the South Atlantic sinkings? What about the Japanese Red Brigade, whose wild terrorists had worked with the PLO before, dealing out murder and mayhem in airports and in hijackings throughout Europe? That was a possibility that had to be seriously considered. Perhaps it was the dreadful gang of German revolutionaries. Had they joined forces in partnership with the PLO?

As Hansen saw it, the only other possibility—if Arafat was to be believed—was totally unbelievable. It was that the Soviet navy's submarines had done it.

By late afternoon on April 26, so much more disturbing information had come in and so many puzzling questions remained unanswered that the President decided that he must have an emergency meeting of the executive committee of the National Security Council. If the worst possibility was true, that the Soviets were responsible for the deliberate sinking of fifteen American-owned super-tankers with all hands . . ! But there was no link to the Soviets, except that the PLO had used Russian-made mines. The Haifa patrol boat blast had proved that. The fifteen Atlantic ships could have been mined anywhere weeks before, in the Persian Gulf or while they were in Europort, wherever. It was apparent that each target had been carefully selected: American owned and under a foreign flag. More than that: foreign and non-NATO. Further-more, their positioning off the west coast of Africa in ballast in the time frame of one or two days could easily have been calculated weeks in advance through published schedules of the ships' movements.

While his basic logic would not let him believe that Soviet submarines were responsible—an act that could bring down retaliation and would take them to the precipice of World War III—there was, nevertheless, a nagging question in President Hansen's mind. He needed the fine brains in his National Security Council to pick over the bones of evidence with him. On the other hand, this was an overt act of aggression against United States in-terests and property. Whether it was the PLO, the Japanese Red Army, or the Soviet Union, action had to be taken. Everything possible had to be done to make sure that it did not happen again. At that point, the president had no idea what could be done.

On the other hand, all the ships were foreign flag and non-NATO. They were in international waters. They were American-owned ships, but their hulls and cargos would be covered by insurers, Lloyd's of London and the new American group that had moved into the Lloyd's field. So why should the president of the United States get involved? John Hansen couldn't fully answer that question until he and his top National Security Council people took a look at the situation. But as long as there was even the slightest possibility that the Soviets had a hand in the simultaneous sinking of the twenty-five American supertankers, the matter had to be of top priority and utmost concern to his administration.

Immediately after a luncheon he hosted for a visiting African head of state, he had words in the Oval Office with Jim Crane and Peterson, the White House press secretary, who told the President that in his judgment he had never seen such a public reaction of indignation since the hostage-taking incident in Iran. As far as the people and the press were concerned, those were American ships, regardless of the flag they flew. Their sinking, no matter who did it, called for action by the president and if necessary, the armed forces. That was Peterson's assessment of the telephone calls and telegrams that were being sent to members of Congress and were flooding into the White House. In fact, it was the same kind of reaction that John Hansen himself felt. There was no way those PLO bastards were going to get away with it. The United States would retaliate somehow.

The National Security Council executive committee met in emergency session at five o'clock that afternoon. All members were present, except General Young. The President had instructed Crane not to invite him, but to tell the chief of naval operations, Admiral Taylor, to stand by his telephone.

When the executive committee had assessed all the available information, it came to the unanimous conclusion that, in spite of Arafat's repudiation of responsibility for the Atlantic sinkings, he was probably responsible for the destruction of all twenty-five tankers as he originally had claimed. His later denial was probably the result of the hostile world reaction. It was noted that the Soviet Union had yet to make any statement condemning the action or, for that matter, approving it.

A request would be made to all NATO members with naval forces to participate in an American navy coordinated program for the mine inspection of the hulls of all the tankers operating along the Cape of Good Hope shipping route from the Persian Gulf. Examining ships in port on the American and West European coasts and in the Persian Gulf would be relatively easy to do. But the handling of those at sea would be difficult and time consuming. Of the world tanker fleet of some 3,300 vessels, only 710 were in the supertanker class of 200,000 deadweight tons or more. It was decided to concentrate first on American-owned supertankers carrying the Liberian or Panamanian flags.

The executive committee shared President Hansen's view that if Arafat's denial of responsibility for the fifteen supertankers sunk in the Atlantic was valid, it meant that some other organization was working with his on a coordinated basis. It had to be the Japanese Red Army, or the German revolutionary group, or some new revolutionary organization. The final possibility was that submarines of the Soviet Navy had carried out those sinkings using the PLO as cover.

Difficult as it was to believe that the Russians would perpetrate such an act of aggression, the executive committee nevertheless unanimously recommended to the president that he should discuss the matter with the Soviet government, to ask for their assurances that they were not involved. Hansen had accepted that recommendation, saying that he would talk to Chairman Romanov on the hot line as soon as arrangements could be made. The president ended the executive committee meeting at that point, saying, "Even if I get his assurances they weren't involved, I don't know whether I can believe him any more than I can believe Arafat."

27

27 April   5:00 P.M.

Moscow

Chairman Romanov expected that President Hansen would soon want to talk with him on the hot line. He was, therefore, not surprised when his principal secretary entered his office to advise that the President had put in a bid for a talk in one hour, 6 P.M. Moscow time, nine o'clock in the morning in Washington. The secretary reminded the chairman that he had an appointment at six o'clock to meet a delegation from the Georgian party and Politburo member, nonvoting, Shevardnadze, who was responsible for the supervision of that group. They could wait. His conversation with the American would not last long.

At six o'clock Romanov was at his desk, the hot line television transmitter-receiver in front of him. To his right sat his interpreter. At the end of the desk between it and the wall sat a communications technician. Opposite the chairman sat his three key men, Gromyko, Andropov, and Ustinov, each dedicated to the cause and purposes of Marxist-Leninist communism, the party, and the domination of the world by the Soviet Union. These were experienced men and jealous perhaps in their own way of the younger Romanov, but loyal and trustworthy—at least until some face-losing situation transpired, as with Khrushchev.

At the appointed hour, all sat silent, impassive, waiting for the initiating contact, which came a few seconds after the hour when the face of the new president, Hansen, with whom none of them had any previous contact, appeared on the television screen. Hansen's opening remarks were friendly, as protocol demanded between the leaders of the world's two ascendant superpowers. The preliminaries between the two men, both of an age, were quickly disposed of. Each knew an enormous amount about the other through briefings by their respective intelligence agencies, supplemented by the State Department in America and Gromyko's own foreign affairs ministry in Moscow. It was, therefore, a challenge in evaluation and assessment for Chairman Romanov as he listened to the deep, modulated voice of the towering six-foot five-inch man speaking to him from his Oval Office at the White House. The challenge for John Hansen was equally trying.

But it was not so difficult for them as such discussions had been for their predecessors because, for the first time, the encounter was televised through a special satellite recently launched in a space venture jointly mounted by both countries. Even though the words and images were scrambled for security during transmission, they appeared at both ends in the clear. Thus, for the first time in history, the president of the United States and the chairman of the Soviet Union could see each other during a hot line discussion, an advantage to both in the critical business of long-distance negotiations concerning matters of world-shaking import.

From the very outset, Romanov was favorably impressed by the handsome, white-haired Hansen. As they began their conversation, he could sense that in other circumstances there could be a good rapport between them.

The conversation moved slowly because of the necessary intervention of the translators. Finally, both men knew that it was time to move to the main arena.

"And now, Mr. President, I assume you wish to talk with me about Pakistan and to tell me that the United States is prepared to abandon this indiscreet act of aggression. If so, perhaps there is some form of quid pro quo that might be considered. I can tell you in no uncertain terms what has already been related to you through our diplomatic channels: that I regard the United States intervention in Pakistan in the same light as President Carter regarded any intervention we might have made in Iran or the Persian Gulf countries. He said the United States would use military force to prevent us from so doing. He regarded any such action on our part, therefore, as being a *causus belli*. I want to make it perfectly clear that my colleagues and I look upon Pakistan as a vital area of interest to the Soviet Union and any military intervention there by the United States will be regarded as a *causus belli*."

Hansen nodded. "I understand your position. I do not believe you're justified in taking it. But I understand it. However, Pakistan is not the reason for my call. Perhaps we can talk about it in the next few days . . ."

"There are not too many days left, Mr. President."

"There are enough. I want to talk about the tanker sinkings yesterday. Mr. Chairman, I'm sure you and all of your colleagues have been fully briefed on the PLO action yesterday, the blowing up of the ten loaded tankers in the Indian Ocean and the other fifteen in the South Atlantic, the ones that were in ballast and apparently sank without trace, although some confirming debris has been found at each of their plotted locations."

Hansen paused to let Romanov's interpreter do his work.

Romanov acknowledged. "Yes, Mr. President, we have been fully briefed."

"You will know, therefore, Mr. Chairman, that Arafat has disclaimed any responsibility for the fifteen that went down in the Atlantic."

The chairman's acknowledgment was a nod. But he followed with a question: "But what is your interest in these vessels, Mr. President? They weren't American and they carried the flags of Liberia except one which was Panamanian. And if I recall my facts correctly, they were all in international waters, thousands of miles away from the United States."

Romanov could see the novice president shift uneasily.

"You're quite right. But every one of those ships was owned by American corporations or individuals."

Romanov held up his hand. "It is a capitalist device, an American capitalist device, to register ships in Liberia and Panama in order to avoid your law that requires American registered ships to use only American crews, a law which, if not avoided, would double or even triple the crew cost. Furthermore, Mr. President, most of those ships are owned by multinational corporations who range across the world plundering its economies. They have their head offices of convenience, like their flags of convenience, in the United States, the country that provides the most advantages and luxuries for their management groups. Those multinationals do no more than suck on the economic blood of the oil producers, of your government, and of the people of the Western world."

He went on when the interpreter was finished. "So I find it difficult, Mr. President, to accept the validity of your position that you are interested in the fate of those tankers simply because they are purported to be owned by U.S. interests."

The chairman could feel a touch on this left hand, a finger asking for attention. He turned to listen to Gromyko, then looked back at the screen and with it the television camera. "I have also been reminded that none of the crews of any of the ships were American. So I ask, Mr. President, what is your interest, what is the interest of the United States, in this matter?" He held up his hand to indicate that he had an addition to that question when the interpreter was finished.

"And if you have an interest that I am prepared to recognize, then the next question is, what is it that you want of me?"

Hansen responded, choosing his words carefully. "The

fact of ownership of those vessels, American ownership, not only gives me a legitimate interest but very deep concern. The mass destruction of American property anywhere in the world through an act of war or an act of aggression must be viewed seriously by the Government of the United States and is a matter of substantial concern. That is a fact, regardless of your apparent wish to reject it. But quite apart from the legalities, it is of vital interest to us that the flow of oil from the Persian Gulf to the United States not be cut off or, for that matter, that the supply of oil from any of the OPEC countries, whether in the Persian Gulf, Venezuela, Malaysia, or elsewhere, not be cut off by blockade or threats of naval aggression. We constantly face the possibility of a major supplier nation terminating its flow of oil because of political instability, as in Iran. That risk is inherent in dealing with most OPEC members. We could probably compensate, make up for the flow of lost oil from one country by getting increased supplies from others. Really, what I am concerned about is the preservation of the transportation system, the world tanker fleet, that carries the OPEC and Mexican crude oil to our shores. As you know, we import more than forty percent of our consumption and all of it comes in by tanker."

"I understand your concern about the tankers," Romanov assured him, "but surely you don't think the PLO could threaten the world's tanker fleet?"

"No, I don't. They might try to blockade the Strait of Hormuz by mining it, but we could look after that situation quickly. Or they could sink a group of tankers with your support, just as they did yesterday."

Romanov bristled. "Are you accusing us of being involved in those sinkings?"

"I'm not accusing you of anything, Mr. Chairman. But we do know that the mines the PLO terrorists used were of Soviet manufacture. The same PLO terrorist group used the same type of mine at Haifa early last month."

The chairman waited for Hansen to drop the other shoe about the leader of the PLO group, whom the Israelis had killed in Durban, being a KGB officer. But that did not come. He wondered whether the president knew.

"We also know that the Soviet government has been an active supporter of the PLO for many years. There is a difference between support and direct involvement in an action. I am not making any accusation that there was a Soviet involvement with yesterday's sinkings.

"What I'm concerned about . . . the reason I want to talk with you is this: Arafat has denied any PLO responsibility for the fifteen tankers that went down in the South Atlantic. If the PLO didn't do it, perhaps it was another revolutionary group. But if it wasn't such a group, then the only country in the world with the capability of sinking those ships and at exactly the same time as the PLO blew up the group in the Indian Ocean, is the Soviet Union. Let me hasten to assure you, Chairman Romanov, that I don't believe Arafat. I think he was responsible for the whole thing. On the other hand, it would be helpful to the government of the United States if I could have your assurances, sir, that the Soviet Union . . . your navy has a large number of submarines in the South Atlantic at this time . . . if you could assure us that the Soviet navy did not sink the fifteen tankers in the Atlantic."

Stunned by the bluntness of the question but showing no evidence of it, Romanov made his response immediately. He knew what the answer was. It was part of the Andropov Plan. Furthermore, there was precedent for it, in the assurances Chairman Khrushchev gave to President Kennedy as the Cuban missile crisis was developing in 1962.

"You should know, Mr. President, that I deeply resent the arrogance implicit in your belief that I should account to the United States for any action that the Soviet navy might or might not have taken. But having said that, and in pursuit of the goal of peaceful coexistence, a goal which the Soviet Union has always sought, you have my assurance on the question."

28

1 May

Atlantic Ocean

The surface of the Atlantic fifty miles west of Cape Town on the morning of the first of May, May Day, had a heavy roll but was without waves. The sky was dotted with flat-based cumulus clouds sitting at about 3,000 feet, their white tops brilliant in the morning sun as they moved eastward, carried by the steady five knot wind.

Splendid, still keeping 150 feet, was pronounced by Pilot at 08:36 Zulu to be abeam Cape Town, fifty-two miles west of her light. At that moment the communications officer appeared in the control room to hand the captain a signal. "It's from the flag officer submarines, sir."

From the flag officer! The pink sheet of paper marked Top Secret had Commander Marcus Leach's immediate and full attention. The body of the signal read:

Splendid will make rendezvous with VLCC *Esso Atlantic* to carry out inspection of her hull for limpets. Technical instructions to deactivate and neutralize Soviet-type expected to be found will follow. The *Esso Atlantic*'s real time position is 14° 10' 15" east, 34° 8' 2" south, making 16 knots.

She's very close. Should be on the sonar screen any minute now, thought Leach as he read on:

Approach *Esso Atlantic* with maximum caution. Cause of mass Atlantic sinkings April 26 still not certain. Largest ever deployment of Soviet submarines now in South Atlantic and Indian Ocean. Positions on them cannot be plotted.

You're bloody right they're here! Leach's mind agreed. From the time *Splendid* had entered the tanker lane off Durban on the twenty-seventh, her active sonar had picked up twelve of them, one for each hundred miles of the distance from Durban to Cape Town. Furthermore, they appeared to be running slowly, as if on station, and were spaced roughly one hundred miles apart. Leach didn't like it one bit. But it was up to the brains at Whitehall to figure what was going on. They still hadn't.

Recommend *Splendid* reconnoiter *Esso Atlantic* area carefully before surfacing to carry out inspection. Urgent you report any Soviet submarine activity. Captain *Esso Atlantic* expects contact. Report ETA for rendezvous soonest.

"Keep seventy-five feet." He would go to periscope depth and raise the radar mast so he could transmit.

"Pilot give me an ETA for us from here to . . ." he rhymed off the latitude and longitude set out in the signal. "Subtract one hour's steaming southbound at sixteen knots in your calculation." That would take care of the *Esso Atlantic*'s southbound progress toward them during a one-hour period.

"Aye, aye, sir."

The communications officer stood ready to take the captain's message. Without looking up from his chart table, Pilot quickly came up with the answer. "Fifty-two minutes, sir. ETA 09:32 Zulu."

"Good!" To the communications officer he said, "Make a signal to the flag officer submarines. Message re *Esso Atlantic* received. Wilco. ETA 09:32 Zulu. That's it." The communications officer scuttled out of the control room.

"Keeping seventy-five feet, sir."

"Up search periscope. Pilot, what's the heading to the location I gave you?"

"Three degrees port will do it, sir."

"Right. Three degrees port."

"Three degrees port, sir." The boat swung imperceptibly to the left to take up the new heading.

"Sonar, keep an eye for a contact. Should be dead ahead coming on your screen shortly. Let me know as soon as you've got it." Leach realized that was a useless order. The sonar watchkeepers would give it to him almost the split second it appeared on the screen without his having to tell them to do so.

To the messenger of the watch, Leach said, "Smith, get Chief up here, chop, chop." It would be up to the ship's technical officer to get the divers organized and to sort out the instructions on how to handle the limpet mines when that message came in.

The periscope handles were in his hands. He scanned the horizon, looking intently ahead through the clear morning air. Still nothing. A precautionary sweep of the entire horizon showed the same result.

When Chief arrived in the control room the captain left the periscope to show him the message. "We have two clearance divers on board, have we not?"

"Yes, sir, Parkin and James, but I have half a dozen men who can operate with our scuba diving equipment. The same men who cut the cables."

"How many sets of scuba diving gear, oxygen bottles, that sort of thing, do you have?"

"Six, sir, and at least six men."

"Right. Ask for volunteers. Tell them what they're going to have to do. And tell them it'll be risky as hell."

At that moment Pots appeared with the technical signal from the flag officer submarines outlining the method of neutralizing the limpet mines and the device that would have to be used to do it.

"Simple," Chief pronounced. "It's a quarter-inch square metal rod nine inches long. I can make a dozen of those in ten minutes."

Leach clapped Chief on the shoulder. "Good chap. Now hop to it. We haven't got much time. Get your volunteers. Brief them. Get them into their wetsuits in half an hour. Our ETA for the tanker is 09:32 Zulu but I'm going to spend perhaps an hour doing a wide swing around her and run alongside of her a bit before we surface."

The captain then picked up the broadcast microphone and told the ship's crew what was going on. He believed that as part of his team they should know everything he knew—well, almost everything. His discourse to the crew was cut short by words from the sonar watchkeeper.

"Contact dead ahead, range forty-five miles." The sonar man did not hear the captain's briefing message over the broadcast system because his ears were glued to his headset. Thus he did not know that his target was one of the largest tankers in the world, the *Esso Atlantic*, 1,334 feet long. "And Christ, sir, she's big. The biggest thing I've ever seen on the screen!"

Leach chuckled to himself. He then ordered active sonar. He wanted to see if there was a Soviet submarine lurking in the area, waiting silently so that passive sonar would not pick her up. The pinging active sonar would find her but at the same time it would give away the presence of the British submarine. He timed three minutes. Then, picking up the action broadcast microphone he said, "Report, sonar crew."

The watchkeeper replied immediately. "Listening all around, sir. No contacts."

He was satisfied for the moment. "Secure active sonar."

"Secure active sonar, sir."

Beckoning to the first lieutenant and also the officer of the watch, Leach went to the chart table to stand just to the right of Pilot who was seated, busily working. With the other two gathered so they could see, he outlined his tactics as his finger stabbed at the chart.

"Here's the position of the *Esso Atlantic* and here we are. What I propose to do is to keep periscope depth and do a wide swing out to the west about ten miles beyond her. Then we'll turn north and sweep around behind her, coming up alongside keeping 150 feet. I want to run alongside her about fifty yards out to her port." He didn't say so but he intended to keep *Splendid* running parallel to and in formation with the *Esso Atlantic*'s stern where her mighty engines and propeller generated maximum ship noise.

"We'll stay at periscope depth. I'll have attack scope up but not above the surface. I'll use it to keep station with the tanker. During this part of the maneuver we'll sit next to her for probably an hour, perhaps an hour and a half."

The first lieutenant ventured, "What's the game, sir? Surely if a Russian sub attempts to move in to attack the *Esso Atlantic* it won't attack if we're on the surface or if it sees us. Shouldn't we be on the surface?"

Leach explained. "We've been ordered to try to find out, if the opportunity presents itself, if it's the Soviets who are doing the Atlantic sinkings. The point is, if they see us they won't attack. If they don't see us, then we'll soon know whether they're going to attack or not."

"And if we're in the way, sir?"

"No sweat. We'll just put on the brakes." His officers laughed and Leach with them. But in his own mind he was deadly serious. Besides, it was impossible to think that the Russians would risk starting World War III by sinking tankers. They just wouldn't do it. In any event . . .

"I want to make absolutely sure that before we surface and get both the *Esso Atlantic* and ourselves stopped and into a totally vulnerable spot, totally immobile . . . I want to make sure we haven't put ourselves into the station area of a Russian submarine."

"But, sir," said Pilot, "even if we do, surely they're only going to be there to watch us and monitor what we're doing."

The captain looked down at the naive young face. "Of course that's all they'll do, Pilot. But remember, there's something afoot out here. Five days ago fifteen tankers disappeared without trace in these waters. Like everyone else, I'm quite certain that the PLO is responsible. But right now, the way the world is going . . . Today is May Day, the big day for the Russians. Six days from now the

Americans start landing in Pakistan whether the Russians like it or not . . . As a matter of fact, I think it's safe to say that the next six days will be the most critical between the Americans and the Russians since World War II.

"Today, Pilot, I'm taking nothing for granted, least of all any goddamn Russian submarine captain. If there's one in the area he'll make his move either when we're doing our big circle or in the period that we're running in formation with the tanker, up close." A flaw in his tactics occurred to Leach. "On second thought I think that instead of being on the port side—that would blanket our sonar's ability to see out to the starboard side of the tanker—I think we should be in formation with her in line astern as close as we can get. That way we'll be able to see with our sonar in all directions except dead ahead and perhaps thirty degrees to either side of that position."

To the messenger of the watch he called, "Fetch Lieutenant Pritchard."

When Pritchard, the sonar officer, arrived at the control room the captain explained to him where he wanted to position the submarine behind the tanker. Would that interfere with the operation of *Splendid*'s passive sonar? No, it would not. Nor would it interfere with the active sonar.

"From this moment, I do not intend to use the active sonar. It would give away our presence and our position. One final thing, old chap. When we're in position behind the tanker, tucked in right up her bum, if we get a contact with a Soviet submarine, say from the port side, then as soon as we do we'll move up to the port side of the tanker in the station that I originally told you about, next to the engine and propeller and about fifty yards out. Vice versa if the contact's on the starboard side. That'll make doubly sure the Russki can't tell that we're there. Any questions?"

There were none.

"Right, we will go to diving stations immediately. First Lieutenant, have the attack team close up at the double. Bring all tubes to the action state. Let's go, gentlemen!"

In short order H.M.S. *Splendid* was at full fighting

pitch, ready to attack or counter an attack. The captain was at his position in the control room. All communications channels in the ship were open to the sound of his voice, which could demand immediate response from sonar, the tube stations, or whatever compartment he wanted to talk with.

"Now what's our heading, Pilot?" Leach demanded.

"Three-thirty, sir. The tanker's on a reciprocal."

"Sonar, what's the range of the tanker now?"

"Coming up to twenty miles, sir."

"Right. We'll take a fifty degree cut to port to begin our wide circle around her. Steer 290."

"Steer 290, sir." *Splendid* began banking gently to the left to begin the planned sonar sweep westward of the *Esso Atlantic*.

At 09:32 Zulu, her advertised ETA, the submerged *Splendid* was ten miles to port of the *Esso Atlantic* and abeam her. Leach went into the sonar room to take another look. He was still amazed by the size of the white blob the huge tanker made on the screen.

"Bloody marvelous!" he muttered.

Back in the control room keeping an anxious, overseeing eye on everything going on, he said to Tait, "That poor bloody tanker captain will be wondering what's happened to us. By the time we surface . . ."

"About two hours from now?"

"Right. He'll have given us up for lost. Pity."

One hour later *Splendid* had completed her sonar sweep of the waters to the west and north of the *Esso Atlantic*. No contacts were reported. Leach began to move her into close line-astern formation behind the tanker.

For an undistorted view ahead as he prepared to execute this most delicate, precise station-keeping maneuver, Leach had put up his attack periscope with its nonmagnifying lenses. Its eye sat only two feet above the top of the tower. He calculated that at that position he would be able to judge accurately where the uppermost part of his boat and, most important, her nose were in relation to the *Esso Atlantic*.

Leach caught his first glimpse of the roiling turbulence from the tanker's propeller when *Splendid* was some 800 yards astern of the *Esso Atlantic*. By the time he had closed to 400 yards, with an overtaking speed of two knots over the tanker's sixteen, the captain realized that the foaming white turbulence from the big ship's screw was blinding him. He would have to settle for tucking the *Splendid*'s nose up under the keel so that his periscope eye sat perhaps ten feet below and behind the rudder, clear of the vision-destroying turbulence. He was satisfied that, sitting in that position, his own boat's cavitation noise would be lost in the sound of the *Esso Atlantic*'s 45,000-horsepower steam turbine power plant and her enormous propeller. *Splendid* would be safe from the prying sonar eyes of any Soviet submarine.

Taking his boat below the wake of the tanker, he gradually edged her forward. Sonar called one hundred yards range. At that moment Leach had his first glimpse of the *Esso Atlantic*'s stern gear. He was amazed at the scale of what he saw. Her rudder stood as tall as a six-storey building. Immediately behind it was her five-bladed propeller, thirty feet in diameter. At eighty revolutions per minute it rotated so slowly that he could distinctly see each of its gleaming blades.

The crew of *Splendid* had picked up the propeller and engine noise of the massive tanker at maximum range. Now, as the submarine edged her nose under the big vessel's stern with the periscope sitting exactly where Leach wanted it, ten feet down and slightly back from the rudder, the thumping roar from above was deafening. So loud was the noise that Leach, who could not for one second take his eyes away from the periscope, had to scream out his instructions. The first lieutenant stood immediately next to him in order to hear what his captain was saying so he could repeat it. As they approached the stern of the tanker, Tait had realized that the volume of noise coming up would probably destroy all normal voice control over the ship, so he had broken out the ship's bullhorn. Thus, when Leach screamed out an order, the first lieutenant boomed it through his bullhorn over the pervasive din of the *Esso Atlantic*'s machinery and screw.

When *Splendid* was in the exact position, close under the *Esso Atlantic*, that Leach wanted, he screamed out a request for a stool to perch on. While that was being tucked under his butt, he asked, "Is sonar scanning all right?"

The first lieutenant shouted in his ear, "I'll check."

Tait quickly took the few steps to the sonar compartment, had a shouting conversation with Pritchard and returned to his post beside the captain.

"Sonar's scanning okay, sir. Pritchard will bring me any contact as soon as it's made."

"Good-o."

For close to an hour the *Esso Atlantic* and *Splendid* moved in tight formation like an enormous gray whale with her calf tucked under her belly.

"Coming up to one hour in thirty seconds, sir," Tait bellowed into the captain's ear.

Leach started giving the orders that would move *Splendid* down fifty feet and then swing her out to the port to surface running alongside the tanker. "Keep 125 feet." He shouted the order to take her down. But there was no bullhorn repeat from the first lieutenant at his elbow. Instead, over the din he could hear scraps of screamed words. Then Tait's mouth was at his ear.

"Contact, sir. It's another Victor at range forty miles. Bearing green one hundred. Closing at thirty-five knots. Course 110 degrees. She's headed right for us."

No doubt about it, she was on an intercept. Leach calculated the Victor would be in an ideal attack position at say three miles in about forty minutes. Time to move.

He took *Splendid* down to 150 feet, well clear of the tanker's gargantuan keel. Then he swung his boat off to the starboard side of the big craft until the submarine was about fifty yards away, running in line abeam of the propeller and engine room at the stern. Next he eased her up to periscope level, maintaining the positioning of his attack periscope eye just above the tower. He would not put either of his periscopes above the surface. At the right moment he would raise only the radar mast.

Leach had *Splendid's* propeller and motor exactly where he wanted them, fifty yards away from the thundering engines and propeller of the *Esso Atlantic* and in a direct line between those powerful noise generators and the oncoming Victor. As the Soviet submarine's position changed he would maneuver his boat to maintain that line.

At her new station, the volume of the tanker's noise inside the hull of *Splendid* diminished considerably, sufficiently that Leach could give his orders directly to his control room crew. He turned the periscope over to the first lieutenant and picked up the broadcast microphone.

"All compartments, this is the captain. We have a Victor class submarine moving in from the starboard. She is at 095 degrees to our heading and about thirty-five miles on an intercept course. We're running next to the *Esso Atlantic*, as you can hear. We're about fifty yards to her starboard beside her propeller and engine room and in a line between them and the Russian submarine. The tanker's noise will mask our sound so the Victor won't know we're here. I expect she'll be in an ideal attack position in an hour from now, at 11:40."

He then told the crew what his plan of action was, depending upon what the Soviet submarine did. From that moment it was a matter of watching and waiting. At 11:30 the Victor, approaching the three-mile range, changed from its intercept course to run parallel to the *Esso Atlantic* and moved ahead until it was abeam of the tanker. There it sat, a constant blip on the sonar screen. At 11:34 the radar watchkeeper reported, "Periscope, sir. Green 085. Range 3 miles." The Soviet captain was ready for visual contact with the supertanker.

At 11:55 the Russian submarine altered its heading again to an intercept course.

In the control room of *Splendid*, Marcus Leach received the report he wanted to hear.

"All tubes reported in the action state, sir. Guidance systems in computer control, sir."

Leach acknowledged.

"Up radar mast."

"Up radar mast, sir."

"Communications center."

"Communications center. Go ahead, sir."

"Be prepared to transmit in the clear a running account of everything you hear if the Victor attacks. But don't transmit unless I tell you to."

"Aye, aye, sir."

Throughout the length and breadth of *Splendid*, the next words of the captain caused everyone to tense.

"Stand by to start the attack and watches." *Splendid*'s complex computers, electronic equipment, and instruments had been locked onto the advancing submarine by the attack crew, the sonar information being fed into the system giving it the Victor's depth, speed, range, and course. That information was fed directly into the torpedo control settings. When he made his final decision to attack and gave the order to launch the torpedos, the timing watches would be started to clock their estimated run time to impact with the target.

Finally, on the fire-control computer the five red Torpedo Ready lights flashed on.

The *Splendid* was set. If Leach had to shoot, the torpedos would leave their tubes in the bow of the boat, then turn on their computer set headings to the target. Their own sonar and heat-sensing devices would lead them into it for the impact. In case something went wrong and a torpedo turned back against *Splendid* itself or the *Esso Atlantic*, the torpedo's warheads would not be armed until they had run several hundred yards.

It was coming up to 12:00 Zulu. Leach watched the sweephand go by on the control room clock.

In the control room of the atomic submarine 501, its captain, Boris Chernavin, kept the hairline aiming cross on the exact point on the *Esso Atlantic*'s bridge where he wanted his submerged-launch SS-N-7 surface-to-surface rocket to strike, enter, and destroy. His clear eyes absorbed the scene presented to him through the boat's periscope, as he listened to his executive officer's voice giving him the countdown of seconds to 12:00 noon. On the precise second he gave the order: "Fire!"

Instantly there was a growling, rumbling sound from the forward launch compartment. The surface of the sea immediately in front of the periscope burst in a showering cascade of foam and smoke as the rocket, flung out of its tube by compressed air, ignited its propulsion pod. Its retracted wings sprang out as it began its flat trajectory toward the tanker. Trailing behind it was a guidance wire that was optically and electronically locked to the periscope sighting mechanism controlled by the eye and hands of the captain.

As the clock recorded 12:00 Zulu aboard *Splendid*, the radar watchkeeper shouted, "A rocket, sir. She's launched a rocket!"

Leach couldn't believe it. But he had to.

"Hard to starboard!" If torpedos were to follow the rocket to the *Esso Atlantic*, he had to be out of their path.

"Stop engines! Up attack periscope," Leach had to track the rocket. "Paul, get on the periscope. Tell me what happens with the rocket!"

The combination of the hard bank to starboard and the quick pulling off of power put the *Splendid* astern of the tanker. But would it be enough?

At the instant Chernavin observed the rocket's impact exactly on target he called out, "Fire all torpedos!" He could feel the submarine shudder as she disgorged her lethal package of eight computer preset torpedos toward the helpless supertanker. At that moment, its entire stern superstructure was being ripped apart by the devastating explosion of the powerful rocket. No one could survive that blast. As planned, the communications center of the *Esso Atlantic* was destroyed without warning.

The *Splendid* was only halfway through her turn to face the Victor head on when Leach heard the sonar report,

"Torpedo HE, bearing 040." Pratt's voice was edged with anxiety. "I have eight of them running, sir. Range three miles!"

That was it. The rocket and now the torpedos. It was the Soviets who had sunk the fifteen on April 26!

"Communications center, start broadcasting!"

"Aye, aye, sir."

At that instant the sound of a heavy explosion shook the hull of *Splendid*. At the same time the first lieutenant shouted, "Christ, it hit just below the funnel. It's taken the whole bridge area out and her communications center would be right there." The Russian tactic was clear: hit the communications center first. That explained why there was no word from those that disappeared six days before.

Leach looked at his Torpedo Ready lights. They had gone out as the attack team reset their information. Suddenly they glowed red again.

"On, sir . . ."

"Shoot!"

The impact of having the five torpedos leaving the bow of *Splendid* finished off her remaining forward motion.

"Torpedos running, sir."

"Running time?"

"Two minutes fifty-two seconds to three minutes, sir."

Within ten seconds after the Victor II's torpedos had been launched, all eight tracking with deadly accuracy toward the hull of the tanker, the sonar michman's voice on the loudspeaker system had cut through the hot fetid air of the control room with words that jolted the captain.

There was a contact just behind the tanker. The computer said it was British of the Swiftsure class. It must have been running beside the tanker. The submarine was falling behind the *Esso Atlantic* rapidly. Its bow was swinging toward the 501. The michman's voice did not stop but its pitch became higher as he began to realize what was happening. The port torpedo originally programed to strike the *Esso Atlantic* in the stern, engine room, rudder, propeller area, had locked onto the British submarine and was tracking directly for it.

Then came the chilling shock when the sonar michman's voice with a high shrill of panic screamed that the British sub had just launched five torpedos at the 501.

Captain Second Class Boris Chernavin reacted quickly. He shouted an order to the wheelsman to turn hard to the left. That would put the 501's bow head on toward the running torpedos, minimizing their target profile. That order was followed in the same breath by "Full speed ahead! Dive! Dive!"

That done, the captain said to himself, "It can't happen to you, Chernavin!" He could do nothing now but wait.

On *Splendid*, Pratt's voice again contained a hint of panic. "Sonar, sir. Torpedos halfway to tanker. Seven are tracking to the tanker and one of them is heading for us!"

Leach's reaction was instantaneous. "Dive! Dive! Full ahead!"

In the two minutes left of the Soviet torpedo's running time, diving was the only escape maneuver left to *Splendid*. Agonizingly slowly the ponderous bulk of the huge submarine began to move forward. The planesman had the hydroplane control wheel shoved hard forward as the main ballast tank inlets opened wide to allow emergency flooding in the desperate attempt to avoid the oncoming torpedo.

In two strides Leach was in the sonar room, eyes fixed on the screen, its winking lights instantly conveying the story to him. There was the torpedo, two miles away, speeding toward *Splendid* with the accuracy of an arrow. His own torpedos had completed their turn toward the Victor and were almost a quarter of the way to it. Tracking toward the *Esso Atlantic*, already half a mile south of the stopped British submarine, were seven dots running fast and parallel. They would strike the tanker at spaced intervals from the bow to the stern.

In the communications center, the communications officer was monitoring the voices in the control room. He knew exactly what was happening and he was broadcasting it to the world.

Commander Marcus Leach RN, the captain of H.M.S. *Splendid*, his eyes fixed on the image of the lethal torpedo hurtling through the water toward his boat, thought for an instant about warning the crew. But why panic them? If they were going to buy it they were going to buy it.

Watching the white streak on the sonar screen traverse the last inch toward the bright, shining *Splendid* dot on the sonar screen, Commander Marcus Leach's thoughts raced. "It's going to miss us. Surely it's going to miss us. After all, it's only a Russian torpedo. Primitive construction. Probably a dud. It can't happen to you, Leach. No way."

29

1 May   5:40 P.M.

Moscow

The scene in Chairman Romanov's office was much the same as it had been five days before. The players were the same, the chairman in his dark suit behind his desk looking grim, the translator by his side, the communications technician, and opposite, Marshal Ustinov looking splendid in his uniform, Gromyko bland as ever, and General Andropov looking agitated, nervous.

It was May Day, glorious May Day, the day the Soviet Union celebrated the victory of the revolution, the day that thousands of army, navy and air force troops paraded proudly through Red Square, marching with their tanks, guns, missiles, and all the modern paraphernalia of war, while overhead screeched squadrons of the newest fighters and bombers. It was a showcase into which, through the magic of television, the eyes of the world could look in awe at the increasing might of the Soviet armed forces.

The parade that day had lasted for three hours as it moved past the saluting base where Romanov and his colleagues stood in their formless, dark overcoats and matching wide-brimmed fedoras worn by all except Ustinov, who was in uniform. The spectators that day and the world press were quick to notice that instead of fourteen Politburo members standing behind the white balustrade to take the salute, there were only ten. That was the first clue to Romanov's emerging ruthlessness. On April 28, four members of the Politburo, Pelshe, Kirilenko, Suslov, and the premier, Kosygin, all in their late seventies and old men even by Romanov's standards, had asked for an audience with the chairman and were promptly received. Romanov was horrified when he found that they wanted to abort the Andropov Plan even though they had earlier approved it and stage one had been executed with huge success. The old men were shaken by the devastation wrought by the sinking of the American supertankers on April 26, stage one of the plan. They had convinced themselves that the consequences of stage two would be suicidal for the people of the Mother Country and contrary to the previously established pattern of securing Marxist-Leninist world domination by the socialist peoples in carefully planned and managed incremental steps rather than by the giant step that was implicit in the Andropov scheme.

Unable to dissuade the little group of patriarchs, Romanov decided that he simply could not have in the Politburo a clutch of weak-kneed old men who were totally opposed to any change in the status quo. Such men would chew away at the vitals of the successful execution of the Andropov Plan. He needed men of iron will and determination who were prepared to accept the prospect of a thermonuclear war, knowing that if it occurred, the Soviet Union would be victorious, that its society would survive and that of the enemy would be totally destroyed. He needed men who, at the same time, had total faith in the Andropov Plan and had faith that it would take the Soviet Union to a glorious victory over the capitalistic imperialists of the United States and their NATO and Western world minions. He would replace those old fools with such men. He had so informed them. The flabbergasted four had slunk from his office with no hope of turning back the clock. The next morning, as Romanov had judged, his motion to terminate their membership was carried in a full session of the Polit-buro. The decision was unanimous, the victims being unable to vote on their own fates. By May Day, however, Romanov had not yet decided which among the nonvoting members of the Politburo, or for that matter, from his loyal friends and supporters outside it, he would nominate to replace the four purged ancient ones.

Thus, only ten members of the Politburo had stood that May Day to receive the salute of the passing military might. During the parade Romanov stood in the center of the line of Politburo members, assured now that all the others knew how ruthless their chairman was. That quality would soon be discovered by the president of the United States.

The completion of stage two of the Andropov Plan was scheduled for three o'clock in the afternoon, Moscow time, noon GMT. Romanov had, therefore, asked for a hotline conference with President Hansen for three hours later, six o'clock in Moscow and 9 A.M. in Washington. In the three-hour interval he would have confirmation that stage two had, in fact, been executed. He and his colleagues would have a chance to rest after the grueling hours-long stand on the inspection platform, and he could polish his notes for the message he was going to deliver to the presi-dent. From his perspective of history it would probably be the most important statement delivered by one head of government to another in the history of mankind.

The chairman had been working at his desk alone in his office at 5:35 P.M., carefully going over his statement, when his principal secretary burst in, saying that Hansen urgently wanted to speak with the chairman. It was of the highest priority and could not wait for the appointed hour of six o'clock. Romanov agreed.

"Tell the Americans to give me five minutes." He waved his hands at the television gear at the end of his desk. "Everything is set. Fetch my colleagues."

At 5:42 when contact was established and the face of each leader appeared on his respective television screen, Romanov's trio, Gromyko, Andropov, and Ustinov, were in place opposite him, witnesses to the impending confrontation.

This time Hansen wasted no time on preliminaries.

"Mr. Chairman, I have in my hand," his huge right hand thrust toward the camera a single, long piece of paper, "conclusive and absolute evidence that, just forty minutes ago, one of your Victor class submarines not only sank a British submarine, it also, and without warning to the crew, sank the American-owned *Esso Atlantic* using a rocket and torpedos. My evidence is a broadcast from the sub before it sank. And I also have evidence that as of this moment, another twenty American-owned supertankers have disappeared in the South Atlantic. They were sunk by your submarines just as the fifteen were sunk five days ago." His thundering, accusatory voice rose in pitch and volume. "You lied to me, Romanov, you lied to me—just as Khrushchev lied to Kennedy—when you assured me that the Soviet Union had nothing to do with those sinkings. You have committed an act of war against both the United States of America and Great Britain and don't give me that business about flags of convenience and international waters!"

Romanov was tempted to taunt with "What are you going to do about it?" but he denied himself the pleasure. After all, he held the winning cards. Instead he replied passively, coldly.

"You must understand, Hansen," he would reciprocate the president's rudeness by also using his surname alone, "that if it serves the interests of the nation I lead, I am as prepared as any of my predecessors to say truths which are not true and even to die in the cause of our Mother Country."

Romanov intended to take the initiative away from the emotionally overwrought president. "The United States, you, Hansen, are in the process of committing an act of aggression against the Soviet Union by your entry into Pakistan. You refuse to back off. We have given you every opportunity to do so. The United Nations has censured your action. Yes, 110 countries voted to censure you, whereas

only 104 censured us when we entered Afghanistan to protect our own interests on our own borders. We have given
you every opportunity to retreat from your active military
madness of putting a hundred thousand men on Asian soil
in Pakistan at our very throat."

His eyes dropped to his notes as he began to follow
them, from time to time looking up into the television
screen where President Hansen's haggard image sat clearly
before him. Hansen made an effort to intervene in protest
but Romanov waved him down, saying, "It would be best if
you heard what I have to say. Hear me out and you will
have every opportunity to respond."

Hansen remained silent as the Russian went on.

"As a result of your intended act of aggression in
Pakistan, and for other reasons which I will outline, the
Soviet Union has decided upon a course of action to
preserve its own security, to preserve the peace of the world
and, at the same time, to gain permanent access to a commodity essential to the economy of the Soviet Union and its
East European allies.

"That commodity is crude oil. As far back as October
of 1979, economic analysts of your Central Intelligence
Agency—and we have the highest regard for the CIA, Mr.
President, it is almost as good as the KGB—those analysts
told a congressional committee that the Soviet oil industry,
then a net exporter of a million barrels a day to Eastern and
Western Europe, had peaked in its production and the supply was starting to fall off. Those analysts testified that by
1982, in the face of increased Soviet demand and resources,
Moscow would be forced to import 700,000 barrels of crude
oil a day and that there was only one place to obtain it—the
Middle East. There was much controversy in your country
about the validity and accuracy of the CIA estimate, but I
can assure you, Mr. President, they were wrong. Our daily
shortfall is not 700,000 barrels a day, but 1,200,000, and
rapidly rising to crisis figures for our economy and that of
our European allies. On the other hand, the CIA analysts
were also right. We have had no new major discoveries in
the Soviet Union in recent times and the prospects do not

look good and, therefore, the only place we can secure the crude oil we need is—as the CIA put it—the Middle East.

"It is apparent, therefore, that assured access to Middle East oil is a matter of paramount concern to the Soviet Union at this moment, just as continued access must be of paramount concern to the United States and to Western Europe, which receives ninety-three percent of its crude oil from the OPEC producers of which sixty percent comes from the Persian Gulf. It is obvious that if that supply of crude oil from all the OPEC countries was cut off, Western Europe would face the total annihilation of its industrial and economic base and indeed the civilization that it now knows. To a lesser degree, but only slightly, the consequences of the cut-off of Persian Gulf oil to Western Europe would be similar. For you in the United States, the result of a cut-off of your oil imports of nine million barrels a day out of a consumption of twenty would be no less catastrophic. Even the termination of your supplies from the Persian Gulf alone would be a major disaster.

"However, at this moment I speak to you not of a termination of the supply to you of Persian Gulf crude but a termination of all crude oil supplied to you and to Western Europe by tanker from whatever source in the world, Venezuela, Mexico, Malaysia, and for that matter, even from Alaska in your own country, where you made the foolish decision to take the production there, 1,200,000 barrels a day—the equivalent of our shortfall at this moment—by tanker down the west coast of Canada rather than in a secure pipeline by land."

Hansen had slumped back in his chair, totally absorbed in what he was hearing. There would be a punch line. Of that he was certain.

Romanov pressed on. "At this moment I have 381 submarines of all classes at sea, my entire serviceable fleet. At this moment 256 of them are locked on to tanker targets in the Cape of Good Hope route from the Persian Gulf up into the South Atlantic."

Romanov was happy with the look of appalled astonishment on Hansen's face when he heard those numbers.

The president sat up instantly, looking off camera to his people as if for confirmation or denial. Apparently, he had no satisfaction. Relentlessly, Romanov pressed on.

"Similarly, I have thirty-five submarines locked on targets moving between Venezuela and the United States, and Mexico and the United States. In the Pacific I have another thirty on targets running in from Malaysia. Of the world tanker fleet of 4,200 vessels, the supertankers of more than 200,000 tons, which carry most of the crude oil on the major runs to your country and to Western Europe, number only 700. In the last five days, quite apart from the PLO sinkings of ten in the Indian Ocean, my submarines have sunk thirty-five of them. All were swiftly dealt with, disappearing below the surface of the ocean within a minute or two minutes of being hit."

Romanov no longer glanced up from time to time. He pushed his gold-rimmed glasses further back on his nose and went on. "The reason for those sinkings? It was to demonstrate to the Government of the United States and to the NATO powers in no uncertain terms that the Red Navy has the capability of destroying in short order the entire supertanker fleet upon which the economy and future of the capitalist world depends. Mr. President, you and your NATO allies are powerless to stop us. Your numbers of surface and submarine antisubmarine vessels are far from sufficient. Furthermore, even if you had adequate numbers they would not be in place because of the NATO restriction at the Tropic of Cancer. The fact is, there is no defense against our capability to destroy the Western world's energy lifeline from the OPEC countries."

Romanov shifted and straightened then bent back again to his paper. "Mr. President, the United States has put us in a position where we have no choice but to act in defense of our Mother Country and to secure our position in the Middle East so that we can have a guarantee of access to its vast reservoirs of crude oil. Accordingly, I am authorized by the Supreme Soviet to inform you as follows:

"At 1200 hours Greenwich mean time tomorrow, the second of May, 0800 hours eastern daylight saving time in the U.S., the Soviet forces in strength will cross the borders into Iran from the Soviet Union and from Afghanistan, and from Afghanistan into Pakistan. Those forces are under orders to take those countries and to drive on through Iraq, Kuwait, Saudi Arabia, Yemen, Oman, the United Arab Emirates, Qatar and Bahrain. In other words, to seize the entire Persian Gulf."

Romanov paused to let that statement have its fullest impact on the reeling mind of the inexperienced president.

"You should know that my authorization from the Politburo is irrevocable. In the interests of the security of the Soviet Union and in the interests of its urgently needed energy supply, we will begin our military action precisely on the time scheduled, noon GMT tomorrow.

"You have some choices, Mr. President. Let me spell them out to you. First, you can go thermonuclear between now and then. You can order the pushing of the button that will rain nuclear warheads down upon our cities and military installations and ports, knowing full well that the instant you do our ICBMs will be launched in immediate total response. Millions upon millions of our people, yours and mine, will die. That is your first choice.

"Your next is to attempt to stop us in the Middle East by conventional warfare. I pause to add here that any use of nuclear tactical weapons will be tantamount to the use of intercontinental nuclear missiles and will be responded to accordingly by us. You can attempt to land your Pakistan Task Force on the seventh of May. You can attempt to throw in your 82nd Airborne Division as soon as you can get it ready.

"The final choice is to not intervene in our Persian Gulf initiative and to recall your Pakistan Task Force."

Romanov's hands moved as he shifted to the next page of his notes. "I suggest that you and your advisers give the utmost consideration to that course of action, Mr. President, because if you do intervene in our Persian Gulf initiative with military forces of any kind—air, sea, or land—then I will forthwith proceed to sink every super-tanker on the high seas, all 700 of them, and sufficient of the remaining smaller and medium capacity ships to ensure that all OPEC crude oil supplies to you and Western Europe are cut off for the foreseeable future. Bear in mind, also, Mr. President, that if I destroy those tankers, neither you, Western Europe, nor Japan will have the industrial capacity even to begin to rebuild that fleet for the next ten years.

"So as I see it, you can go nuclear, or you can go conventional, or you can abstain. If you choose to abstain, if you leave us a free hand in the Persian Gulf, stay out of Pakistan, then I will give you this quid pro quo.

"I can assure you that, firstly, my navy will sink no more tankers; secondly, the Soviet Union will guarantee the United States, Canada, Western Europe, and Japan a continued flow of crude oil from the Persian Gulf countries in amounts equivalent to those being shipped today, less an amount equal to the shortfall between the Soviet Union's domestic output and its overall demand including those of its Eastern Bloc allies calculated yearly. The price will be the equivalent of today's average OPEC contract price plus an amount equal to the annual inflation rate averaged between the United States, United Kingdom, and West Germany calculated every six months."

It was done. The future of the civilized world lay squarely in the hands of John Hansen, president of the United States of America. The lives of tens of millions of people, unknown to them, were dependent on his decision.

Romanov slipped off his glasses, looked into the television screen and camera and asked in an arrogantly condescending way, "Do you have any questions, Hansen?"

The big man in Washington was shaken to the core. He sat erect in his chair. "You've lied to me once, Romanov. How can I trust your promise not to sink the tankers and to provide a continued supply of crude oil?"

Romanov shrugged. "The answer to that is for you to decide. No matter what conclusion you come to, the armed forces of the Soviet Union will begin their move toward the Persian Gulf at midday tomorrow."

Romanov ordered the communications technician to

turn off the set as President Hansen belligerently leaned forward shouting, "Romanov, you're a lying, unprincipled, inhumane, absolutely ruthless . . ."

As the screen went blank, the chairman could not but agree with the president's harsh description of him, except that he did not consider himself to be inhumane. On the contrary.

30

1 May   10:28 A.M.
The White House
Washington, D.C.

The eyes of the president and everyone in the Oval Office—Vice-President James, Levy, Kruger and Crane—remained on the television screen for many moments after Romanov's image had disappeared. The five men sat speechless, stunned by what they had heard. It was beyond belief.

Slowly, the president turned to look at the others sitting across the desk. "Gentlemen, some decisions have to be made and quickly. There's no doubt in my mind that Romanov isn't bluffing." His mind was turning over what had to be done. He said to Crane, "I want a meeting in half an hour in the cabinet room. I want the director of the CIA, Cootes. There isn't time to get the approval of Congress, but I want the majority and minority leaders of both the Senate and the House and the Speaker of the House and," to the others present, "all of you."

The secretary of defense asked, "What about General Young?" It was a suggestion.

Crane broke in. "He and the three chiefs are at Colorado Springs, the North American Air Defense headquarters. I checked with his secretary this morning. Something about a conference with their senior generals and admirals."

The president waved a hand. "It doesn't matter. Get hold of him immediately. Tell him what's going on. I want him and his people to stay put next to a telephone and keep the line clear so we can talk to him any time. And get Peterson to arrange time with all the television networks. Say six o'clock. Fifteen minutes. The American people have a right to know what's going on. By the time we're finished, I may have to tell them to evacuate the cities."

"You don't really think it's going to go that far," John Eaton protested.

The president pointed toward the blank screen. "You heard what the man said."

The secretary of state had no further comment.

Hansen flicked his secretary's switch on the intercom box sitting at the end of his desk. "Margaret, get Prime Minister Thrasher and the West German chancellor for me on a conference call immediately. It's urgent. Top priority. We'll talk in the clear."

"What about Canada? If we go, they'll be involved." Eaton knew how sensitive the Canadians were.

"Okay. Include the Canadian prime minister. You'd better get going, Jim." As his chief of staff left the Oval Office, the president said to his colleagues, "There used to be a sign on this desk, 'The buck stops here.' Right now I'd like to have old Harry Truman looking over my shoulder."

Half an hour later, when the president entered the cabinet room to get the emergency meeting underway, he was relieved to see that all the people he had asked for were present. They were standing, waiting for his appearance. There were no amiable greetings. Hansen went directly to his chair at the center of the table and lowered his huge body into it. As he did so, he turned to Crane standing behind him, then pointed to the telephone on the table to the right of his place. "Did you get General Young?"

"Yes, sir, he's standing by with the three chiefs. They can hear what's being said and can talk without the phone being lifted."

Hansen opened the meeting with a thorough update on the situation, going over in detail the ultimatum that Romanov had given him.

"What I have to decide is how we respond. And when I say 'I', I mean just that. We have until 12:00 GMT, 8 A.M. our time, tomorrow. There's no possible way I can get any approval from Congress for whatever action I propose to take. There just isn't time. So I'm most grateful to the congressional leaders, my old colleagues, for being here and I hope they'll support whatever I decide to do."

It was the portly, white-haired old Dan O'Brien, the Speaker of the House of Representatives, who spoke for his colleagues, saying, "We're pleased that you asked us to sit in, Mr. President. It seems to me that what Chairman Romanov said to you, the ultimatum, is, in fact, a declaration of war against the United States. Would you agree with that, Mr. President?"

Hansen shook his head. "Not quite. I see it as a statement of intent to declare war or create war, if certain things are or are not done. The Russian sinking of the fifteen American-owned ships I technically regard as an act of war against Liberia and Panama and not against the United States. And it's a clear act of war against the British. Whatever the legal technicalities are, Dan, the fact is that the Russians are going to move against Iran and the Persian Gulf countries tomorrow morning. They're not going to attack the United States, but they are going to attack the Persian Gulf countries."

Secretary Eaton interjected. "But surely the sinking of the world tanker fleet, the sinking of American ships flying the American flag, would be an act of war against the United States."

"It would indeed. And it would be an act of war against any other nation whose ships were sunk—the United Kingdom, West Germany, France. There's one point I want to get cleared up." He pointed toward the telephone saying to Crane, "Jim, can I talk to Admiral Taylor on that thing?" Admiral Crozier Taylor, the chief of naval operations, was at NORAD headquarters in Colorado Springs with General Young.

"Yes, Mr. President. Just talk at the machine. Ask for him."

"Admiral Taylor, this is the president speaking. Can you hear me?"

"Yes, Mr. President." The admiral's voice came clearly through the loudspeaker attached to the phone.

"Good. Then you've heard my briefing on what's going on. We know the Soviets have some 381 submarines at sea at this moment. Romanov says he can sink the world's tanker fleet. In your opinion, admiral, could he do it?"

There was no hesitation in Taylor's reply. "No question about it, sir. We believe he has close to 300 of his submarines locked onto target ships right now. He could take out almost half the world fleet of 700 on the first shot. I would say that within a week, the Russians could destroy between eighty and ninety percent of all the supertankers and probably thirty percent of the smaller tankers, that's between eight and nine hundred of those. You see, Mr. President, none of the tankers that are at sea, and there are hundreds of them, have any protection whatsoever. With their satellites, the Russians know exactly where they are. Each sub carries between twelve and twenty-one torpedos, say an average of fifteen torpedos per sub. With 300 tasked for tanker sinking, that gives you 4,500 shots. In two weeks there probably wouldn't be a single supertanker afloat and probably three-quarters of the smaller ones would be gone."

"Couldn't we stop them?"

Once more there was no hesitation. "Not a hope, Mr. President. In a week or ten days, we might be able to take out say eighty out of their 381 at sea. We have 148 submarines. Only seventy-six of those have antisubmarine capability. Furthermore, the Soviet submarines are on station right now and ready to shoot. Our antisubmarine subs are thousands of miles away. I think we have thirty at sea at the moment, and all of them are in the North Atlantic."

"You've got nothing in the South Atlantic?" The President shook his head in frustration.

"No, sir, but I have six working with the Fifth Fleet in the Arabian Sea."

"What about the British? They're in this with us. The Soviets' sinking of their submarine today took care of that. At least they nailed the Russian sub at the same time."

"The Brits have a few antisubmarine submarines. They've got lots of surface ship capability but, like ours, they're not deployed. Their surface ships at sea are in the North Atlantic and there's a flotilla working with the Fifth Fleet. The problem is, Mr. President, the Soviets have taken us by surprise. If we'd only known they put their whole submarine fleet to sea . . ."

"They aced us, Admiral, with their goddamn sonar interference and dummy submarines to fool our satellite cameras. They aced us. Thank you, Admiral. We'll be back to you if we have other questions."

The president had earlier been fully briefed by his experts on what would happen if the Red Navy destroyed the world's tanker fleet. He had been appalled by what he had been told. He summarized the main points of the report for the men assembled that morning.

"The U.S. imports nine million barrels a day out of a consumption of twenty million. The loss of imported crude would, within six months, cause the shut-down of at least fifty percent of the industries that rely on petroleum products for their operation and maintenance or on oil derivatives for their raw materials. Gasoline would be even more severely rationed to allow the consumption of only five gallons per week by any automobile and heavy restrictions would have to be placed on the transportation industry and agriculture. Food production would be cut by more than half.

"The automobile industry, the heart of America's economy, would be forced to shut down because of the inability of suppliers to manufacture parts, either metal or plastic, and because the market for new cars would totally disappear. Exports of manufactured goods would drop by between eighty-five and ninety percent because of the total collapse of the economies of Japan and Western Europe except for that of Great Britain, which is now self-sufficient in crude oil. Norway, with its North Sea reserves, is also capable of self-sufficiency. Unemployment throughout the United States would be in the fifty percent range, with inflation rising to an annual rate of between thirty and forty percent.

"Ninety-three percent of Western Europe's consumed crude oil is imported. The result of a cut-off there would be a total collapse of the economy of all the constituent countries except Norway and the U.K. Eighty percent of the work force would be unemployed. Automobiles would not be driven. All petroleum would be needed for the operation of basic utilities and the transportation of people and goods. The export and import of manufactured goods would cease because of lack of domestic manufacturing capability and the lack of money in the hands of consumers caused by the eighty percent unemployment level. For Japan, which relies totally on imported crude oil, the effects of a cut-off would be even more devastating than in Western Europe. All manufacturing would cease, including the building of tankers and ships of all classes.

"The shut-down of ship building, not only in Japan but elsewhere in the Western world, would preclude the rebuilding of the world tanker fleet for several years. The keel of the first replacement might be laid in some country, perhaps the United States, within a year after the destruction of the world fleet, but it would take about twenty years to reestablish world tanker tonnage capacity that would be equivalent to the amount destroyed.

"Domestic air travel in the United States would be cut back by eighty percent with travel permits having to be secured justifying travel for business or compassionate reasons. In Japan, all domestic and international flights would be stopped. A similar situation would prevail in Western Europe except for those airlines that could refuel in the United Kingdom or Norway inside a safe radius of operation."

The president took off his glasses and rubbed the

bridge of his nose between the thumb and forefinger of his right hand.

"As I see it, if the world tanker fleet were destroyed, there would be a total economic collapse in Western Europe and Japan. It would be of such magnitude as to mean the end of today's civilization and lifestyle in those parts of the world. It would mean poverty, starvation, revolution, violence. It would mean, certainly in Western Europe, that communism, which thrives on poverty and unrest, that communism would prevail in a short period of time. Furthermore, the military forces of our NATO allies and indeed our own, standing before massive Soviet forces across the Iron Curtain, would quickly be immobilized. You can't operate an army or an air force without fuel.

"In my judgment, the sinking of the world's tanker fleet and the resulting total cut-off of crude oil to the Western world and Japan would be a calamity, a disaster of the first magnitude, its consequences almost equal to those of an all-out thermonuclear war . . ."

Eaton broke in. "Except that tens of millions of people would not die."

"But life for more millions would be a living hell," Hansen responded.

Vice-President Mark James, who usually said very little at such meetings, decided to speak up.

"I wonder if it would be useful to take a look at the options that are open. First, we know that Romanov is going to act tomorrow morning. Let's take that as a fact. He says that no matter what we do, he's going to put his troops into Iran and Iraq, Saudia Arabia, and all the rest of those countries. If we don't interfere, he will continue to supply us with crude oil, but on a sliding downward scale as his own requirements increase. Frankly, Mr. President, I don't think that option is worth a damn. The man is a congenital liar. He lied to you on the twenty-sixth when he gave you assurances that the Russians weren't involved in the tanker sinkings. Once he has the Persian Gulf under his heel, he could make the Western world dance to any tune he wanted. So as I see it, making any deal with that son of a bitch is out, absolutely out." Uncharacteristically, he pounded the table with his right fist to emphasize his point.

He cleared his throat and went on. "If that's out, then the only way to go is to meet force with force!"

The defense secretary jumped in. "I agree. But if we go conventional, we're in real trouble. We've got ourselves handcuffed and Romanov knows it. By straining everything to the absolute limit in an all-out effort, we've scraped together a task force of 120,000 men. And where is it? It's sitting on ships in the Indian Ocean, 2,500 miles south of Pakistan. That's where it is, steaming toward where the Soviet Indian Ocean fleet has been doing its big OKEAN exercise. The only thing I could throw in would be the 82nd Airborne and two marine battalions. We'd have to put them in God knows where. Maybe even the Iranians would let us in if they knew the Soviets were going to attack, which I'm quite sure they do by now . . ."

The president nodded toward John Eaton. "Secretary Eaton's people notified the embassies of all Middle East countries as soon as I was off the hot line."

Secretary Levy continued. "The 82nd is on standby readiness, but it would still take two days to get there and the Russians are going to launch tomorrow at noon GMT. Aircraft from the Fifth Fleet haven't got the range to reach the Soviet-Iran border, or to get into Afghanistan, for that matter." Levy had been addressing his remarks to Vice-President James. Now he shifted his gaze to look at the man who would make the decision.

"What I'm saying, Mr. President, is this. If we use force against force, the conventional route is hopeless. There's nothing we can do to stop them. Even if we did get to Pakistan by the sixth, we'd never get ashore because the Soviets would have taken the entire country by then."

The president held up his right hand momentarily to ask for silence. Speaking toward the telephone with its ear and mouth piece unit sitting in the trough that enabled a two-way conversation, he asked, "General Young, have you been able to hear what's being said?"

The general's clipped voice came back immediately. "Yes, sir."

"Do you agree with Secretary Levy?"

"Yes, Mr. President, I do, and so do my colleagues."

The president looked across the table at Levy. "I think you're telling me that the only force option we really have is thermonuclear. Do I read you correctly?"

There was total silence in the cabinet room. Not one man in that room ever believed he would live to hear that question put by the president of the United States of America. Thermonuclear? Absolutely unthinkable—up to that moment. Surely the answer could not be yes.

There was a long silence as Levy, confronted by that horrific question, decided how he would handle the answer. Finally he replied, "Before I say yes or no to that question, Mr. President, I want to put some numbers on the table that will help me to give you a qualified answer. The numbers have to do with cities and people."

It was Levy's turn to put on the reading glasses. From the pile of material he had brought with him, he extracted the notes he wanted and read from them:

"The Soviet Union stands a chance of surviving an all-out nuclear war. The United States does not. The Soviet population is much more thinly spread than ours. Nearly half our people are close together in big cities. If we wiped out the nine Soviet cities with more than a million people, they'd only lose 8.5 percent of their population. They lost twelve percent in World War Two and survived. And they're more used to losing people than we are, with all the famines, purges, and wars they've been through.

"I find it difficult, Mr. President, to cope with the thought of one hundred million Americans dying in an instant."

The somber president did not smile when he said, "You have no monopoly on that difficulty, Bob."

Levy was ready to state his position. "But my answer to your question, Mr. President, is yes. If we're going to use force, the only alternative now is the ICBM or the submarine-launched ballistic missiles. However, I think we should confine ourselves to the military option. Under the military option, our missiles are targeted only for army bases, airfields, and naval installations. Those military targets that are associated with cities, such as Leningrad or Murmansk, are not included. So we stay away from all the cities. Also included in the military option are the major Russian crude oil production centers and fields in the Pechora and the huge Samotlor field in western Siberia."

Vice-President James could sense a problem. "Surely if you took out their major oil production fields, wouldn't that tempt the Soviets to do the same with the Persian Gulf in retaliation?"

"The very point I wanted to make," Levy acknowledged. "If you go for the military option, Mr. President, I suggest you take out the oil field targets."

The president wondered, "Could we go for targets of opportunity—the Soviet divisions along the Iran border and the Soviet surface fleets in the Atlantic, Indian Ocean, and the Pacific?"

"No problem, Mr. President," Levy assured him. "Although we should stay away from the Indian Ocean. Right now there's far too much traffic in the Arabian Sea. Our Pakistan Task Force is in the area and our Fifth Fleet with the British flotilla."

The president said he had one final question. "If I decide to go thermonuclear, take the limited military option, what should the timing be and should I try to threaten Romanov, get some leverage on him to force him to give up his Persian Gulf invasion? Having put the question, let me give you my view as to time and we'll see if anybody has any comments on it. And I can tell you, gentlemen, that right now I haven't decided what to do except I know that we've got only two choices: We can let the Soviets move into the Persian Gulf without a fight, in return for which they will refrain from sinking the world tanker fleet and allow the Western world continued access to the crude oil supplies in the area, subject to their own escalating requirements. Or we can take the other choice, the limited military option, the thermonuclear route."

The others nodded grimly.

"The crucial time is eight o'clock tomorrow morning," the president went on. "If we go thermonuclear, we should start immediately to get our people out of the cities in case the Soviets retaliate by an all-out attack against us. I've already asked for network time for six this evening."

"With great respect, Mr. President," it was Mark James, "whichever of the two paths you choose to follow, I think the American people should be warned immediately. They should be told the Russians have given us an ultimatum; that the possibility of an all-out thermonuclear war is a real one; that there is truly no need for panic, but that between now and tomorrow morning by six at the latest, they should get out of the cities."

Eaton suggested, "The time limit for completion of the evacuation should be the time you set for launching our ICBMs, which I suggest should be as late in the game as possible. If the ICBMs take roughly twenty minutes from time of launch to time of arrival on target, you want to give Romanov time to consider and to hold his troops back. I think seven o'clock should be your time of launching, Mr. President, and the absolute deadline for all people to be out of the cities. They should know enough to keep away from military installations."

Tom Jackman, the Senate majority leader from Florida, his voice thin and reedy like his body, spoke up. "I agree with the vice-president. It's now quarter to twelve. To wait until tonight to warn the people means that millions of people who could be on the move will have lost six precious hours. I'm sure the networks will clear for you anytime, Mr. President, anytime."

Hansen agreed. "You're right, Tom." He turned to Crane. "Get Peterson to tell the networks I want to go in half an hour, at 12:30." Crane practically ran to the door.

"Now what about bargaining with that bastard Romanov? If I elect to go nuclear, should I threaten him first or just go?"

Old Dan O'Brien, reputedly the best poker player on Capitol Hill, harrumphed from his seat down the table.

"From where I sit, Mr. President, you and Romanov are playing a game with the highest stakes the world has ever seen. He's sure the United States hasn't got enough guts to go nuclear, thermonuclear or whatever you want to call it. He's sitting there positive about that. So he's going to be the most surprised son of a bitch in the world if his radar and surveillance screens tell him at seven tomorrow morning or whenever it is you decide to go, that a hundred or two hundred ICBMs are on their way. You'll catch him with the most important weapon in any battle—surprise. Get him on that hot line two minutes before you launch. Then the moment your big birds are up and on their way, let him have it, then tell him that you're putting in a limited military strike but you're ready to go with a mass attack if he retaliates. And tell him you want three things. Number one, no nuclear retaliation; number two, no submarine attacks on the tankers; number three, no invasion of the Persian Gulf."

"Your scenario sounds good, Dan." Defense Secretary Levy liked what he heard, but it opened up another possibility. "If you're right, the president would have more bargaining leverage in those critical moments if he was able to tell Romanov that even though he could have taken out the Soviet troops massed along the Iranian border in his first ICBM shoot, he had held back. The president could tell Romanov that if he didn't immediately agree to his terms, the ICBMs to obliterate his entire force in that area would be launched."

The president, who had been concentrating totally on what was being said, his body tensed, his mind working at its maximum, decided he had heard enough. "Gentlemen, I'd like about ten minutes to talk this over with the vice-president. If all of you will wait here, please."

With that, President Hansen stood up, as did everyone else around the table. With his vice-president by his side, he made his way out of the room toward the temporary sanctuary of the Oval Office. There he was informed by an agitated Crane that the CIA had reported that the Russians had started to evacuate their cities.

At the stroke of twelve noon, both men returned to the cabinet room. The decision had been made.

When he was settled in his chair, the president spoke toward the telephone to confirm that the chairman of the Joint Chiefs of Staff and the chiefs were on the line and listening.

For the record, the president gave an explanation of his line of reasoning. That done, he stated his decision. "For those reasons, I have decided that at 7 A.M. Washington time tomorrow, I have no choice but to launch an intercontinental ballistic missile assault upon limited military objectives in the USSR. In the first strike, ICBMs programed for the Soviet-Iran border will be withheld, subject to immediate launch in the event negotiations with Chairman Romanov fail. Those negotiations will commence on the hot line as soon as the ICBMs are launched. At that time I will demand Romanov's agreement that there will be no nuclear retaliation; that no Soviet forces will invade Iran or the Persian Gulf; that all troops concentrated against the Soviet-Iran border and Afghanistan will be forthwith withdrawn; that there will be no further submarine attacks against any of the world tanker fleet; and that there be a personal meeting between Chairman Romanov and myself at the earliest possible moment. If he agrees, I will disarm our missiles before impact."

"Let's hope you can," someone muttered.

The president of the United States could scarcely believe the words he himself was uttering. It was like a vivid nightmare.

"General Young?"

"Yes, sir."

"You heard my decision?"

"Yes, sir."

"I'd like you to be in my office here tonight by nine with a list of your recommended military targets and maps showing the locations. Unless countermanded by voice personally by me, you will launch the ICBM attack at precisely seven o'clock tomorrow morning."

The president waited for the general's acknowledgement. When none came, he demanded, "General, did you hear what I said?"

When the general's voice came through the telephone it was filled with contempt. He could not hide his feelings for the bungling, inept politicians he had been listening to.

"Yes, Mr. President, I heard what you said. All four of us here heard what you said. While you were having your ten-minute session with the vice-president to decide what *you* were going to do, we had a little meeting at this end to decide what *we're* going to do. Mr. President, in our opinion, you've been badly advised by people who don't know what the hell they're talking about. If we launched an ICBM attack on limited military targets, the Soviets would blow the United States off the face of the earth. Being able to disarm them at the last minute wouldn't matter a damn. The Soviets would put up a retaliatory launch the instant they saw ours coming. You don't know what you're doing Mr. President!

"What I'm telling you is that the Joint Chiefs of Staffs Committee of the United States of America has decided that there will be *no* launching of any ICBMs or any other ballistic missiles against the Soviet Union tomorrow morning at eight or at any other time until *we're* satisfied it is in the interests of the people of the United States that the launch button should be pushed. In other words, when we're damned well good and ready!"

The president could not believe what he was hearing. "You're telling me you refuse to carry out my order? That's treason, general, absolute naked treason against the Government of the United States."

The general's harsh voice filled the cabinet room. His words stunned his listeners.

"Not if it's a military government, Mr. Hansen. Not if *we*—my colleagues and I—take over."